S.J. MARTIN

Vengeance

Passion. Perfidy. Pursuit.

I am dedicating the final book in the Breton Horse Warrior series to the many amazing 'Beta Readers', ARC Readers and proofreaders who take the time to give me feedback on each book. Just some of the regular ones are:

Alison Hodgson -Historian & Author

Ruth Wainman

Andy Mitchell

Greg Albrighton

Kay De'Ath

Stephen Spencelayh

Love Parker - Author

Theresa Hupp -Author

Tim Walker –Author

Jake Frood – CEO of History Addicts

Contents

Prologue   1
Chapter One   4
Chapter Two   10
Chapter Three   19
Chapter Four   26
Chapter Five   37
Chapter Six   45
Chapter Seven   57
Chapter Eight   64
Chapter Nine   75
Chapter Ten   86
Chapter Eleven   94
Chapter Twelve   103
Chapter Thirteen   111
Chapter Fourteen   117
Chapter Fifteen   126
Chapter Sixteen   138
Chapter Seventeen   147
Chapter Eighteen   154
Chapter Nineteen   164
Chapter Twenty   176
Chapter Twenty-one   185
Chapter Twenty-two   192
Chapter Twenty-three   199

Chapter Twenty-four   208
Chapter Twenty-five   215
Chapter Twenty-six   224
Chapter Twenty-seven   230
Chapter Twenty-eight   236
Chapter Twenty-nine   244
Chapter Thirty   252
Chapter Thirty-one   259
Chapter Thirty-two   264
Chapter Thirty-three   271
Chapter Thirty-four   276
Chapter Thirty-five   283
Chapter Thirty-six   289
List of characters   295
Glossary   298
Author note   301
Maps   305
About the Author   308
Also by S.J. Martin   310

Prologue

November 1085

William, King of England and Duke of Normandy, lay spread-eagled on the floor of the Abbaye-Aux-Dames in Caen. He pressed his cheek and palms against the cold, hard slabs of stone in front of the altar. He could feel the numbing cold spreading through his body but still, hour after hour, he lay there, his stomach knotted with emotion. This was the third year in succession that he had come to prostrate himself in grief.

Finally, he slowly pushed himself into a kneeling position and sat back on his heels, breathing in the heady incense and listening to the bishop intoning the prayers and psalms he had requested for his wife. It was over two years since Matilda was suddenly taken from him; a brief summer illness and she was gone. Fortunately, he had been here in Normandy with her and not in England. He had held her hand tightly as she gave her confession and then took her last breath.

At first, he had refused to believe that she was dead, locking himself away in his chambers, distraught with grief as he had loved her dearly to the day she died. She had been a ray of light in his life, giving him ten children, and he had listened and acted on her guidance and wisdom, often leaving her to rule Normandy in his stead.

The huge Abbaye-Aux-Dames where Matilda was entombed was empty, save for the clergy and choir on the altar and the two guards standing in the entrance archway with its impressive twin, iron-banded doors. As William sat back on his heels, eyes closed, he reflected on the difficult last two years without his Queen. As usual, there was dissent and warfare on his borders. He had somehow lost the important strategic alliance with Duke Hoel of Brittany, and now King Philip of France was again poised to take advantage of any weakness and invade Normandy.

William, listening to the soaring voices of the choir, raised his eyes to the vaulted roof above him and thought about his sons. William Rufus was in England and would inherit the throne upon his death, a capable man. His youngest, Henry, was a clever and careful young man who would be financially well provided for after his death. His eldest son, Robert Curthose, gave him the most concern. Yet again, father and son were at odds; Robert had demanded that his father make him Duke of Normandy before his death, and William had refused. Robert had left his father's court straight after his mother's death, and he had not seen him since. He received news that Robert had travelled the courts of Europe, garnering support for his case to be Duke. Recent reports were even more alarming—Robert had again gone to Paris. He was now openly conspiring with King Philip of France against William.

This thought angered him and brought him to his feet. He bowed his head curtly to the bishop in thanks and, crossing himself, strode down the wide, echoing nave to the doors at the end. Pushing the left one forcefully open, he emerged into the winter sunshine. He decided that he would send cool shadows waiting for them. She recognised the tall, dark warrior with his signature crossed swords on his back. It was Luc De Malvais, Morvan's brother. She had not seen him since her days in Paris nearly seven years ago. He was a few years older than Morvan, but he had hardly changed except for a slight touch of silver at the temples. She did not know the older, tall, grey-haired warrior, but she felt unease as the third man stepped forward into the sunshine.

Piers De Chatillon had been a good friend to Morvan and her, certainly improving their fortunes, but he was dangerous to know. He was one of the most powerful and influential men in Europe, with the ear of the Vatican and most princes. Nevertheless, the crow of death was said to fly at his shoulder, and his presence here on the quayside would not be by accident.

Morvan suddenly caught sight of them and let out a shout of joy. 'What is this, a welcoming party? If so, you're far from home.' He greeted his brother and Chatillon with a warrior's arm clasp, but he enveloped the older man in a bear hug. 'Gerard, I have missed you. It has been far too long.' After much back-slapping and greetings, a smiling Morvan brought his wife and the children forward to greet them. 'My beautiful wife Minette, who we all call Ette,' he said proudly. 'This is Gervais, who is three years old, and Marie, who is four.' Both children bowed their heads being well-taught by their mother. They all greeted Morvan's family, and Luc smiled to see his brother so settled and happy.

'Come, I have rooms prepared and dinner waiting for us at my house in Ghent,' said Chatillon. Morvan shouted directions to the servants and then followed his brother while asking numerous questions about his home at Morlaix, about his mother, Luc's family and finally…

'How is my son Conn, Luc? I can't wait to see and meet him. I believe you said he was very dark like me but with Constance's clear blue eyes. Is that right?'

The silence hung in the air, and Ette caught the look that passed between the three men, as did Morvan. 'What is it? Is he ill? Is he dead?' he asked in a whisper, afraid of the answer.

They stopped, and Chatillon looked over his shoulder and around them to check that no one was too close on the busy quayside. He placed a hand on Morvan's shoulder. 'This is no conversation to have here, a place where many people are paid to listen. We will discuss this back at the house.'

However, Morvan wasn't to be put off, and he gripped Luc's arm. 'Just tell me whether he lives,' he demanded.

Luc sighed and turned to face him, pulling him to the quay's edge away from the crowds. 'We believe so, Morvan, but we don't know. I promise we'll explain all, back at the house.'

Morvan shook his head and turned to look into Ette's large brown concerned eyes as she reached for his hand. 'So he isn't at Morlaix, Luc?' At that point, Gerard stepped forward and lowered his voice. 'He was taken, Morvan. He was kidnapped from us. All three of us have searched from here to the French Alps to no avail, but I swear we will never give up. We will find him.'

'Conn was taken? By whom and why did they take him? When did it happen, and how long have they had him?' he shouted at them.

Chatillon could see a crowd gathering, and he urgently pushed the group towards the horses before turning back to confront the angry Horse Warrior. 'Be quiet now, Morvan, before you land us all in danger, or I swear I will shut you up by booting you off this quay,' he growled at him, his face inches away, his black eyes glittering, his hand ready on his dagger.

Morvan had not seen Chatillon that angry or threatening for many years, so it brought him to his senses, and he stepped back and stood staring at the ground, before turning stricken eyes to Ette.

'Someone has taken my son, Ette. They have stolen Conn.' She put her hands up to touch his face in reassurance as she could feel the anger and dismay and see the confused look in his eyes. She realised he had now found himself in a situation he had no control over, and she had never seen that before. 'We will find him, Morvan.'

Morvan nodded and reluctantly followed Chatillon to the horses. He would do as they asked because he wanted to know more. He would hear what had happened, find out who was responsible and make them pay. He would find his son.

Chapter Two

It had been seven years since Morvan had been in Chatillon's house in Ghent, and it brought back bittersweet memories. His then-lover, the beautiful Italian widow, Bianca da Landriano, was murdered by one of the assassins sent to kill him in revenge—assassins sent by Alan Fergant, the heir to the Dukedom of Brittany. Morvan blamed himself for her death, as did Chatillon, who had also loved Bianca and had planned to marry her—he blamed himself too for allowing her to become involved with Morvan. They were both devastated by her brutal and sudden death.

Now Morvan sat around a table laden with food, surrounded by family and friends, but still, he could hardly eat, his stomach knotted in frustration and anger. Someone had taken his son, the son he had never seen. His son's mother, Constance, now the Duchess of Brittany, did not even know Conn lived. She believed that he had been killed at birth, exposed on a hillside by her husband, Alan Fergant. These thoughts went round in Morvan's head as he watched the faces around the table and listened to snatches of their conversation.

Ette could see the emotional turmoil that Morvan was experiencing, and she reached over, put her hand on his thigh and smiled at him. 'Wait until the servants have gone and ask your questions. But eat something—you'll need your strength.' He sighed and speared a large slice of succulent beef just as Chatillon clapped his hands and cleared the room of everyone, with the exception of Edvard, his Vavasseur and right-hand man. The man who knew all of his secrets and who carried out many of his assignments and assassinations. Chatillon steepled his fingers and gazed down the table at Morvan while conversation slowly died. Then he began...

'This is what we know about the kidnapping of young Conn so far. Monseigneur Gironde planted a spy at Morlaix. It was a clever plan. The man's name was Brian Ap Gwyfd, and he was what they call a horse whisperer. Before long, he was happily entrenched in the stables at Morlaix. He was a consummate horseman, but he also made friends easily and took everyone in.'

He paused, and Sir Gerard jumped in. 'He even had that wild black mare of yours eating out of his hand; he backed and rode her within a month of arriving.'

Chatillon nodded. 'He was very good. He purposefully tracked the movements of Luc, and he developed a relationship with the children's nurse, Hildebrand. Before long, he had somehow worked out that Luc wasn't, in fact, Conn's father, probably through Hildebrand as she had been the child's wet nurse since he was born at Falaise.'

Morvan sat forward, his hands on the table. 'And the nurse? Did she go with him when he snatched Conn?'

Luc answered. 'Yes. She had always been with Conn, and she loved him, which has been a small comfort. Brian Ap Gwyfd chose his moment well to snatch him as Gerard and I were away, so he had several days start on us when we finally learnt the truth. We had no idea even in which direction they had gone. Fortunately, Chatillon found that they had sailed down to Bordeaux through his network of contacts. We tracked them from there across Brittany and France, riding day and night. Before long, they were only eighteen hours or so ahead of us. We thought we had them in Montpellier, but they moved swiftly to Marseilles, and we lost them there. We searched the port and its hinterland for weeks!'

Silence reigned in the room as Morvan absorbed all this. Ette watched a gamut of emotions chase across his face. Then he pushed the chair back and got to his feet, unable to sit still any longer. 'So who is behind this? Monseigneur Gironde is the personal chaplain of the Dukes of Brittany, is he not? I remember him as a cunning and devious cleric. So is this the work of Alan Fergant again? Did he somehow find out that Conn still lived? Did he snatch him to kill him?' His voice becoming more strident as he kicked his chair out of the way, realising that his son could now be dead.

Chatillon shook his head and waved Edvard to pick up the chair while gesturing to Morvan to regain his seat at the table. 'There is more... this is a much bigger and far more devious plot than you realise. Think for a second about exactly who your son is. He is not only the child of you and Princess Constance. He is the first male grandchild of King William, a possible heir to Normandy if Robert dies childless, and possibly to England as well. He may be born out of wedlock, illegitimate, but remember that King William was also the bastard son of Count Robert of Normandy, and look what he has become. Your child is a pawn in the hands of those ambitious individuals who wish to use him as a figurehead in the future.'

Listening to this, Ette sat wide-eyed. She had not considered that connection before, and she turned to Morvan. 'Mon Dieu, no wonder they have him so well hidden.' She could see that none of this had ever occurred to Morvan as he turned a questioning gaze on Chatillon.

'So if this isn't Alan Fergant out for revenge, who is it? King Philip of France? Count Robert of Flanders? He hates William. Or, God forbid, could it be Fulk of Anjou?'

'We know who it is, Morvan, but he has yet to admit it to me. It's the man you know as Cardinal Dauferio, the one you spied upon at the monastery in Paris when they were plotting against King William. We now know that he sent men out to scour Normandy and the Vexin for the child when he discovered his existence. Our problem lies in the fact that he has been clever. No evidence or trail leads back to him. We captured Gironde, his creature, for a while, and we extracted every iota of information. Unfortunately, he did not last as long as we hoped. Next month, I'm going to Rome, and I will confront him while I am there.'

'Dauferio,' spat Morvan in disgust, 'that cunning, manipulative priest. Why would he do this?'

'You're behind the times, Morvan. The Cardinal Dauferio was also the powerful Abbot of Monte Cassino, a post that gave him influence, position and access to the Holy See in Rome. On the death of Pope Gregory, Dauferio, albeit reluctantly, accepted the nomination for Pope. The votes were cast, and Cardinal Dauferio is now Pope Victor III and untouchable, he believes. In addition, it's now five years since the horseman and Hildebrand took the child. I think the Pope believes that the kidnapping has been forgotten. I intend to disabuse him of that fact and stir up a hornet's nest that might bring results.'

'How could they just disappear?' asked Morvan. 'Gerard said that the horseman had distinctive body markings.'

'Yes, Brian Ap Gwyfd is covered in blue Celtic tattoos from his druid heritage. When we could find no sign of them along the southern coast of the Mediterranean, I even sent men to Wales, to his island home of Ynys Mon. I sent messages to Ireland, a land of horse breeders where he has friends. But everywhere, it was the same. He hasn't been seen for years.'

Morvan turned to his brother, who sat back in his chair, listening to what was said. 'Is there anything we can do, Luc?' he implored.

Luc's steel-blue eyes met the amber ones of his brother in sympathy. 'Morvan, Gerard and I have spent nearly six months away from Morlaix searching for Conn every year for the last five years. Nothing has been seen of Brian Ap Gwyfd, Hildebrand or the child; they have just disappeared and must be lying low in some obscure remote place. Both Chatillon and I have spread gold along the quaysides, in the marketplaces and at horse fairs all over Europe. Any sightings of him and they will send for us immediately. We must wait and see if anything comes from Chatillon's meeting with the Pope. If he becomes rattled, he may send a message to the people holding the boy, and we will be waiting.' Morvan was clearly dissatisfied and frustrated, but he could do no more than settle for that at present.

'Now let us raise the mood slightly,' said Gerard raising his wine goblet. 'Here is a toast to the newest members of the Malvais family. A warm welcome to Ette and your children, Gervais and Marie. May there be many more little footsteps around the castle's corridors at Morlaix now that Alan Fergant has lifted your banishment.'

Ette turned a delightful shade of pink at Sir Gerard's toast. She knew how important the older knight was to the family. Originally a squire to their father, he had taken the boys under his wing when they were very young, becoming their swordmaster and friend. Their father died at Hastings, and since then, Gerard has been like a father figure to them. He had never married, and Morvan was convinced it was because he had always loved their mother, Marie. He would never admit it, although his eyes followed her everywhere at Morlaix.

The rest of the evening was pleasant as Morvan talked of the campaigns in Scotland. All three men laughed at the description of Ette stabbing Morvan's foe Robert De Belleme through his thigh, pinning him to the ground when he tried to rape her.

'You know that he has never recovered? He is even more bitter and unpleasant than he was before if that is possible. He limps and walks with a stick and rarely appears in court anymore. Apparently, he is courting Agnes of Ponthieu, a wealthy heiress.' added Chatillon.

'God help her,' muttered Ette to more laughter. Ette joined in with her tinkling laugh, and Luc smiled. He could see why his brother had fallen for this captivating French girl. His mother, Marie, who was also brought up in the French court, would love her.

However, it had been a long day, especially for those just disembarking from a long sea journey, and so Morvan and Ette retired to bed after checking on their children, fast asleep with their nurse in one of the attic rooms. The other three sat for a while around the table, the firelight glittering on the polished wood.

'Do not give him too much hope, Chatillon. We would surely have found them if they were still alive by now.' Chatillon narrowed his eyes at Luc. 'The boy is alive, Malvais. I know it because Dauferio had a plan for him, his life mapped out. He is too valuable for them to kill. I will find him for Morvan no matter how long it takes.'

Closing their room's large oak door, Ette wrapped her arms around Morvan's waist and pulled him close. He kissed the top of her head and let out the long breath he held. She did not say a word; she knew there was little she could say. If the combined forces of Luc De Malvais and Piers De Chatillon had not found the child over the last five years, there was only the slimmest chance that Conn was still alive. Therefore, she did the only thing she could under the circumstances. She lifted Morvan's dark blue linen tunic and slid her hands over his body to firmly stroke his muscled torso. She swept her hands round to his back and, reaching up, kneaded his tense shoulder blades, moving up on tiptoe to do the same in his neck. She felt him relaxing against her, and so she moved her hands down to his buttocks and clenched her fingers into his muscles, pulling him against her body.

With one hand, he lifted her chin and gazed down into those huge, dark eyes, the firelight flickering across her face, and he saw her give a mischievous grin as she brought her hands slowly round to the front of his body to stroke and hold his hardening manhood. 'You have been neglecting me, my Lord,' she whispered as she unfastened his chausses and linen braies to enable better access to him. He gasped as she dropped to her knees and used her tongue to torment him. He gave a growl of desire and peeled his tunic over his head before grasping her wrists and pulling her back to her feet. His mouth descended firmly on hers, his tongue probing her mouth while his hands began to loosen the cross-woven ties at the front of her gown. However, he quickly became impatient with that, and he grasped the fine linen and ripped it apart.

Ette squealed in surprise and mock outrage. 'I'll buy you another one,' he said as his lips descended onto her breasts, gently biting and licking her nipples. Ette closed her eyes, currents of pleasure and desire running through her body. Her gown hung around her waist, and she smiled down at the naked warrior caressing her body, her Horse Warrior.

He ripped the rest of the dress apart, lifted her and dropped her on the bed. 'So. Neglecting you am I, Minette De Malvais?' he said in a threatening tone as he grasped her ankles and pulled her towards him. Ette gurgled with pleasure as his large muscular thighs forced her legs apart, and she ran her hands over his powerful shoulders. He guided himself swiftly into the warm wetness of her body with a groan of pleasure. She threw her head back and closed her eyes. She wanted him so much that her body rose to meet him. She wrapped her legs around him as he plunged inside her and lost himself in the desire and passion of the embrace...

Afterwards, they lay sated, her head resting on his shoulder as Morvan dropped into a deep and satisfying sleep while Ette trailed her fingers across his abdomen. She loved this man so much, and she would do everything in her power to stop him from getting hurt. She needed to talk to Chatillon. She needed to know the truth. Was the child still alive? Was there a chance of finding him? On the other hand, was this just a wild goose chase that would scar Morvan forever? She needed to prepare herself and him for the outcome.

swordsmanship and warfare will begin.'

Conn could feel the waves of apprehension emanating from the boys beside him. Their lives were hard enough; their training every day with wooden staves was brutal. His body was covered in new and yellowing bruises from hand to hand combat, and Conn knew that he was one of the best, fleet of foot with perfect balance, speed, and hand to eye coordination. He did not know it, but he was certainly his father's son.

Scaravaggi eyed the kneeling boys with satisfaction. He viewed the coming years with pleasure; he would turn these boys into a weapon of God to wreak havoc and deliver punishment to those who defied the word of Christ. When they became young men of sixteen or seventeen years, they would train and develop seven disciples of their own so that the numbers would build. With the wealth and backing of the Holy See, they would be sent out into the world to make their mark. They would infiltrate all levels of society, gathering wealth and power. They would become leaders and experts in many fields, some becoming diplomats and strategists. Doors would be opened for them. They would have respect and influence. But they would also be feared. Working with his mentor Dauferio—the leader of the Christian world—they were creating an army of warriors, all moulded into Scaravaggi's image: intelligent, highly educated, fearless, unstoppable Knights of the Cross.

Like these boys, Scaravaggi was given to the church at an early age. His father owed money to the church, and the handing over of his youngest son to the Warrior Monks cleared the debt, wiping the slate clean. Scaravaggi had been dragged from his screaming mother's arms in Tuscany. He never saw his family again and now had no interest in finding them. He had been taken to Monte Cassino to begin his education, and there he was put under the wing of a fast rising monk called Dauferio. In only a few years, that rising star in the church had become the Abbot of Monte Cassino and was now Pope Victor III.

Unlike some of these boys, Scaravaggi had loved his new life. He had excelled at everything he did whilst receiving the best education and training in swordsmanship, which turned him into a formidable warrior monk and future leader to carry out Dauferio's vision. He felt honoured and privileged to assist Dauferio in putting his vision into practice. He glanced at the kneeling boys and left them, turning on his heel. Five pairs of eyes followed him, this tall, muscular statuesque monk with his shaved head and the distinctive, large, tattooed cross on his neck.

Two days later, the two older boys arrived, confident and boastful. They described themselves as lieutenants. Conn sighed and shook his head in dismay. To the five boys, this was just going to be another layer of bullying they had to contend with each day. The rather exotic monk, Father Mezzi, who had brought them, was the one good distraction. Short and squat with ink-covered fingers, he sang and hummed lilting foreign songs and tunes to himself as he wandered around the stone walls and corridors of the large Hermitage. He was also a storyteller, and during rest periods, the boys sat at his feet to hear tales of ferocious wild beasts, mermaids and even dragons he had encountered on his travels. Conn was surprised at the tolerance shown by Scaravaggi to Father Mezzi. Conn thought the monk must be a prized scribe or illustrator to be treated so leniently. A few months later, Conn was to discover exactly what the monk did, and he was to carry the marks of it for the rest of his life.

Chapter Four

Robert Curthose strode confidently through the corridors of King Philip's residence on the Isle de France on the River Seine. He had been there numerous times and having courted the support of princes and counts across Europe, he had now returned to see what Philip could offer. He was not to be disappointed as he received the offer of both funds and troops from the French King.

Robert was a spirited and likeable man. Unlike King William, he was popular and welcomed everywhere. However, he wasn't naïve; he might be impetuous, but he knew that King Philip planned to split the Anglo-Norman empire. Philip wanted King William in England, out of the way, and Robert installed in his stead as Duke of Normandy.

Robert smiled at the thought that King Philip might not find him so malleable or easy to control once he had the Duchy of Normandy. Robert would use the French King's resources to defeat his father as he had done once before at the siege of Gerberoi. Robert was using Philip the same way the King was using him, both trying to gain their ends and weaken William.

King William had lived a life of incessant warfare. He had enjoyed a successful military career in England and Europe with only two minor defeats, at Dol and again facing his

in several conflicts. He did not want to face him and his formidable Horse Warriors in battle.

Chatillon could see the emotions cross Robert's face. 'I believe he intends to take a few months' leave to visit his mother and family in Morlaix—he hasn't seen them for over seven years. That will give you all a few months of breathing space. Can I ask when and where you intend to attack?'

King Philip answered for the rebel Prince. 'Robert is determined to claim his rightful place as Duke of Normandy, and so he will be attacking the Norman Vexin in the early spring—with our support, of course.'

'Of course,' replied Chatillon, a mischievous glint in his eye. 'Yes, the Vexin, a constant thorn in King William's side. The eastern half of the province is now French, since you annexed it when he was busy elsewhere, and the western half of the Vexin is still Norman. The people there, what's left of them, must be decimated and exhausted by this constant warfare.'

King Philip raised his eyebrows and pursed his lips. 'Do I hear a note of censure, Chatillon? If so, is that from you or your Master in Rome?' he snapped.

Chatillon approached a couch near the window. 'May I? It has been a long and tiring ride.' The King nodded his permission, and Gervais proffered wine while they settled into the chairs opposite.

'There is no doubt,' continued the Papal Envoy, having taken a long draft from his goblet, 'The Pope is becoming weary of these endless skirmishes that produce little result. Robert is as likely to become Duke of Normandy as I am. Unless King William dies, of course. Is there an appetite for assassination amongst the three of you? For that could be easily arranged,' he suggested, his head on one side as he watched the reaction to his suggestion.

Robert Curthose was the first to respond. 'God's bones, Chatillon, what do you think we are about? We are not murderers. I may dislike my father, and I find it difficult to forgive him for how he treats me, but I don't hate him. I respect him and intend to defeat him in battle. But he'll not die by my hand or by the knife of an assassin I employ.'

Chatillon expected that response from Robert, but as he watched under hooded lids, he was far more interested in the enigmatic smile and expression on King Philip's face. *Yes,* he thought, *you would happily have him killed without a second thought, but you would never admit that to us.* The other two men immediately agreed with Robert's sentiments.

'I'm glad to see that some filial affection still exists, Robert. Your father is one of the greatest men of his time. However, there is no doubt that he has been sorely affected by your mother's death.' Robert found he had to look away; he couldn't meet the man's eyes as he seemed to probe into his very soul. Chatillon continued, 'Not that it has affected his judgment in any way.'

Gervais stood and placed another large log on the fire; it was cold in the high ceilinged room. 'We hope to time the attacks on the Vexin to coincide with William being in England,' he said, turning to retake his seat opposite the Papal Envoy.

'Ah yes, of course, the possible invasion and attack by the Danish fleet,' Chatillon said in an amused tone that unsettled the three men.

'It does exist. My men have seen it. They say over two hundred ships lay ready at anchor,' stated King Philip.

'I don't doubt its existence, Sire. I also know it exists. My man, Vannson, is the Captain of one of these longships. I just doubt whether the ships will ever sail. King Canute is an ambitious man, but he is somewhat unstable and has numerous problems at home with revolts and rebellions. I just give you a reason for caution when launching your plans, for you may find William back in your midst when you least expect him. What a shame you don't have Morvan De Malvais by your side. His strategies seem always to win battles.'

Robert nodded. 'If he has given his allegiance to my father, there is little I can do, and the Horse Warriors from Caen are my father's troops—not mine to use.'

'Pope Victor is happy to supply you with funds, Robert. He is sending you two hundred Genoese crossbowmen at his own expense. They are the best in Europe; use them well.' Robert thanked Chatillon effusively and said he would personally write and thank the Pope.

Chatillon shook his head, 'I don't think that is wise, Sire. The new Pope does not like to keep or receive written records of such a transaction.

'Now I must go,' he said, standing and bowing to the men by the fire. He moved away and then turned at the door. 'Oh, Seneschal, your daughter Minette will be here shortly. Morvan and the Horse Warriors go to Caen. She, however, is bringing your grandchildren to Paris to see you and her mother. Your namesake, young Gervais, is a lively, adventurous boy, always in trouble. A good mix of both of his parents.' He laughed as he left the chamber.

There was silence in the room for several minutes as they considered the information that Chatillon had shared. Then Robert spoke. 'I don't relish my men facing Malvais and his Horse Warriors in the Vexin, especially if my father requests that his brother Luc De Malvais joins him with his troop from

Brittany. Few could stand against such as them.'

King Philip leant his chin on his hand as he stared into the fire. 'I wasn't going to mention this, but reports tell me Luc De Malvais has been absent from his home in Morlaix a lot over the last few years. I have heard reports of a missing child. A child that has been taken. It's hard to hide such a quest when an instantly recognisable figure like Luc De Malvais on his huge black Destrier is searching southern Europe with his men. Rumour has it that it's his by-blow, a Malvais bastard, but now I am beginning to wonder as I hear there may be others searching for the child.' King Philip looked directly at Robert Curthose as he said this, but he could see that the Prince had not made any connection, and he wasn't sure himself. He intended to watch what happened when Morvan returned to his home in Morlaix.

The Horse Warrior in question was riding through the gates of Caen with his Captain, Garrett Eymer, to rapturously cheering crowds. The city knew they had defeated the Scots King, Malcolm, and deserved a hero's welcome. After the four-day ride from Ghent, they had stopped at a river a few miles from Caen, where every horse was washed and brushed until it shone. Tack and breastplates were cleaned, and it was an impressive troop that entered the city, riding in threes on the narrow streets and then lining up on parade once in the bailey. The crowds pushed in but were held back by the guards as the King and his courtiers came out to welcome his troops home.

Morvan dismounted from his huge, black stallion, Midnight Shadow, to kneel before William, but the King opened his arms and clasped Morvan by the shoulders. 'Welcome home,' he shouted in his booming voice while raising the Horse Warrior's fist in the air to resounding cheers from the crowds. Morvan was a popular and famous figure in Normandy—they conveniently forgot that he was a Breton. He was *their* Horse Warrior.

The King gave a short speech to the assembled warriors, praising their courage and bravery on the field and in maintaining peace on the borders for several years. Now they were home.

William took Morvan into the huge keep while the men outside were mobbed by their families: parents, siblings, wives with children that were no longer babes. Some hearts were broken: girls who found that their warrior had married and had children with women from the borders of England while away; men who came back to find their betrothed had not waited and had married someone else; wives clutching a new babe that couldn't be their husband's child.

The servant poured the wine and left them. William sat with Morvan in what had been Queen Matilda's solar. 'I was sorry to hear of the Queen's death. She was a very wise and astute lady.'

William looked away for a moment. 'Yes, I still miss her. I moved my things up here as it was her favourite room, so light and airy. Also, I can still feel her presence in the tapestries she sewed, the embroidered cushions, her prie-dieu in the corner. I have given Prince Henry my old room as his own, and he is delighted. He sits in there reading, making notes, ordering the servants around. He was always the scholar amongst us. I should have had him ordained and made him a bishop; he would have done well in the Church,' he laughed.

Morvan decided to take the bull by the horns. 'And what of your other son, Robert. I have heard little or nothing from him since his mother's death. I believe he travelled widely.'

William's face darkened. 'For a while, things improved between us, but I could not and would not make him Duke of Normandy with so many threats on our borders and so few alliances. I was afraid that he would just become the puppet of King Philip, who would annex the rest of the Norman Vexin. The western Vexin is our land.'

Morvan sighed and inclined his head in agreement. He could understand that, especially as Queen Matilda was no longer there to influence and guide her impulsive eldest son.

'I know you have been away for over six years, Morvan, and I realise that you'll need to look to your estates. You'll also want to see your family in Morlaix, especially with Yuletide upon us, but I do have need of you and the Horse Warriors. I have been informed that Robert intends to attack the Vexin next year. I know you'll find it difficult to fight against my son—he is your friend—but I need you to help devise the strategies to keep them at bay in the Vexin. I will be away in England for at least the next three months, if not longer, dealing with a possible attack from King Canute. He has allied himself with my brother in law, Count Robert of Flanders, who hates me and supports Canute's ridiculous claim to the English throne.'

Morvan met William's hard questing gaze for a few moments and then sighed. 'Long ago, I swore fealty to you, Sire, when I rescued you from the Siege of Dol. I will renew that vow to you, as, although Robert is my friend and my Prince, I believe you have the right of it in the Vexin. I believe your cause is just, and there is no doubt that King Philip will be manipulating Robert. However, do not underestimate your son; he is ambitious, brave and courageous in battle.'

William nodded in agreement, but Morvan's decision brought a ready smile to his face.

'Now, I believe several pressing family matters need your attention.' William laughed, and standing, he slapped him on the back. 'Not least of all is a very pretty French wife, I believe.' Morvan grinned back at the King, but just then, the door to the solar opened and Constance, the King's married daughter, walked into the room.

Morvan froze. She had been the love of his life, his first love, and he had lost her and his child.

'Ah Constance, an old friend of yours has arrived. I'm sure he'll keep you amused while I see to other matters. My daughter has been staying with me for a few weeks. She leaves to return to her husband in a few days.' Then he was gone, leaving the two former lovers to stand and devour each other with their eyes.

They had both changed, were seven years older, and events in their lives had taken their toll on them. But to Morvan, nothing mattered and, opening his arms wide, he scooped her up as she ran into them. Her arms wrapped tightly around his waist, he dropped his face to her hair, just breathing in the smell of her. Lifting her face to his, he gazed into her huge, blue, tear-filled eyes before his lips descended on hers.

'Where can we go?' he whispered, picking her up in his arms. She laughed with joy and pointed to the door in the corner, leading to her mother's old, unused sewing room. Ette and his children were now forgotten as he carried Constance across the room.

Chapter Five

Chatillon approached the Lateran Palace in Rome with determination and a touch of trepidation. So much was resting on this meeting. As he strode across St John's Square, the winter sun lit up the front of the building that had been the principal residence of the Popes since the fourth century, if the archivists were to be believed. To the right was the imposing Lateran Basilica, the Cathedral of Rome. As a young papal legate, he had been interested in the city's history. He had been overwhelmed by the might and glory of Rome—the scale of the buildings they had constructed. He had trawled through documents that told him the hill had previously been the property of the Laterani family, but their rebellion against Emperor Nero had resulted in the confiscation of their properties and land. So the imposing basilica had been built here by Emperor Constantine, who then gave it, and the Lateran Palace beside it, to the Pope.

Chatillon knew the palace well. He had been based here for several years, as his uncle's secretary, and knew the dark secrets buried in the halls and walls of this building. He had resisted the push by his uncle, the Cardinal, to take holy orders. He did not want to be a priest; he wanted a secular life as he recognised his earthly appetites early on. In his twenties, he knew he wanted to forge a role for himself in the Papal enclave, so he watched, listened, and he learned his craft.

He entered the imposing archway and made his way into the triclinium. This had been an addition by Pope Hadrian, a huge dining hall decorated with fabulous mosaics. Most mornings at this time, the well-lit room became a gathering area for those with business at the palace or awaiting a much-sought-after audience with the Cardinals or the Pope. He hoped to find his uncle, Cardinal Odo De Chatillon, here, and he wasn't disappointed.

Odo was deep in conversation with other Cardinals and clerics, but he immediately embraced his nephew. 'Piers, you're a sight for sore eyes. I have not seen or heard from you in months.'

Chatillon bowed to the assembled group, who knew his reputation and regarded him warily. 'I have been occupied, Uncle, with a distressing business, but more of that later. How is the garnering of support going?' he said, inclining his head towards the group they were leaving.

'It seems to be going well. I have most of them in my pocket at present. A few won't budge; they have their own candidates, and we may need to find information against them. Others may be wavering and need to be persuaded with your help,' he said with a questioning look. He never took his powerful nephew for granted.

'Of course, Uncle, I have Edvard with me. Send me a list of the names, and we will arrange a visit. I promise that you will be Pope within a year.' Odo smiled and whispered, 'I know the Holy Father isn't a well man. He has a debilitating recurring illness that no doctor and no amount of prayer can seem to cure.'

Chatillon gave a thin smile. 'Yes, his time is almost up. I just need some urgent information from him first. Then I'm afraid his illness will consume him. He'll be gone within months.'

Odo blinked and stepped back. He narrowed his eyes and met his nephew's hard, glittering gaze. He had to admit that Piers made even him nervous and uneasy at times. 'You have a hand in it? What did you…I don't want to know on second thoughts,' he added, turning away to re-join his friends. 'Join me for dinner,' he shouted over his shoulder as he walked away.

Chatillon smiled. His uncle would make a good Pope. He was not too much of a reformer to upset the traditionalists, as Pope Gregory had done, but he had plans to modernise and take the Holy See forward into the future. With his uncle as Pope, the De Chatillon family were surely in the ascendancy, and there would be no saying what they might achieve together.

Now to deal with the current problem, he thought as he made his way towards the private apartments of Pope Victor III. He had no appointment, but he knew that he would be seen immediately. Monseigneur Benedict, the Pope's secretary, sat working at his desk in the anteroom. He paled when he saw Chatillon leaning against the marble archway.

'At your convenience, Benedict, but the Holy Father has requested my presence with some urgency.' The secretary looked surprised and flicked his eyes from the double doors behind him to the dark figure walking towards him.

'I wasn't aware of that, Seigneur. I will see if he is available?'

Chatillon laughed at the man's discomfort. 'He does not tell you everything, Benedict. I could tell you secrets about him that would make your hair stand on end, or even that useless thing between your legs. I assure you he'll be available to see me now.'

Minutes later, he emerged and waved Chatillon to enter. 'He has a short time before the Bishop of Ostia arrives; I hope that will suffice.' Chatillon inclined his head and entered the impressive room.

This was the third Pope he had visited here. As a very young acolyte, he had undertaken tasks for Pope Alexander II. He was succeeded by the cantankerous and ambitious Pope Gregory VII, who had made enemies everywhere with the strict Benedictine rules he imposed. Now Chatillon confronted the most recent incumbent, Dauferio. He was the powerful Abbot of Monte Cassino, now known as Pope Victor III.

He had not seen Dauferio for nearly a year, and he had to admit the change in him was dramatic. He had been a big, imposing man, but he must have lost a third of his body weight. His skin had a grey tinge, and his hands showed a slight tremor. Chatillon was impressed; his man had been slowly poisoning the Cardinal for several years with an occasional drip feed into his wine and food to debilitate him. It was nearing the end, and he intended to finish it soon. He just needed to find out the whereabouts of the young Malvais boy first.

The Pope waved Chatillon to a chair. 'Chatillon, my friend, I can see the shock on your face at my condition. I am a shadow of my former self, am I not? This illness, this disease, is eating away at me. The physicians can do little; they purge me and bleed me to no avail. However, enough of my woes, tell me what is afoot with Robert Curthose. How are our plans progressing?'

Chatillon related the plan of the French King to use Robert

to defeat his father, King William. The Pope rubbed his hands together. 'So we may have the Norman wolf cornered and then defeated at last. I hope you told them about the Genoese crossbowmen I am sending to Paris.'

'Indeed I did, your Eminence, and King Philip was very pleased and impressed. It has proved very useful to us to keep this French King onside. However, I believe we may have another problem,' he said, fixing the Pope with a penetrating stare.

Victor sat back in surprise while waving his manservant forward. 'Franco, pour us some wine—the Madeira.' The servant placed there by Chatillon many years ago met the envoy's eyes and slightly shook his head. 'Franco, I would prefer mulled ale if possible?' he asked as the servant smiled and moved away.

'The Horse Warriors, the second cohort based in Caen, have returned to Europe summoned back by King William. He isn't stupid—he knows what is afoot with Robert in the Vexin.' Dauferio nodded in agreement. 'William is a cunning strategist, but one of the only defeats of his career was at Gerberoi, fighting against his son Robert.'

Chatillon shook his head. 'As you may remember, your Eminence, the architect of that defeat, wasn't Robert. It was Morvan De Malvais. Now he is back with his men in Caen, back at William's side.'

Dauferio put out a shaking hand. 'You must go and speak with him, Chatillon. You must persuade him to fight for Robert again. Tell him I command him to do so. That it is the wish of the Holy See in Rome.'

Chatillon stared down into the swirling liquid in the tankard. He did not reply for so long that the Pope found himself asking, 'What is it? What do you fear?'

Then he pulled his chair forward so that his knees were almost touching the Popes. 'Why would Morvan De Malvais follow any request or order of yours? He knows, your Eminence. He knows you have his child, and I fear it'll not be long before Morvan and his very formidable brother Luc decide to ride to Rome.'

What little colour that was in the Pope's face now drained away. 'How does he know?' he whispered.

Chatillon drained the tankard. 'I believe that Luc De Malvais found and tortured Monseigneur Gironde to death. As we know, Malvais isn't a patient or forgiving man. My men found the body; it was unrecognisable. Gironde gave up everything he knew and implicated you as the man behind it.'

The Pope's eyes widened in horror. 'But Piers, remember it wasn't originally my plan to find and use the child. It was Pope Gregory's, I was just carrying out his wishes.'

Chatillon slowly shook his head. 'That won't wash with the Malvais brothers. He was taken nearly six years ago—you have held him since. I have heard they are very close to finding him.'

A panicked expression flickered across the Pope's face. 'Is the boy even still alive?' asked Chatillon, sounding disinterested. The Pope seemed to have difficulty answering. His tongue darted out to try and moisten his lips. Chatillon refilled his goblet with wine, which the Pope downed in one. 'Where is the child?' he asked.

The Pope raised his eyes to meet his gaze, and he could see that he was assessing how much to tell him. 'I'm not sure if he is alive. It's some time since I heard from the Master, but I think I would have been told if the boy had died.' Then the

Pope's eyes narrowed, 'Why the interest Chatillon? Are you again getting too close to your protégé, Morvan De Malvais?' he spat.

Chatillon sat forward again. 'This illness is addling your thoughts, Eminence. If you die soon, which is a possibility, I want to ensure that the child does not fall into the wrong hands. King Philip asked me questions about a child that Luc De Malvais was searching for—he knew something.'

The Pope looked alarmed. 'Then we must ensure that he does not find him, Chatillon, if he is alive. I will think about this and send a message to check on the boy's welfare. Come again tomorrow.'

The door opened at that moment—the worst possible time for Chatillon, who had been about to threaten the Dauferio. Benedict ushered in the Bishop of Ostia and, glaring at the secretary, he had no choice but to kiss the Papal ring, bow and leave.

He stalked down the corridors towards the sunshine of the Lateran square. As he emerged, he made for the huge obelisk brought, at great expense, from Egypt by Emperor Constantine. He stood and regarded the inscription on its base, but he did not really see it. The boy was still alive. There was no doubt of that, hence the urgency of the Pope to contact whoever held him. The term 'Master' was a clue. People who used that title were rare. It had to be earned in the Catholic Church to be bestowed exclusively. As he had previously suspected, it brought to mind hard teaching in a military establishment of some description—back again to the Warrior Monks who had told him they knew nothing. Well, he would see how much they did know.

He was determined to find this 'Master' who held the boy,

and he swore he would have vengeance on this Pope. He set off at a fast pace back towards his house. He needed to get Edvard and his entire network onto it immediately.

He ran up the steps and into the imposing entrance hall, throwing his cloak at a servant and shouting for Edvard. Within minutes, he relayed what he had learned from his conversation with the Pope. Edvard looked thoughtful and then suggested various contacts who might know more.

'Go to it, Edvard, send out the pigeons. With over a thousand informers, someone out there must know something, or someone must have heard the title *The Master*. Also, warn all of my contacts inside the Lateran Palace. I want to know who the Pope sees and what messages he sends. We will be staying here for the next few months, and we will be watching him like hawks. We need to know everything Dauferio does,' he said, rubbing his hands together.

Edvard smiled—this was more like it. The chase was on. A boy's life was at stake. Edvard wasn't fooled, though, he could hear the concern in his master's voice. He knew there was a reason for haste. Chatillon thought that the boy would be disposed of if the Holy See feared that he would bring disgrace and retribution to the Pope's door. They just needed to find him first before they killed him.

Chatillon returned to seek an audience with the Pope each day for several days, but Pope Victor's health deteriorated. When he finally gained admittance, Victor's obstinate lips were sealed. He swore he thought the child was dead and was just waiting to confirm that fact.

Chapter Six

For three days, Morvan had spent as much time as he could with Constance without causing too much comment. They had reinstated their early morning rides. At first, all he felt was euphoria, Constance was the love of his life, and she told him that she had never stopped loving him. They had held each other and kissed without restraint as if they had never been apart, but although they both wished to make love, they exercised restraint. They were both married to other people, and Morvan loved Ette. He wouldn't betray her.

The time came for Constance to leave and return to Alan Fergant. So, on that last day, they had ridden out to the cave where they had first made love and conceived their child. Morvan unrolled the horse blankets and built a fire. They wouldn't make love, but he held her, and he told her the truth, that their child, Conn, was still alive.

Constance sobbed into his doublet. 'I'm so happy that he lived but full of sadness that I will probably never see him. He will never know that I am his mother.' Morvan was unsure what to say. 'It's for the best, Constance. It would put your life in danger and his if he knew.'

She had wiped her eyes and surprised him by saying, 'Tell me about Ette.' So he had described his lively, pretty, elfin-like wife, who was fearless in adversity. 'You really love her, do you not?' she asked, her eyes filled with tears.

'Yes, I do. Ette came after you, but I dearly love her and our children.' He had taken her face in his hands and kissed away the tears. 'Now, we must return to Caen before we are missed.'

As they reached the long meadows beside the river, she suddenly pushed her spirited chestnut gelding into a full gallop. Morvan laughed and set off after her. Soon Shadow's long stride closed the gap, and they burst in through the castle gates while scattering people and animals. 'A draw, I believe, Morvan De Malvais,' she shouted, laughing.

'I will give you that one, Constance, even though you cheated initially,' he said, leaping off and raising his arms to lift her down from the saddle. They had gazed hungrily at each other for a few seconds until he swung her out of the saddle onto the ground, reluctantly letting her go. Each of them wrapped up in their thoughts and the moment's sadness. They led their horses to the long, stone stable block in silence.

Ette had managed to travel from Paris to Caen very quickly, in a carriage and with outriders provided by her father, which meant she had arrived more than a day earlier than expected. King William and his courtiers were hunting, so Morvan wasn't there to greet her. She had not been to William's stronghold in Caen before, the new capital of Normandy, so she explored the great keep and bailey. Then she walked in the direction of the training ground, and stood for a while watching Garrett, Merewyn's Saxon brother, put his men and the great war Destriers through their paces.

The Horse Warriors greeted her with smiles, waves and whistles. She had spent several years with them in New Castle on the wild borders of northern England. Garrett had walked over to stand beside her. As a natural horseman and courageous commander, he recently took over as Morvan's Captain, relishing the role.

'Well met my Lady. I hope you found your parents well in Paris,' he had said, smiling at her.

Ette nodded. 'I presume that Morvan is riding out with the King?' she had asked.

Garrett had looked uncomfortable for a few moments and stared at the ground before answering. 'I believe that he has ridden out, but that was several hours ago, and he should be back soon.' Abruptly he left her and went to shout at one of the newer recruits. Ette had stared after him in surprise.

As she came through the small stone gate and archway from the training ground by the river, she froze as she saw them gallop in. She had stepped back into the shadows to watch them. Her hand came involuntarily to her mouth. There was no doubt who this was, the beautiful auburn hair tumbling down her back in waves. This must be Constance, but she wondered why she was here and not with her husband in Nantes. As Morvan raised his arms, she could see from their faces that they still loved each other—the way he looked at Constance had made her breath catch in her throat.

As they disappeared into the stables, she found that she had to put her hand on the stone wall for support. Suddenly a hand came to support her. She whirled around in alarm to find a Captain in the livery of the Duke of Brittany standing just behind her. She had been so preoccupied with what she was watching that she had not heard him arrive. His mouth was in a grim line, and she realised that he must have seen it as well. She drew herself up and looked him in the eyes.

'I am Minette de Malvais, and I am Morvan's wife. They are just old friends,' she had found herself saying. Even after seeing them together, she was still defending and protecting him.

The man said nothing, he just narrowed his dark Breton eyes, and she walked briskly over to the stable block, moving out of the bright winter sunshine into the dark interior. It took a few moments for her eyes to adjust, but then she had seen Shadow towering over the other horses in the far stalls, and she walked down, her feet making no sound in her soft kid boots. She had reached the stall, and then she saw them. Morvan had his arms around Constance, holding her tightly to him, her tear-drenched face tucked under his chin, his lips moving in her hair.

As the anger bubbled up inside, she couldn't help herself. 'I presume that this is the Lady Constance I am sharing my husband with,' she said quietly. The couple leapt apart in shock. 'Does your husband Alan Fergant know of this renewed liaison?' she said, noticing that Morvan could not meet her eyes. 'Well, I am sure he soon will as I wasn't the only one watching your arrival,' she said, and she had turned on her heel and left them just as the Duke's Breton Captain arrived.

Ette heard him say in an accusing tone, 'I wasn't informed that you were riding out with someone this morning, my Lady.'

Ette had needed somewhere to think, and she discovered the small stone-built chapel on the grounds of the bailey. She had knelt there for hours, trying to subdue the anger and the pain she felt. She tried to sit back and view it objectively; this woman had been the great love of Morvan's life, and it had taken him years to recover from losing her and his child. Finally, she wearily stood up and made her way to their room. She knew she had to appear at his side for the King's dinner that evening. When she reached their chamber, it was empty, and she raised her head high. She was Minette de la Ferte, the daughter of the powerful Seneschal of France. She was no peasant to air her emotions in public. She would show them tonight what it meant to have pride.

Having searched for his wife, Morvan had made his way to the Great Hall where the guests were gathering. He noticed that Constance was there, so he made his way to talk to the Earl of Clare.

'Where is that errant son of mine?' he demanded of Morvan.

Morvan bowed and replied, 'Roger escorted my wife to Paris with her brother Ettienne, and I believe he is spending some time with Robert Curthose.' The Earl had looked alarmed at that news. 'God's bones! He had better not join another rebellion against the King, or I swear I will disown and disinherit him.' Morvan secretly hoped the same thing, but he bowed and moved away just in time to see Ette descending the stairs on the King's arm.

Ette had dressed in a deep blue silk gown embroidered in gold thread. Her long, dark hair had been brushed until it shone and was held back with a matching band. Her huge dark eyes in her petite elfin face shone in the light of the hundreds of candles in the Great Hall. She smiled at the assembled gathering, and she had never looked more beautiful. King William brought her to his side.

'The rumours were true, Malvais. Your French heiress is just as beautiful as they say, and she is witty with it. She has kept me amused in the solar for a while. The arrogant Belleme stabbed through the thigh and pinned to the ground? What I would have given to see that.'

His laughter had boomed around the Hall, and heads turned to see who was amusing the King. Morvan looked at Ette. She smiled, but it did not reach her eyes, and he felt his mouth go dry as he led her to the top table.

The meal had been interminable for Morvan, while Ette talked and laughed with the King. Ette had put on the performance of a lifetime, and everyone loved her. She clapped her hands and laughed at the jugglers and acrobats, she teased and danced with several knights at the side tables, but she said hardly a word to him.

Constance, who sat in a sea of misery, had sent her a glance of pure admiration. Morvan's wife had shown them that this was how a woman trained in the courts of Paris behaved when faced with her husband's possible infidelity. Ette had watched her mother doing the same when faced with the numerous affairs of her father, Gervais.

Later, she sat fully clothed in a chair by the bed, waiting for Morvan to appear. He entered and moved to stand by the fire, unsure what to say. The silence had continued, so he crossed and dropped to one knee beside her, taking her cold hands in his. 'I'm so sorry, Ette. I swear I never intended or wanted to hurt you. You know how much I love you.'

She gazed down into his eyes. 'How can you say you love me when you have betrayed me? You have certainly made love to Constance—it was written all over your faces.'

Morvan had found that he had to look away. It seemed impossible to explain, but he shook his head. 'We never got the chance to say goodbye, Ette; she was just dragged away from me by Luc. It was a shock to find her here when I arrived, and we just could not help ourselves. Yes, we held each other, but I swear we did not make love. I would never betray you like that with another woman.'

Ette had found that she could no longer hold back the tears. They ran down her cheeks from her closed eyes. 'Leave me, Morvan. I need to think about what you have said.' She pulled her hands out of his, and he had risen to his feet, leaving to find a bed elsewhere, while Ette sat and sobbed that he still obviously loved Constance so much. Had they all meant so little to him? she asked herself.

Morvan had not returned the next morning, and Ette had dressed in a sea of misery. They still had several days here, and she decided to keep her brave face, but it was hard. She had been just about to leave when Constance had appeared. 'He isn't here; you have wasted your time,' she said, ready to close the door in her face.

'It's you I have come to see,' Constance replied, coming in and closing the door behind her. She stood just inside the door, twisting her gloves in her hands. 'I have come to say that I am sorry. I know that will be no consolation to you, but he told me how much he loves you. Please don't let this ruin your marriage, Minette. Mine has been a living nightmare for the last seven years with Alan Fergant. Often, night after night, he forces himself on me and then publically berates me for not being with child. He calls me barren, but we both know that isn't true. A few months ago, I snapped back that it was perhaps his fault as I had successfully borne another man's child. He beat me so badly that I could not leave my room for weeks. If you tell him Morvan and I have spent time together, I know he will kill me. He is insanely jealous and tried to have Morvan killed before,' she finished in a whisper.

Ette had moved back beside the fire as she considered her plea. 'Do not fear Constance. No matter how angry I am, I won't be the one to tell Alan Fergant, but you must know that his Captain certainly will by his demeanour, while he was watching you both.'

Constance had paled and turned for the door. She stopped her hand on the latch. 'If they find our son, Conn, please try and love him, Minette. I can't imagine what he must be going through, snatched from the people that loved him.' Ette nodded, and the door closed.

She found herself in a quandary. She hated that they were still so much in love, but she also had sympathy for what had happened to them and their son.

It had been nearly eight years since Morvan had set foot in his home in Morlaix, the imposing castle of the Malvais family that sat on a bluff, overlooking the busy little port and fishing village on the estuary below. He had hoped to ride in here with joy in his heart at seeing his mother Marie and his family. However, there was a weight on his shoulders. His son, Conn, had been kidnapped, and his beautiful wife Ette had hardly spoken a word to him since they left Caen over four days before. He knew that the latter was his fault.

They were arriving at Morlaix, something Ette had longed for, but it was bittersweet. Relations between her and Morvan were cold and strained. They had not shared the same bed since, and she hardly spoke to him as she still tried to come to terms with what had happened.

Their party of twenty clattered into the large, partly cobbled inner bailey, accompanied by two covered wagons, one of which contained the children and their nurse wrapped up in rugs and furs. Garrett was here in Brittany for the first time, but many Horse Warriors were returning home to their families in Morlaix, so it was a chaotic scene of cheers and raised fists as crowds gathered.

Ette sat on her horse and surveyed the impressive castle, the Malvais coat of arms and motto carved above the huge entrance. A cry of greeting broke out above the clamour, and there was Sir Gerard de Chanville, loud as ever and large as life, coming down the wide stone steps. He was still a tall, handsome, muscled man with sweeps of grey hair and piercing grey eyes. He was entering his fiftieth year but was still a very fit and formidable warrior, having taught the Malvais brothers everything they knew. He slapped Morvan on the back and whisked Ette out of the saddle like a feather.

Beside Gerard, with a smile on his face, was a very hand-some young man with a shock of black hair and large green eyes. There was no doubt whose son this broad-shouldered young warrior was. 'You must be Lusian, Luc's son,' she said, proffering her hand. He smiled and inclined his head while bowing over her hand like a French courtier.

Morvan grabbed him by the shoulders as he straightened up. 'God's bones, Lusian! I would hardly have recognised you. If you keep growing at this rate, you'll tower over your father and me, and we will have to make the doorways bigger.' Lusian, shaking with laughter, hugged his uncle.

'Where is your father?' Morvan asked, glancing around.

'He is out on patrol, Morvan. I even dealt with a few raids while he was away, but he wanted to see the damage to the cottar's houses. It's Yuletide, so we expect him back tonight.'

Morvan smiled at the confident young man and nodded. A tall, elegant figure appeared at the top of the steps. Morvan raced up them two at a time to greet his mother, Marie De Malvais, still a beautiful woman in her fifties, who flung her arms around the son she feared she might never see again. Ette followed and bowed deeply to her when she finally released Morvan. Ette brought the two children forward and had them bow to their grandmother.

Marie clapped her hands in joy. 'They are delightful. Come inside out of the cold. You must all be chilled, and you must meet Luc's wife, Merewyn, who is waiting impatiently inside with her other children, Chantal and Garrett.'

Once in the Great Hall, Ette was overwhelmed by the warm welcome. She could feel her eyes filling with tears; this should have been such a joyous occasion, but she found that she could still hardly look at her husband and experienced a gnawing pain every time she thought of him and Constance...

'So this is the nephew I have not seen before,' said Morvan, sweeping young Garrett up in the air while the others settled around the huge fireplace. 'Well, I have a surprise for you, young man, for I have brought your namesake with me!' He turned and waved to the young man leaning against a pillar at the side of the Hall. 'This is your Uncle Garrett, who has come from New Castle in the North of England to see you.'

Merewyn squealed with delight and ran to hug her brother, who she had not seen for ten years. She held him at arm's length and looked at him. 'You're looking well, Garrett. Being a trained knight and now a Horse Warrior Captain certainly suits you. Tell me, how are our father and brother Durkin? He must be nearly twenty now. Does he look like you?' she asked, impatient for news from home in Ravensworth.

Garrett laughed. 'As you know, father married again, and he is very happy. Durkin is very like father, a warrior through and through. He was desperate to come and fight the Scots with us, but I told him that as I was signing my inheritance over to him, the Manor and estates would be his when our father dies, so he had to stay and manage it. After an initial outburst of temper, he threw himself into the landowner's role and is now courting a wealthy thegn's daughter from Richmond.' Merewyn clapped her hands in delight.

There was suddenly a cacophony of barking as the many great dyerhounds raced to the doors, and servants began running to help as the Steward announced that Luc De Malvais had arrived home. Minutes later, he strode into the Hall in full Horse Warrior regalia, his crossed swords still on his back, filling the Hall with his presence. Ette could feel the strength and power emanating from him. It was easy to see why so many men feared and were intimidated by him.

He smiled, greeted his guests and called for the massive Yuletide log to be lit as Merewyn served everyone with the heady Yule-spiced wine. Ette settled happily into the chair beside Merewyn and Marie as the men questioned Luc on what he had found on patrol.

Marie placed a hand on Ette's knee. 'This will be your home now, Minette, until Morvan decides where you'll settle. As I am sure you know, he has inherited the large estate in Vannes from his father and brother. Still, he also has other smaller estates on the borders of Maine that King William has given him, and I believe he was recently left a wealthy estate near Milan, is that correct?'

Ette couldn't help herself as she bitterly answered, 'Ah yes, Morvan and his women. He had a dalliance with a wealthy Italian widow, Bianca Da Landriano. She fell in love with him and left him one of her many estates. Chatillon has arranged a competent Bailiff and Steward to manage it, but we hope to visit it. I have never been to Italy.'

Merewyn and Marie glanced at each other as Ette looked away. They could sense there was something amiss between Morvan and his pretty wife.

Chapter Seven

They spent several happy days at Morlaix with the usual family Yuletide activities: feasts, games, musicians, and players who entertained them with plays and jests. Morvan had gone to their chamber each night but always left to sleep elsewhere, once the family had retired. He often slept down in a chair in the Great Hall. This situation, however, couldn't continue; they were staying here for several months, and the Steward and servants were beginning to notice.

The next night he asked Ette to sit on the bed and listen to what he had to say. 'Ette, I know that you can't forgive me, but can we please be civil to each other for the semblance of normality with my family?'

She narrowed her eyes at him. 'I am sure that I will forgive you in time, for you may not have physically made love to her. But I could see that you wanted to, and she wanted it too. You are my husband, the father of my children. I still love you with all my heart, so yes, we will rub along amicably for the sake of your family.'

Morvan found that he had to look away as guilt consumed him. 'I can only repeat that I'm sorry, and I promise I will try and make it up to you, Minette. I don't blame you for being angry,' he said, quickly changing his tunic in silence. After a few moments, he left.

Ette found that she no longer felt angry. She felt numb as if all feeling had left her. The future she had seen for them together seemed to have a bleak pall hanging over it.

Morvan entered the solar and found his mother and Gerard there, sitting close together and very companionably by the fire. Marie was delighted to see him. She had thought she would never see him again, banished from Brittany by Alan Fergant and banished from his home by his brother, for betraying the King. She had been devastated when Conn was stolen from them, and she prayed every night at her Prie Dieu that they would find him. Now, Morvan was here with a pretty French wife. Marie was looking forward to long conversations in French about the gossip and scandals of the French court where Ette had spent all of her adolescence.

At dinner, Ette felt Garrett's perplexed eyes on her and Morvan. He had lived with them for years in New Castle, and he knew that something was seriously wrong. He did not doubt that it was to do with what happened in Caen, but he had no idea what to do. He decided to talk to Merewyn; she had always been wise beyond her years.

The meat courses had just been removed when Sir Gerard rose to his feet, goblet of wine in hand. The family sat back expecting an amusing yuletide speech; however, they were to be surprised.

'I am delighted that we are all here again as a family, with some new additions,' he said, raising his goblet to Garrett and Ette. 'However, Marie,' he said, bowing towards her, 'and I have some news. I have finally raised the courage to ask her if she would deign to become my wife, and I'm delighted and amazed to say that she agreed. I am sure the boys know that

I have loved her since I arrived here nearly thirty-five years ago as a young squire. Still, I never thought she would agree to marry a mere knight such as I.'

He sat down with a thump while a cacophony of cheering and clapping broke out, and Marie leaned over and kissed him soundly, to the delight of the giggling children. Morvan couldn't have been happier for them. His mother's eyes shone, and Gerard had always been like a father to them.

He looked over at Luc, who grinned back. 'He came and asked my permission. They will be married in a month,' he said in a stage whisper that made everyone laugh, as they all raised their glasses in a toast to long life and long love.

Later that night, everyone had retired apart from the two brothers and Garrett, who, after much wine, bravely decided to broach the subject that had been troubling him. 'Morvan, has something happened to Minette? Is it her father?' she seems very troubled, and I have never seen her like this. This change is since her visit to Paris.'

Morvan felt, rather than saw, Luc's gaze suddenly focus on him. He sighed. 'I am in sore need of your advice, for I have yet again done something of which I'm ashamed. But I couldn't help myself. When you hear what it is, I assure you that you can't berate me any more than I have berated myself. It is a situation of my own making, and I don't know how I can put things right.'

Luc, who rarely looked any the worse for the alcohol he drank, leaned forward and placed his hands on the table. 'Tell me,' he said softly.

Morvan sighed again. It was doubly difficult to admit it to Luc, as his love affair with Constance had caused a great rift between them. But it had to be done, so he took a deep breath and told them what had happened in Caen and Ette's reaction. Morvan found that he couldn't meet Luc's eyes.

Garrett shook his head in disbelief. 'But she loves you so much, Morvan. Ette has risked her life for you several times. How could you do that to her?' he protested. Morvan found that his mouth was suddenly dry, and he ran his hands through his hair in nervousness before taking another draft of wine.

'I can't expect either of you to understand what it was like for me to see Constance again, to hold her in my arms again, and she felt the same. We still love each other.' Finally, he risked a glance at Luc's face. To his surprise, he did not see the anger he expected. Instead, he saw disappointment, which was worse.

'Do you not remember, Morvan, that I risked our family here in Morlaix to go and threaten Duke Alan Fergant on your behalf, to demand that he call his dogs off—his assassins—and lift the banishment? I humiliated him in front of his father. He has probably never forgiven me for that and is just biding his time. If he finds out you spent so much time alone with her, it could be a war between our families that won't end well.'

Morvan had no words to answer him. He could hardly explain himself.

'Do you realise that if Ette could see your love for Constance so easily in one day, others could as well? Servants gossip, Morvan. We ignore them because they move silently through and around our lives, but they see, hear, and talk about everything.' Morvan sat forward, his head in his hands. 'I wasn't thinking. I admit I am now paying the price. I will never see her again. We said our goodbyes.'

'As for Ette, you beg her forgiveness, Morvan, and reassure

her that you still love her and your children daily.' Luc sighed in exasperation, pushing his chair back and leaving.

In some ways, Morvan felt relieved that he had told Luc what had happened in Caen. Some of the weight had been lifted from his shoulders, although he still found it difficult to meet his brother's stern glance for at least a week. He felt ashamed, and even Garrett seemed to avoid him, being especially attentive to Ette. Despite this, there were those guilty moments in the dark of the night where he allowed himself to think about Constance—how much he had loved her, how much he still did—and thought of those wonderful days together. He prayed to all of the Gods—Christian, Celtic, and Breton—every night that she might not suffer at the hands of Alan Fergant for her time with him in Caen.

During the day, Ette, as good as her word, responded to him with the family banter and interactions of old. She smiled at him, but it never reached her eyes. He apologised and begged her forgiveness repeatedly. He swore he loved her above anyone else and always would, but they both knew he still loved Constance.

Things came to a head on the lovely spring day of the wedding. Marie De Malvais and Sir Gerard de Chanville were to be married in the castle chapel. Luc opened the castle's gates and had announced a holiday for all the estate workers, apart from the cook and his poor servants who slaved over hot stoves and fires all day, to produce the mountains of food necessary, to feed the multitudes from the town and the estates. Several fire pits were dug and now hosted roasting wild boar and beef.

A dozen huge casks of beer and wine were set up under the watchful eye of the Steward and his staff to make sure some people did not take too much advantage of the generosity. There was entertainment from jugglers and exciting fire-eaters. The monks had come from the local abbey to sing in the chapel, and they would chant and sing psalms outside during the promenade when the married couple made their appearance and thanked the people for coming. More importantly, the Horse Warriors were to perform acts of daring and danger in a performance that afternoon.

The boys and young men of the village could hardly contain themselves, as there had been little in terms of fun over the dark winter months. There would be dancing to an array of musicians outside, in the early evening, with fires lit to provide warmth and a ring of torches to provide light. There would be the opportunity for a stolen kiss or fumble in the shadows. The women and girls were in their Sunday best and looked forward to watching the brave Horse Warriors; many girls from the villages and town had their eyes on the newly arrived recruits.

Despite all that excitement, the simple but beautiful cere-mony in the chapel brought Ette to tears. Watching Marie's shining face as Sir Gerard plighted his troth was too much for her. Tears ran down her face. Morvan put his arm around her and pulled her into his shoulder. To his surprise, she did not resist but tucked her head under his chin and stayed there for a while. 'It'll be all right, Ette. I promise you that I will do everything to deserve your love again.'

Sir Gerard had never looked more handsome in full chain mail, his bright tunic with its coat of arms worn over and his sword buckled by his side. He looked younger than his fifty years, and both Malvais brothers knew he could still see off every knight and Horse Warrior at Morlaix. A courageous, fearless warrior, they were pleased that he had chosen to spend the rest of his life at their mother's side. Marie looked radiant. Early spring flowers decorated her headband, and her long, dark grey hair hanging down her back shone with the perfumes and oils massaged into it. As the priest blessed their union, they turned and faced the packed chapel, and a roar of cheers went up. The couple had never looked so happy.

Chapter Eight

March 1087

As Morvan left Ette and his family behind in Morlaix to return to Caen, his son, Conn, faced some of the hardest challenges of his short life at the Hermitage. As he expected, the two older boys, Verachio and Gustav, had set out to make the lives of the other five boys a misery. They had stolen their food for months and tormented and beaten the younger boys. Now Conn decided that enough was enough. The new additions had been allowed to get away with this under the watchful eyes of the Master and the other monks. When the younger boys complained, they were told to toughen up.

They waited for a night when Father Bruno had imbibed more wine than usual. Conn had plotted his revenge. Everything was ready.

In the darkness, in groups of two and three, carrying ropes and gags, they padded quietly over to the pallets of the older boys. Conn had planned this carefully, and each group carried a small wooden box with a sliding lid.

Conn was the largest of the five boys, and so with Georgio, the two of them tackled Gustav, the biggest boy. Each group stood poised over the intended victims, the moonlight streaming through the high grilled windows, lighting the scene. On the whispered command of 'Go' from Conn, the boys stuffed a gag into the open mouth of each of the sleeping boys and quickly bound their flailing arms and legs. Conn nervously glanced down at Father Bruno at the far end of the dormitory, but he was still snoring. He looked down at Gustav, who glared back up at him in a fury, making threatening noises. Conn delivered a punishing blow to his head, and he quietened.

Conn told both boys that they were taking no more punishment from them—it ended tonight. Gustav snorted with derision until Conn picked up the wooden box and indicated to the boys standing at the next pallet to do the same. They simultaneously slid back the lids, showed the contents to their trussed victims, and quickly turned the box upside down on the victims' stomachs. They thrashed around and tried to scream and shout through the gag until numerous punches descended, and they quietened.

'As you can see, these are yellow fat-tails, the most poisonous scorpions in the world. I keep them as pets, and they know my smell. I feed them scraps. If we bang on the box like this,' he said, tapping it a few times, 'they get angry. If we keep doing it, they will sting everything around them. If one stings you, there is no doubt you will be dead by sunrise. We tried it on Father Bruno's old milking goat. As you know, it died, he was very upset.'

Conn let the silence hang for some time. 'If you do not stop bullying us, I promise you they will be in your bed one night or wrapped in your tunic when you pull it over your head. Do we have an agreement?'

Both boys, the sweat of fear on their brows, nodded quickly. The lids were slowly re-inserted under the scorpions, and the boxes removed. The three boys on the other bed found that Verachio, always just a follower of Gustav, had wet himself in fear. He was cringing with embarrassment, and the boys were shaking with laughter as they undid his bonds. The noise disturbed Father Bruno, who began to stir, so they ran back to their beds.

Early the next morning, as they washed by the well, the difference was noticeable as Gustav deferred to Conn and let him go first. All of the boys received and ate their food unmolested in the refectory. The monks noted this and reported to Master Scaravaggi, who took Gustav to one side and extracted the story. It took a small amount of vicious persuasion for the older boy to admit his fear, not something you did lightly to the Master.

The Master watched the training for a while afterwards, particularly watching Conn with interest. Gustav had been convinced that Conn would happily kill him without a qualm. There was no doubt in the Master's mind that Conn had been the leader and instigator of the plan. The many bruises on the two older boys showed that he was also happy to deliver a beating. It seemed that Dauferio was right. The boy had the potential to become a great leader and then a Master in his own right.

Later that day, the boys were delighted to find that there were large portions of meat on the plates of the five friends. Conn glanced at the monk who served them and caught a half-smile. So the Master knew about what had happened, and he would reward such courage, thought Conn.

The next day began differently with a sermon from the Master. 'You are here because your families gave or sold you to the church. They were assured that you would get the best education and training. Today you'll move up a level in your education and training. It will become more intense. You, the chosen seven boys, will be no mere foot soldiers. You will be future leaders and masters for the Holy Father. You will be respected and revered but also feared.' He let that sentence hang in the air and then turned on his heel and left them to break their fast.

Shortly afterwards, a new, younger monk appeared. He had arrived with Father Mezzi, but they had seen little of him. Like the others, he was a warrior monk with a large blue tattoo of the cross on his neck, but something about him was different. He had dark eyes, but they were alive with interest and vitality.

'I am Father Franco, and I am from Spain. Today we will begin to learn about the history and politics of Europe. We will begin with France and King Philip. Knowledge is everything, and each of you needs to know about the power struggles in the past that shaped Europe today, but also about our present-day rulers and princes—what drives and motivates them and how we can use that knowledge to manipulate them in the future.

This then was their new day—an hour with Father Franco instead of the monotonous learning of psalms. Conn absorbed the knowledge like a sponge and asked more questions than the others, when he was permitted. He would often reach a conclusion or see the implications before the other boys had even thought of it.

Father Franco was impressed and reported this to Scaravaggi. 'He is very bright, very quick, but more importantly, he reasons, he understands, so he questions the decisions taken by former princes. He is a long way ahead of the other boys.'

Conn's outlook had changed with the arrival of Father Franco. He had enjoyed the basic geography and history they had learned previously, but this was different. Working out and understanding European politics and diplomacy, he began to see this as a skill to be developed, a necessity. His heroes became successful emperors and rulers who had defeated their foes with their intellect and armies: Attila the Hun, Alexander the Great, Charlemagne and the more recent King William of England and Normandy, not realising for a moment that this hero was his grandfather and that royal blood ran in his veins.

Only one thought troubled him as he lay awake under his thin blanket at night. The Master had said that they were here because they had been sold. It went round and round in his head, sold or given away, unwanted. So why had his family not wanted him? Who were his parents that he had been given away? A feeling of loneliness and loss settled inside him, creating a knot in his stomach as he weighed up the Master's words, and he knew he could only depend on himself in the future to make his way in the world. The events of the next day confirmed that to him.

When they woke the next morning, they hurried out to wash and were taken to a large room used as an infirmary. Father Mezzi, the odd little monk, and two others waited for them.

'Today is the day of crossing over the river from boyhood to manhood. You may experience a small amount of pain today, but we all have to face pain in our lives and learn how to deal with it, to rise above it. It'll also show me your strength of character as you face these trials.' Conn glanced at his friend

Georgio beside him and raised his eyebrows; some of the recent training sessions with the heavy wooden staffs had been nothing but pain.

'Who will go first? Who will show me they could make a leader?' asked Master Scaravaggi.

There was hesitation as all of the boys stared at the ground. Volunteering usually meant humiliation, but the word 'leader' held an attraction for Gustav, so he stepped forward.

Scaravaggi gave a smile. 'Take off your tunic.' The older boy did as he was bid, and he stood naked and shivering on the cold stone floor. The two monks stepped forward, and taking his arms, they led him to the table behind them. The other boys watched in horrified fascination as they secured his arms and legs with straps.

Meanwhile, Father Mezzi, humming a tune to himself, unrolled a leather bundle to reveal an array of instruments, knives of different shapes and a dozen long needles. Conn's eyes widened as the monk picked up a short knife and made his way to the table. The monk held the knife's blade in a candle for a minute and then plunged it hissing into a tankard full of liquid.

Are they going to torture Gustav? he wondered, his anxiety increasing. *Is this a test of character to see how much we can take?*

Gustav, seeing the monk and the knife, began to thrash about and then, to the embarrassment of the others, he began to whimper. Quick as a flash, the monk wielded the blade and removed the boy's foreskin. 'Now you are a man, Gustav, so cease that noise,' spat Scaravaggi in disdain.

Conn's fear lessened slightly. He knew they did this in many cultures—the boys had talked about it. The two monks were now cleaning away the small amount of blood and spreading a thick green herbal salve on the wound. They released Gustav, who made his way shakily to his tunic. He couldn't meet the eyes of the other boys.

'There will be no training today, so go and break your fast. This afternoon, you'll be back here to receive your tattoo now that you're a man.'

Conn's eyes went to the large blue cross on the necks of all of the Warrior Monks. It was a badge, thought Conn, like wearing the colours or carrying the shield of your Lord or Patron. Except this time, it was for the Holy Father, for God.

Father Mezzi was now cleaning the blade, and Conn couldn't help himself. 'Why do you do that, Father Mezzi?'

Scaravaggi whirled around to rebuke, but the monk held up his hand. 'An enquiring mind is healthy, is that not so, Master?' he said, head on one side and Scaravaggi reluctantly nodded. 'I have learned much about medicine on my travels, young man, particularly from our Arab friends, who do everything they can to avoid infection in a wound as it so often kills. So I clean the knife before every procedure.'

Conn nodded in understanding and then stepped forward. 'I will be next. I don't need straps. I will not move now I know what is to be done,' he said, climbing up and lying down on the table. Father Mezzi looked at Scaravaggi and raised his eyebrows, and the Master understood that look. This boy was indeed his father's son, and his grandfather's courage ran in his veins. Father Mezzi was the only other monk who knew Conn's parentage and Dauferio's plans for the boy.

The boys were in some pain and discomfort, but they were still expected to be with Father Franco, to study, for several hours before returning to the infirmary. The table was still there but covered with an old stained cloth. Father Mezzi

70

still had his roll of instruments on display, but there were numerous ink pots.

'As a brotherhood, you'll all have the same tattoo, which will be the mark of your calling. Unlike ours on our necks, yours will be hidden as you walk the corridors of power in Europe. A tattoo is not a quick process, and you'll all spend an hour in here for several days as it is built up.'

Conn narrowed his eyes, astonished that it would take that long. Father Mezzi, now singing the snatch of a song, chose the needles he needed and moved the tray of inks closer to the table. 'It isn't very painful, just the tiny prick of a needle, and after a few, you barely notice it as your body becomes used to it. You can all watch the first one and then return to your studies. Today I will only be doing the outline.'

The boys watched with some trepidation as the eccentric monk unrolled a large sheet of vellum and gave it to the other two Warrior Monks to hold. Conn's eyes widened in amazement as he gazed at the image on the sheet. This was no small tattoo. Father Mezzi explained that it was a sword of power and faith. Conn stared in alarm at this huge sword. It had been turned into a cross with a widened cross-guard on which rested a crown of thorns. From this dripped seven drops of blood down the blade to represent the brotherhood. At the bottom, Father Mezzi explained, flames of vengeance fanned out from the point of the blade. Vengeance against the enemies of Christ, the infidels, the blasphemers.

Conn went cold. He was fascinated and repulsed at the same time. This image was not a tattoo—it was a work of art and a badge. But it was so big. Where was it going?

Scaravaggi led Verachio to the table and made him lie on his stomach. It was going on their backs, across their shoulders and down to the base of their spines. Conn closed his eyes. He would have to carry this image for the rest of his life. A feeling of hopelessness washed over him as he realised that he couldn't escape this trial. Did his family know about this, he wondered, when they handed him over to the monks? Or did they just want the money? A wave of dark, cold anger grew in him that they would love him so little to put him through this life. One day he would find them when he was older, then he would tell them what he had suffered here in the bleak Hermitage.

Scaravaggi left the boys and headed for his study. It was one of the few rooms at the top of the Hermitage, and it had a small window that looked down over the precipitous drop and the valley to the south. He rolled out a map of the area on the table. There had been several raids on local farms by a bandit group living in a valley close by. Livestock was stolen, women raped, and young men had been taken to swell their ranks. Normally the Master wouldn't concern himself too much, but he had heard that a small group of infidel Turks led the band. That alone made them a target for him, but it would also achieve other things as well. The local community was afraid and wary of the Warrior Monks, which was how it should be, but he was happy to accept their gratitude, as they always needed fresh supplies from these local farmers.

This opportunity would also be a good exercise for the boys; their fighting skills were coming on apace, and a few could now hold their own with grown men. Using stealth at night, he would take them on a raid. They had suffered poor rations and hardship for many months because he wanted them to experience hunger and pain. Now for the last few months, their rations had been doubled. They had wolfed the extra meat and cups of rich goat milk down ravenously, and he could see the difference in them as they were filling out and building muscle.

Father Bruno arrived clutching a pigeon. He held the pigeon out to the Master, who took the rolled lead capsule from the bird's leg. 'From Rome,' said the old monk. Scaravaggi unrolled the message and then sat and decoded it. As he read, his face darkened. 'Is it bad news?' asked Father Bruno.

The Master snorted with derisive laughter. 'I know that Dauferio has been ill for some time, but I think he has finally lost his mind.' Father Bruno raised his eyebrows. 'The Malvais family are still searching for the boy. After many years, his father, Morvan De Malvais, arrived back in Normandy. Dauferio thinks they are getting too close. He wants us to kill the boy or move him to another group near Naples or even to the one outside Monte Cassino.'

Father Bruno shook his head in dismay. 'You can't do that. He is a natural leader, the best in the group. You have invested so much into him already.'

Scaravaggi agreed. 'Do not worry, Bruno. That boy is going nowhere.'

Father Bruno turned to leave and paused. 'And this made you laugh?'

Scaravaggi shook his head. 'No, it was the second part of the message. Dauferio thinks that Chatillon is becoming dangerous, that he knows too much. He wants us to kill him.'

Father Bruno's mouth dropped open. 'Kill Chatillon? He is always dangerous,' he whispered.

'I know. It's a huge joke, is it not? An assassin is sent out to kill the most lethal assassin in Europe. As I said, the Pope must be losing his mind.'

Father Bruno breathed a sigh of relief. 'Good. We must stick to the plan. We don't want to be involved in plots that could endanger us. Those boys are our future. Also, Chatillon and his minions would see us coming, and someone in Rome would have read that message already,' he announced.

Scaravaggi waved him away and sat at his table deep in thought for some time. He had to admit that Dauferio was right. If anyone could find the boy, it would be Chatillon with his web of spies and informers. Had he perhaps found him already? Did he know he was here at the Hermitage? Was he just waiting for the right moment?

Perhaps Dauferio's idea was not quite as mad as it seemed. Maybe they needed to cut the head off the snake. He reached for a quill and began coding a message to Milan, asking them to find out exactly where Chatillon was at present. Once he knew that, he would think of how to deal with him.

Chapter Nine

Chatillon had, in fact, just arrived in the newly formed Republic of Genoa, a thriving city-state on the northwestern coast of Italy, in the wealthy province of Liguria. After centuries of rule by Lombardy and then the Frankish Holy Roman Empire, Genoa had finally emerged as an independent, wealthy trading power.

Chatillon shrugged off his dusty cloak and opened large wooden shutters, onto an impressive balcony, while Edvard chivvied the servants to unload the chests. He stood for a while, his hands resting on the stonework, looking out over the bustling port. To his right, the city stretched up the hillside where a forest of impressive stone-built towers or Torre, each trying to outdo their neighbour in height and decoration, dominated the skyline. These towers had been springing up in Italian cities for some time. Not only because of the frequency of war between the warring republics, as they vied for power, but also because of the fighting family factions within the cities. With the significant rise of the noble merchant families, they had been drawn into civic politics, each family vying for positions of power.

Most of the towers were attached to the fortified residences of the families. This made for plotting, scheming, feuds, and constant social tumult, so Chatillon limited himself to essential visits to Italian cities. However, Genoa was better than most and was now under the rule of a powerful Signori, Guglielmo Embriaco, an interesting man.

Chatillon was in the city for two reasons. The first—his lost love, Bianca Da Landriano, had left him this large stone Castello, or house, nestling on the southern hillside of the city. It perched on the cliffs, an impressive edifice with extensive walled gardens overlooking the bay. A wealthy widow, she had spared no expense in its decoration with Byzantine mosaics on the walls and marble pillars, with, of course, several balconies to greet the morning sun and watch the sunset.

He had been there only a day when Edvard came to him, concern etched into his face. 'Sire, I have spoken to the Contessa's household. The Steward has done a good job maintaining the Palazzo Castello and in opening it up for your arrival.'

Edvard paused, and Chatillon raised his eyes again. 'And?' he questioned, knowing that Edvard wouldn't usually bother him with this. 'There are twenty servants in total, but fifteen are slaves of various nationalities.' Chatillon wrinkled his face and sighed. This practise was common in most maritime communities, which ran slave markets.

'Give them their freedom Edvard. We do not employ slaves. Those who wish to stay will have a roof over their heads, food and the usual small yearly stipend.' Edvard smiled, his master would cut a throat without a backward glance, but he found slavery distasteful.

Chatillon sat on the balcony in the shade. The day's sun had baked the stones around him, but a pleasant breeze now drifted across the bay. He lifted the carved Venetian glass to his lips and took a mouthful of the dry white wine, cultivated on the slopes above the city. His mind was now on the second reason he had come to Genoa, for Chatillon was here to find a wife.

Signori Guglielmo Embriaco was a naturally suspicious man. He had to be as the head of one of the most powerful families in Genoa. He was not only of wealthy merchant noble stock but was also a successful military commander. He was one of the founders of the new Republic of Genoa. He wasn't a man to be trifled with or taken lightly, and he had a fierce determination to protect the Compagna or, Company of Genoa, from any threat.

Nonetheless, he now had a problem; a Papal Envoy had arrived in his city, not just any Papal Envoy but Piers De Chatillon, a name to send a shiver of fear down the spine of any God-fearing man. He asked himself, *Why was this man here? More importantly, what does he want with me?* Chatillon had requested a meeting, and of course, Embriaco had invited him to dine with other notables at his house that evening. Embriaco's brows drew together. Genoa had spent decades trying to throw off the yoke and interference of the Holy Roman Emperor; they did not need Papal interference in their newly created Genoan Maritime Republic.

Chatillon dressed with more care than usual that evening in an embroidered dark blue velvet tunic with the new, popular, wider sleeves. His neck was adorned with his gold chain of office, and he sported a heavy gold ring with a large ruby at its centre. His dark hair was lightly oiled so that it shone, as did his newly trimmed short beard. He was a tall, handsome, lean but muscular, virile man, and he certainly did not look his forty years of age. Edvard, handing him his blue, silk-lined cloak, smiled as he knew some of what was afoot in Genoa. The sun set behind them in a blaze of glory as they walked up the hill, through the narrow streets, towards the impressive Embriaco residence.

On arrival, they were shown into a grand entrance atrium where servants waited to take their hats and cloaks before leading them through the huge, carved, double doors, which opened into a richly adorned, high-ceilinged chamber. A large company of people were gathered in small groups talking quietly. Word had gone out that Chatillon was in Genoa, so most of the influential members of Genoese society were here tonight, intrigued as to why he was in their midst.

'Monseigneur Piers De Chatillon, Envoy to the Holy Father Pope Victor the third,' announced the Steward in stentorian tones. The nobles bowed their heads in recognition, and Embriaco came forward to greet Chatillon.

'It's an honour to have you here, Monseigneur. It's certainly not your first time in our city, but it's your first time in my home, and we welcome you.' Edvard had left his master's side and stood quietly in the shadows of the pillars, ever watchful.

A very pleasant and interesting evening ensued. Many topics were discussed as Chatillon, well-informed as ever, brought news from the courts of London, Paris and Caen. However, apart from admitting he was now the owner of Bianca Da Landriano's Palazzo Castello and estates, he gave no reason for his visit to Genoa, to the frustration of many who couldn't believe that such a man was there only to view a house.

Meanwhile, Chatillon watched the wealthy and powerful families around him—some he knew, and some he did not.

One woman caught his eye, as she wouldn't immediately meet his glance. Every time he felt her eyes on him, he looked up, but she immediately turned away. As they rose from the tables to mingle and listen to the music, he strolled over to Edvard. Indicating the attractive, richly dressed woman, and said, 'Find out who she is, Edvard. She seems very familiar.' Edvard nodded and moved back to his place.

Meanwhile, the great and good flocked to his side to issue invitations to all manner of events to enliven his stay. Gradually people began to leave as the evening wore on, and Chatillon, talking to Embriaco, suddenly found himself face to face with the woman in question. She had large, clear, grey eyes that he seemed to recognise, but she immediately bowed her head while thanking her host for a pleasant evening. Chatillon had seen the anxiety in her eyes, and he knew they had met before. Had he bedded her? he wondered. She was certainly an attractive, handsome woman with large breasts and a long willowy figure. He sighed; there had been so many married women, and he couldn't remember them all.

'Signora Di Monsi, may I introduce Monseigneur Piers De Chatillon.' He bowed over her hand as Embriaco moved away and left them alone but held on to it longer than was necessary. 'I seem to think we have met before, Signora?' he asked.

She dropped her eyes and shook her head. 'I don't believe so, Monseigneur, although we may perhaps have been at other receptions.' He still held her hand in both of his, and he lightly stroked it while giving her his most engaging smile. 'Perhaps it would be to our advantage to get to know each other better,' he suggested.

She slowly removed her hand, but he could see her breasts rising with her quickened breathing, and there was a slight flush to her cheeks. 'I don't mix in society very much. I am always busy with my business and my daughter,' she said, her large, grey eyes meeting his dark, almost black ones. She had difficulty pulling her eyes away, but she knew she was in danger and had to leave immediately. Therefore, she bowed her head to him in farewell and took her leave.

Chatillon watched her tall, graceful figure sway towards the great doors, her servants rushing to place her cloak around her shoulders. They had met, he was sure—he remembered those beautiful eyes—but where? She was obviously wealthy and influential, or she would not have been invited. He needed to know more. He was intrigued by her, the desirable Signora Di Monsi.

Despite that, he needed to get to the matter at hand. 'Cavalieri Embriaco, can I beg a few moments of your time alone?'

Embriaco smiled and led the way to his study. *Now for the crux of the matter, we will find out why he is in Genoa*, he thought as he opened the door. However, nothing prepared him for the conversation he was about to have, as he poured two glasses of sweet Muscat wine, and they settled into two comfortable chairs near the window.

'So, Genoa is buzzing with activity and business Embriaco. You have successfully set up a maritime republic here that will benefit all your noble merchant families.' Embriaco smiled and sat forward with enthusiasm. 'We are building our own fleet, Chatillon, and building new trading alliances across the Mediterranean.'

Chatillon nodded sagely. 'Yes, a brave move that had come to my attention. What cargoes are you carrying out? Goods from your rich hinterlands, I presume. Grain? Cotton?

Necessary staples for the urban cities such as Rome.'

Embriaco narrowed his eyes. He wondered with alarm clear to see on his face. *Does the Pope want to extend his influence here to tax this wealth for the church somehow?*

'I can see that you have established yourself as a leader, the Signori of the city. I must commend you for such a move. You have come far from your days as a pirate,' He laughed. Embriaco smiled but now felt uneasy at the probing questions and flattery, so he suddenly blurted out, 'Why are you here, Chatillon? What do you want of us?'

Chatillon twirled the wine in his goblet. 'I believe you have two sons and a difficult daughter—what is her name?'

Embriaco's eyebrows rose. 'Her name is Isabella. She is with her mother visiting her grandparents in Milan. They return tomorrow.'

'Do you have many suitors for her hand?' asked Chatillon.

A thought suddenly occurred to Embriaco, but he instantly dismissed it. He knew that Chatillon preferred beautiful, older, intelligent women. He wouldn't be interested in a headstrong girl such as Isabella. Part of him wished that he would be, as his daughter was the bane of his life. She was stubborn and spoilt—her mother's fault. She had turned down half a dozen men over the last year alone. 'There have been several, but none were found to be suitable,' He finally answered with a sigh.

'Suitable to you or to her?' Chatillon asked astutely with a raised eyebrow and amused tone that made Embracio colour up. God's bones, the man was annoying. He seemed always to know the crux of the matter. 'And if I was to offer my suit, would I be found to be… suitable?'

Embriaco's mouth dropped open in astonishment. 'Monseigneur, we would be honoured,' he said quickly, thinking of the advantages for his family, for his position in Genoa and indeed in Italy if he allied himself with this powerful and influential man.

'I will call and meet your daughter tomorrow evening if that is convenient?' suggested Chatillon.

'Of course, Monseigneur. I will arrange an intimate family dinner.' Chatillon drained his goblet and took his leave, pleased with how the evening had gone and certainly leaving his host with food for thought.

Edvard was waiting with his cloak. 'So what did you find out?' he asked.

'I talked with her servants and the Steward here. She is a wealthy merchant and a widow here in Genoa. He believes she has been here for nearly ten years. She has a daughter but has never remarried. She is a very private person who rarely goes out or travels.'

Chatillon thought about this. So, where had he met her? Was she a friend of Bianca? 'Is she Italian?'

'They seemed unsure. She speaks Latin, but they seem to think she came from western Europe—France possibly.'

'Well done, Edvard. For now, it must remain a mystery—we have other things in hand to arrange.' And with that, they set off down through the narrow, dark streets back to the palazzo.

They had not gone far when Chatillon leaned towards his manservant and whispered, 'Have you seen them?' Edvard nodded. 'How many do you think?'

'I have noticed only two so far, Sire. They are clinging to the walls and deep shadows, creeping closer behind us.'

Chatillon gave a quick glance behind. 'Leave them for now.

I want one of them taken alive if possible. I always like to know who is trying to kill me.'

Edvard grunted agreement, and they quickened their pace across the harbour and up the steep slope. On reaching the large wooden gates in the palazzo walls, they entered and locked them behind them. Chatillon called his men from the kitchens and then took the stone stairs, two at a time, to make for his chamber. He stole onto the wide balcony standing back in the deep dark shadows to watch what happened below. He had no doubt they would try to enter—he was their target, after all.

Edvard gave the armed group of men in the entrance hall orders to wound and neutralise their opponents rather than kill them. Some men were the house guards, and others were Chatillon's trained bodyguards, ex warriors who knew how to fight. They would lead the way into the gardens and direct the others. Edvard was confident as he locked the large impressive doors behind them and made his way up the staircase to protect his master.

Chatillon watched as the two assassins climbed over the walls. He noticed that they were tall, lithe, but well-built as they dropped into a crouch on the ground below. A third hooded man then appeared, but he straddled the wall watching what was happening below.

Chatillon's men emerged from the shadows and attacked. Chatillon expected it to be over quickly, but the fighting was fierce, and within minutes, two of his house servants were down and a further man injured. 'They are very good—definitely trained warriors. I must go down,' whispered Edvard standing in the shadows of the shuttered doorway. Chatillon nodded in agreement.

The man on the wall seemed unconcerned with the fighting below as he put up both hands to lower his hood before staring intently up at the balcony, where Chatillon was concealed as if it was daylight and he could see him. Edvard came out of the doors below with a roar, running at the two assassins. He was a huge and formidable sight with both hands holding a large curved Saracen sword, and the attackers seemed taken aback. The slight moonlight shone on the third man's shaven head as he gave a whistled signal for his two men below to withdraw. They had not expected or prepared for a pitched battle, and one of them clutched his middle, wounded in the fray as Edvard had taken on both of them. Within seconds, they were pulled up over the wall and were gone.

Chatillon was thoughtful as he watched his men helping the injured below. Edvard returned, his hand wrapped in a blood-soaked cloth. 'You're hurt?' asked Chatillon in concern.

'A mere scratch. Sire. They were very good. They have killed Michel, and Roget is badly injured but will recover.'

Chatillon did not answer at first. These were his new servants. He did not know them, but they were still his responsibility. 'See that their families are looked after,' he said, moving inside. While Edvard lit the lanterns and the candles, he dropped wearily into a chair. There had been dozens of attempts on his life over the years—it was a hazard of his occupation. Some said he survived these attacks because the devil looked after his own, not that anyone had ever dared to say that to his face.

He waved Edvard towards a chair and the wine. 'Warrior Monks?' he asked.

Edvard nodded while pouring them both a goblet of wine. 'They all had shaved heads, and the one on the wall had a large cross tattooed on his neck.' A feeling of alarm shot through Chatillon, a rare occurrence, but he had a memory, not a pleasant one, of a large, young monk with a tattooed cross on his neck. He was one of Dauferio's protégés in the monastery at Monte Cassino when he was there in training, on the orders of his uncle. A cruel monk, similar in age but a bully, Chatillon decided to teach him a lesson. He nearly lost his life in the attempt because the ruthless, obsessive acolyte was a master swordsman. *Is that where the boy is?* he wondered. *Is he hidden at Monte Casino? Could it be as simple as that?*

He decided to send birds south tomorrow to see what he could discover.

Chapter Ten

Morvan wasn't surprised that Ette had decided to stay in Morlaix with his family. Although things between them were much better, she had hugged and kissed him in farewell. He hoped the time apart would heal the rift further, as he truly loved her. He had found it increasingly difficult to meet the disapproving and disappointed looks from his mother and Merewyn, who now both clearly knew about his transgression. Therefore, it was a bittersweet moment as he rode out with Garrett Eymer at his side, for they could be away for anything up to six months before they returned.

He had received a summons from King William to return to Caen with his men. The King expected to be back at the end of May, so Morvan was pleased that it would give him time to get the men and horses back up to standard and begin training the new replacement recruits. He was surprised to be greeted in Caen by his comrade and dearest friend, Roger Fitz-Richard, the eldest son of the Earl De Clare. 'Well met Roger, have you come to join us?' shouted Morvan jumping from the saddle and grasping his dearest friend by the shoulders.

Roger grinned. 'Unfortunately not, Morvan. I'm going back to England. My father and the King want me at the side of William Rufus with the remains of the cavalry. My wife and children are here in Caen with me, and we sail in a few weeks. I fear I won't be returning to Normandy as my father has insisted that we make our home on our estates in England.'

Morvan still held him by the shoulders, and he smiled into his friend's face. 'It's probably a good thing, Roger. Your father, the Earl, has been the regent here in Caen since the King left, and if you stayed, you might find yourself riding out against our friend, Robert Curthose, as I will have to do.'

Roger smiled. 'I know. I have just spent a month with him in Paris. I am afraid that he is dead set on a course of war against his father again, with King Philip fanning the flames of resentment. They are attacking the Norman Vexin again as we speak. As Regent of Normandy, they believe that my father does not have the stomach for war. They are wrong. He'll ride out, and I'm pleased you have arrived to support him, Morvan.'

At that moment, Earl De Clare appeared in the bailey. He welcomed Morvan and the Horse Warriors back to Caen and added, 'I believe we will have King William back with us sooner than expected. I received a message this morning; he'll be here within weeks. The Danish threat has been neutralised. After all, King Canute's fleet never set sail, so William is returning to lead his forces into the Vexin.'

Morvan was alarmed. This news certainly did not give him much time to get his rested, grass-fed horses out of the fields and into condition. He bowed to the Earl. 'If that is the case, I must indeed go, Sire. There is much to do. I will see you this evening, Roger. You can tell me of your wild month in Paris.' Roger laughed while the old Earl snorted in disgust.

The next few weeks were a frenzy of activity as men and horses underwent a rigorous training regime. Coats brushed of mud, hooves trimmed, shoed and oiled to prevent splitting on the hard, dusty roads. Long ragged tails were docked, and manes were plaited. However, the long hours in the saddle took their toll: charging, attacking, rearing on command, striking out with fore and hind legs. After a gruelling week, they were beginning to work in unison again, the fighting and biting between the stallions in close proximity had lessened, and the new recruits were beginning to spend less time on their backs in the dust.

Morvan rubbed the sweat and dust from his eyes. It was a very warm June day, and they had been training all morning. He walked up the slight incline towards the gate. Shading his eyes, he could see four or five people there, which wasn't unusual. The training of the big war destriers often attracted an audience. He saw Earl De Clare and his son Roger as he moved closer. Beside them was an unmistakable figure—King William had returned, and Morvan paused, for that meant war was now imminent.

'Well met, Malvais, and how are our Horse Warriors?'

Morvan bowed to the King. 'Certainly better now, Sire, than they were five days ago, and that is only the men!'

The King gave a loud bark of laughter. He knew what intense training they would undergo, 'I intend to ride out in three days or so, but I need to discuss certain tactics and strategies with yourself and my nobles first. Roger here tells me that my son has employed a full contingent of Genoese crossbowmen. They could do a lot of damage to your Destriers with those huge ragged metal bolts. I would like to know where he gets the money for these mercenaries. They do not come cheap.'

Morvan looked at Roger with an enquiring tilt of his head,

not lost on William, who pinned young De Clare with a gimlet stare. Roger sighed. 'I did hear it told, Sire, that perhaps Pope Victor had provided them.'

The King banged both of his fists down on the gate with a growl. 'Always the Holy See, interfering where they shouldn't, always trying to extend their influence no matter how much I spend to appease them. I sometimes think that these Popes won't be happy until they take the place of the Holy Roman Emperor across the whole of Europe. I swear I will make sure that this Pope regrets his decision to support my son.'

'I believe that this present Pope may not be with us for much longer, Sire,' said Morvan, to surprised glances from the group. 'I have my own sources who tell me he is ill and very weak. He is moving from the Lateran Palace in Rome back to his original home in Monte Cassino, where he is fully expected never to leave again.'

William looked at Morvan with interest. His Horse Warrior never ceased to amaze him. 'Join us this evening, and you can tell us more, Malvais.' With that, he turned on his heel and left.

Roger remained. 'You're full of surprises, Morvan. I presume this was from Chatillon. I noticed that he was waiting with your brother in Ghent.' Morvan nodded. 'They are still searching for my son, but they think they are getting closer, and once again, it leads to this nefarious Pope.'

Roger could see the anger and frustration on his friend's face. He was the only one, outside of the family and Chatillon, who knew of Conn's existence. 'They will find him, Morvan, I know it's hard, but it's a waiting game.'

Morvan grasped his arm in solidarity. 'It's your last night before you sail for England, so let us break open a cask to friendship, Roger Fitz-Richard De Clare, for you have been the best of friends, and I will miss you and your sage advice when you leave us for England. Now I must rid myself of this sweat and dust.' Morvan strode up through the postern gate to strip off his tunic and sluice himself down under the pump in the stable yard.

Later that evening, a group of men gathered around the table in what had been Queen Matilda's solar. Several weighted maps lay rolled on the table, but the map showing the Norman and French Vexin was spread out and weighted down at the corners. William addressed the group. 'Robert and his forces have attacked and burned villages and manors along the River Epte in the Norman Vexin. Last week it was the larger village of Fourges. They drove considerable numbers of livestock over the river into the French Vexin. We can't let these raids continue. One of my older knights, who maintains two manors in that area, came to plead for my help today. His eldest son was killed in the attack.'

Morvan stared down at the map. He knew some of the background of the provinces. The Vexin was a large, rich, agricultural province to the north of the River Seine. From the time of Rollo, the first Norman ruler, the western part of the Vexin was given by treaty to Normandy. The eastern part had remained under the control of the French Capetian kings. The River Epte, which ran from north to south, was the border between the two parts. Morvan knew that dozens of wars had been fought in this province. The French kings had always seen the Vexin as a vulnerable stepping-stone for others to invade France, and they needed to protect it, as Paris was only eighteen or so leagues away from Rouen.

The Earl De Clare leaned forward and put his finger on the

River Epte near Fourges. 'So do we reinforce the border along here with constant patrols of Horse Warriors, Sire?' he asked.

'That is like plugging a leaking dam full of holes—rushing from one to another. I wasn't thinking of taking a defensive position. I wish to find, punish and defeat their forces. I want vengeance on this French King.'

Morvan followed the province's southern border with his hand, which ran along the River Seine. 'Sire, they have carried out dozens of attacks over the border into the Norman Vexin. Why not take the war to them in retaliation rather than chasing small groups of raiders, as they would expect you to do. I have been to Mantes. It's a large, wealthy French town sitting on a bend of the River Seine. We can cross the border, attack the town, and be back into Normandy before they know we have been there. It's only three or four leagues ride from the border.'

William slammed his palm down on the map, making both the weights jump, as did several of the knights bent over it. 'Now *that* is the strategy I meant. We leave with a small force of five or six hundred men as soon as possible. De Clare, work with Malvais to organise our men and horses. We need to be able to move fast.' In fact, it took nearly a fortnight to assemble the forces and supplies that William would need for such an attack. The delay involved waiting for his cavalry to arrive from England and ensuring that his archers had sufficient arrows; the fletchers worked night and day to provide those.

It was a hot, sultry July day when they were finally on the move. The Horse Warriors were once again going to war, and the people of Caen came out to cheer them and their King on his way to defeat the French. No one dared to mention that Robert Curthose, the King's eldest son, led those French forces.

Robert Curthose was, in fact, deep in the French Vexin. He had set up his headquarters in the southwest at the castle of La Roche, which controlled the river crossing of the Seine, one of the main routes out of Normandy. If his father was indeed going to attack the French Vexin, his followers told him that this crossing would be the place he would use, and Robert intended to be waiting for him. In Paris, King Philip was also dismayed to hear that King William had returned to Caen sooner than expected. 'So Chatillon was right,' commented the Seneschal, Gervais de La Ferte.

'Yes, he usually is. We should have listened to him, but we were too sure that the attack by the Danes would keep William in England. Instead, the Danish fleet never left the harbour, and now we have William gathering his forces to march on the Vexin,' said King Philip, a worried frown on his face.

'Robert has beaten him before, Sire.'

'Yes, but he had the sharp mind of Morvan De Malvais and the strength of the Horse Warriors on his side. Now I believe that Malvais rides with the King. How did we let that happen?' he said querulously.

Gervais tried to reassure him. 'Robert has a strong position on the River Seine, a good defensive position in the huge stone donjon on the cliffs of La Roche. Also, he has hundreds of Genoese crossbowmen who will deliver a blow to the Horse Warriors.' The King did not look convinced as the Seneschal bowed and returned to his chambers.

Gervais found himself in a quandary. They needed Robert to win and defeat his father, King William, so that Robert could become Duke of Normandy. However, Morvan was his son in law; he admired and respected him. He prayed that a bolt from a Genoese crossbow did not find him or that beautiful black stallion he rode.

Chapter Eleven

It was a beautiful early summer morning in Genoa, the sunlight reflecting off the waves lapping at the dozens of ships and boats in the crowded harbour. Two women stood in windows in different parts of the city, gazing out at the bustling, noisy scene below, watching the dock wallopers loading and unloading ships, both not really seeing it as their minds were elsewhere. The dock scene below meant nothing to the younger woman, as she had seen it most days of her life. It was just part of the tapestry of life in Genoa. It was of far more significance to the older woman who had made a considerable fortune in trading goods and investing in several warehouses behind the wharves.

However, this morning, she had other concerns as she pulled the silk shawl around her shoulders and sat down in the carved wooden chair on the balcony. In her early thirties, she was a very handsome woman with distinctive, large, grey eyes. She was independent, proud, and had worked hard to win the respect of Genoese society with her business acumen and ready wit. She had never married again after the death of her husband. Instead, she had focussed on expanding her trading empire and bringing up her daughter, who was now coming up to seven years old and the image of her father.

All of this was under threat because of one man: a tall, dark, wealthy Frenchman who appeared at the Embriaco dinner last night. Piers De Chatillon. She had seen him only a few times nearly eight years ago, but she had never spoken to him. Now she was worried that he had recognised her.

She had been pleased to get the invitation to meet the Papal Envoy, who had now taken a large palazzo in Genoa. As a wealthy businesswoman, she had gone because she was concerned about Papal interference or expensive levies. She recognised Piers De Chatillon as soon as she saw him, and a cold shiver went through her. He was a tall, distinctive handsome man with the darkest eyes she had ever seen. He had an air of supreme confidence about him. Even years ago, she had seen his effect on others, their nervousness and apprehension. This man had a mind like a razor, and he never forgot anything—so quick, always watching and listening when appearing unconcerned.

Now she expected a knock on the door. She was not naïve; she had seen his manservant questioning the other servants, hers included, about the Signora Di Monsi. She realised that he couldn't quite place her, but she thought it was only a matter of time before he remembered. So she set off around the Great Hall, on her own quest, to gently elicit as much information as she could about Chatillon, for forewarned was forearmed. What she heard amplified her fears. Cunning, intelligent and ruthless, he was here in her home, and it wouldn't be long before he realised who she was. He would discover the name she had left behind many years ago, and then what would happen? Would he expose her? Would he blackmail her? Would he hand her over to the authorities?

A knock sounded on the large wooden gates that opened

onto the narrow street below. She heard her servant talking to someone before closing and barring the gates again. She listened to his steps coming slowly up the marble staircase. He knocked on the open door and then entered before bowing. 'A missive Signora,' he said, handing her the neatly folded sheet of expensive vellum. She went cold as she saw the Papal seal on the back.

She broke it and unfolded the thick vellum sheet, smoothing it out on the table and waving her servant away. She read the contents twice and gave a sad smile. *So it begins,* she thought. She must send her daughter, Marietta, into the countryside for a few days. They had a beautiful villa and farm up in the hills behind the city, and her daughter loved it there, riding her horses. She needed the child somewhere safe while she dealt with this, for Chatillon was coming. He had requested an audience that afternoon, and she had no idea if she would have any future in the city that she loved after that meeting.

The younger woman's problems paled into insignificance compared to those of the Signora Di Monsi. They were causing a gamut of emotions: anger, disbelief, frustration and absolute incredulity at the situation she found herself in this morning.

They had returned to their home in Genoa from Milan in the early hours. They had travelled overnight to avoid the building heat and the dust from the very busy road leading into the city, it had been a relief to get out of the bone-shaking carriage, and she had intended to head to her room to wash and sleep. However, her father was awake and waiting for them in the huge entrance atrium, and he had immediately whisked her mother away to his business room. For a few moments, she had wondered what was afoot. Had someone died? However, not long afterwards, her mother had appeared in her room.

'Come, Isabella, sit here on the bed. I have surprising and wonderful news for you,' she said, taking her daughter's hands and leading her to sit. 'You are to be married,' she had announced.

Isabella's eyes widened. 'What? Who to? Has father given in? Will father now accept Alfredo?' she had asked, hope and surprise in her voice.

Her mother had spat the name out with contempt. 'Alfredo Di Lorenzo is a nobody from a debt-ridden family of fraud-sters. Your father and I would never allow such a disastrous liaison with the name of Embriaco.'

Isabella's lips had set in a tight line of anger. 'Well. Mother. I will not be marrying anyone else, I promise you, whoever he is!'

Her mother had ignored her. 'His name is Piers De Chatillon, an important Papal Envoy, a powerful and wealthy man in his own right with estates and property all over Europe.'

Isabella gritted her teeth. If her mother had expected her to be impressed by that, she was about to be disappointed. 'Papal Envoy? You are marrying me to a priest?' she had shouted.

Her mother had shaken her head. 'No. Chatillon never took holy orders. He became a papal secretary and is now a consummate diplomat and politician for the Holy See. He has the ears of many rulers and princes in Europe.'

'So he is old! Did his wife die? Are his children my age or older? How can father even think I would find this acceptable?' she hissed.

Isabella had always found it easy to bend her parents to her will, but she had not liked the mulish expression around her mother's mouth. 'Your father wants to see you in his business room now, and I suggest you moderate your tone, or you may not like the outcome.' Her mother had risen and held the door open for her.

Sometime later, she had emerged, red-eyed, from her father's room. He had never shouted at her like that before—even the servants in the kitchen must have heard him. She had made her way back to her room and flung herself face down on her bed. They were marrying her off to someone she had never met who was undoubtedly as old as her father. A diplomat and politician, a man who would be as stale and boring as week-old bread. Nonetheless, she had no choice; her father had threatened her with the nunnery at the Abbey Di Capodimonte if she refused. Her life was over, she thought, as she sobbed into the bolster and beat it with her fists. She had no idea what the future now held for her.

Further to the west, a third, deeply unhappy woman stared at the stone walls of her chamber. She had been kept a virtual prisoner since her return to Nantes. Hoping to delay her return to her husband, Alan Fergant, she had persuaded her brother Prince Henry to travel with her to Falaise, their father's childhood home. She had tempted him with the thought that if Robert were killed or injured in the forthcoming battles in the Vexin, Henry would inherit the Dukedom. This thought had certainly occurred to Henry, so he gladly accepted the idea of showing himself to the people at their main fortresses. Although Robert Curthose was her favourite brother, Constance knew her younger brother Henry was clever, cunning and quite avaricious, and so they went to spend Yuletide at Falaise together. At the same time, her husband became even angrier waiting for her in Nantes.

The Steward and staff had been delighted to have a royal party arrive at Falaise, although the old fortress held bitter-sweet memories for Constance. She had spent the secret months of her confinement here, and she had given birth to her son, Conn, holding him for a short time before he was taken away. Following that, she was forced into a hand-fasted marriage with Alan Fergant, the powerful Duke of Brittany.

Constance had sent her husband a message inviting him to Falaise for Yuletide, but he refused, demanding that she return immediately to their home in Nantes as she had already been away too long. Constance had ignored his demands; she knew that his sour-faced Captain would report what he had seen her doing, riding out each day with Morvan De Malvais in Caen.

After a pleasant interlude in Falaise, it was mid-January when she had finally returned to a cold mannered, angry husband in Nantes. Within an hour of her return, he had come to her chamber and beaten her so badly that she thought she would die this time. It was only through the intercession of his old nurse, Marta, that she had survived. She had come running into the chamber and spread herself over the top of Constance, telling him that the Lord God would never forgive such a transgression if he killed her and, more importantly, she was King William's daughter. He had stormed out in frustration.

Since then, she had been a prisoner in her chamber, denied access even to the garden or chapel. The only people she saw were Marta, his old nurse, and the chaplain, who came to pray with her every day. Still, her husband denied her the sacrament each Sunday. He accused her of adultery, and he tried to force her to confess on her knees to the chaplain that she had yet again played the whore with Malvais. She denied it repeatedly, but he did not believe her.

She had seen nothing of her husband for the last seven months, which was strange. This man had forced himself on her four or five nights a week, constantly trying for the heir he wanted so badly. To her surprise, he appeared that afternoon. He looked fit, tanned and healthy, a warrior and Breton lord in his prime.

'I hope you have had ample time to consider and do penance for your wanton, whore-like behaviour. I hope you have begged God's forgiveness every day for breaking the sanctity of the sacrament of marriage,' he said in a level, controlled voice while pulling her to him and gripping her chin, forcing her to look up at him. She felt herself colour up at his words, for some were true. She loved Morvan and betrayed her husband in her thoughts. 'Marta assures me that your courses have appeared each month, and you're not carrying another Malvais bastard that I would be forced to kill.'

Constance had to bite her tongue not to say a word. Oh, how she would have loved to throw back in his face that Conn lived, despite his attempt to murder him. However, instead, she raised her head and stared back at him with an expression of defiance and triumph in those huge blue eyes. He stepped back, releasing her chin to look at her. She was so beautiful with those long, curling, bright auburn locks that hung to her waist and that hourglass figure. She looked every inch a Duchess, and he desired her, lusted after her, despite the many mistresses he had taken in the last year and even though he believed that she had lain with Malvais.

'I will be back in your bed tonight and every night. I need an heir, and God help you if you can't give me one. Bring up a tin bath, Marta, with water as hot as she can stand it. I want every inch of her scrubbing until her skin is raw. I want the stench of Horse Warrior off her body,' he snarled, and turning on his heel, he made for the door. Marta followed him out, shaking her head. He was waiting outside in the corridor.

'You watch her like a hawk, Marta. Never leave her alone. Ensure she takes no medicine or herbal drinks. If she gets with child, make sure she keeps it. I beat it out of her maid that she was drinking potions every month to prevent carrying a babe, my babe,' he hissed at her, the anger making the veins stand out on his forehead.

Marta put her hand over her mouth, in shock, as he took a deep breath and continued. 'She has three months. After that, if no child is forthcoming, we will be giving her our own herbal tonic, a special one to aid conception,' he said with a knowing look. Marta nodded, but she knew exactly what tonic that would be. The Duchess would be dead in a matter of weeks if she did not produce an heir.

The door closed behind them, and Constance sat forlornly on the bed. A thin-faced young woman now sat sewing in the corner, another of his servants set to watch her. He would be here every night—that was all she could think. She knew what that meant. She knew just how brutal and forceful he would be. How could she bear it again when she loved Morvan so much. Constance thought about her future; she wanted to run, but where could she go? Her mother was dead. Her father, the King, would never understand—duty to a husband was duty. She would have to suffer it until she found a way out. Perhaps if she offered to go to a nunnery, to let him marry again, he would let her go. This thought gave her some comfort, some hope for an otherwise bleak future.

Chapter Twelve

Chatillon was somewhat preoccupied. He had a busy but pleasant day ahead, with a visit to meet the very attractive Signora Di Monsi. Later this evening, he was to meet his future wife. He knew that she was young and could be somewhat of a handful. Chatillon had always enjoyed spirited women, and he looked forward to shaping her and moulding her while ensuring she kept that fiery spirit.

The door swung open, and Edvard strode in to interrupt his reverie. 'I thought you might want to see this immediately,' he said, handing the small piece of rolled-up paper to his master.

Although it was in code, Chatillon, having used that cipher for several years, grasped its contents immediately. As he read, his face lit up; finally, after no leads whatsoever, they finally found a mariner-come-smuggler who remembered the tattooed horseman and his family. 'Edvard, send a message to Luc De Malvais. Tell him what we have found and get him to meet you in Marseilles. Make sure they keep the man there. Make it worth his while—ply him with silver if necessary. You leave tonight on the evening tide. It should only be a few days' journey.'

Edvard had barely left the room before he was back. 'You have a visitor, Sire,' he said, opening the door. Chatillon's brows creased in annoyance at his manservant. Edvard knew he did not like surprises. Nevertheless, he rose to his feet with a smile as his old friend, Bishop Conrades Mezzanello, came into the room. He had thought the bishop was in Rome supporting his uncle Odo in his campaign.

Conrades was only five years or so older than him. They had spent time together in Monte Cassino and then in Rome, but his friend had taken a different route, taking holy orders which had seen his meteoric rise in the church with the backing of some powerful friends. It wouldn't surprise Chatillon if he became Pope in another ten years or so. He bowed formally to the Bishop of Genoa but then embraced his friend with a laugh.

'Well met, old friend, it has been far too long,' Conrades laughed. 'I heard you paid a fleeting visit to Rome to upset the Pope, he left shortly afterwards for Monte Cassino, and we have not seen him since. I was disappointed to miss you,' he said, settling into the proffered chair.

'Yes, I needed to see the Holy Father on an urgent matter, and I wanted to support my uncle, who we all hope will be the next Pope.' he said pointedly.

Conrades smiled. 'I think there is little doubt of that. He has a lot of support. He is spending his silver lavishly, and I hear that perhaps some pressure has been put on those who might have been wavering?' he asked, raising an eyebrow.

Chatillon laughed. 'Conrades, you always did think the worst of me.'

'Not without good reason, Piers,' the Bishop added with a raised eyebrow, accepting the goblet of wine and plate of fruit and cheese brought by Edvard.

'So I heard the lovely Bianca Da Landriano left you her

Palazzo Castello and extensive estates in Liguria. A sad affair, Piers. I always thought that you two would make a match of it. She brought so much light and laughter into our lives.'

Chatillon looked away across the harbour and did not answer. Even now, her unexpected and pointless death was still raw. Seeing this and understanding his friend's loss, the Bishop changed the subject, 'Tell me what brings the powerful and great Chatillon to my home city of Genoa?'

'I am here to find a wife, Conrades. With her father's permission, I am paying court to Isabella Embriaco.'

Conrades gave a low whistle. 'The biggest catch in the North of Italy from one of the richest and most powerful families. You must know that she is quite... difficult. She must have turned down a dozen suitors, some even wealthier than you.'

Chatillon nodded and smiled. 'You know I don't like insipid women, Conrades. I like a challenge. However, on another note, I need your help.' He then related the tale of the attack by the Warrior Monks with distinctive tattoos.

The Bishop steepled his fingers and leant forward, brow furrowed, before answering. 'Not good enemies to have Piers, but I always thought you worked with them?

'I have, Conrades, many times in the past. They have often proved to be very useful to the plans of the Holy See, but this seems to be a breakaway sect.'

I have been told that half a dozen Warrior Monks had appeared in the city a few days ago. I like to keep my finger on the pulse, but I was unsure why they are here in Genoa. I'm never comfortable with them as they rarely travel anywhere without some reason or task. I have also heard, from various sources, that there have been new communes of these Warrior Monks set up in remote communities across

Europe. However, when I asked about these in Rome, no one was forthcoming—all professed ignorance of their purpose.'

Chatillon nodded. 'I have had a similar problem, and I met with a wall of silence. Someone is protecting them.' They sat considering this for a few moments. 'Do you remember a young monk who trained with us in the early days? Scaravaggi was his name, I think?'

Conrades nodded. 'I certainly do, and I have had several run-ins with him since. He has been attracting, and even taking, young boys from the city and villages in the hinterland as trainees. I challenged him on this, and he said he was obeying orders from above, and if I wanted my career to prosper, I would not interfere.'

'I believe they are creating an army of Christ, calling them Knights of the Cross. They were the words that our veritable leader used.'

Conrade's eyebrows shot up in surprise. 'Pope Victor has sanctioned this?' he asked.

'Yes. Our friend and mentor, Dauferio, seems to have fingers in many unsavoury pies. Can you use your contacts, Conrades, and see if you can locate Scaravaggi for me, as I believe he may well have kidnapped my friend's son for this army.'

'I will do my best, but he has always been an elusive individual, travelling widely and rarely settling in one place for long. In fact, that sounds just like you, Piers.' Chatillon heard Edvard give a snort of amused laughter and frowned across at him. 'I did hear something about him being far north in the mountains, but he has also been seen at Monte Cassino recently, preparing for the return of Pope Victor to his home there, I presume.'

This information gave Chatillon food for thought as he bade

farewell to his friend. The name Monte Cassino kept coming up. Chatillon had spent his formative years there in the old Benedictine abbey and college, perched high on the imposing bluff above the Latin Valley. Most of the Holy See Secretariat did their early training here, pouring over the hundreds of sacred texts and scrolls.

It was here that Abbot Dauferio had taken him under his wing. He had set out to develop the charming young Frenchman with the razor-sharp mind into a young diplomat and Papal envoy, sending him to Rome to work for Pope Gregory. Always with the instructions to report any interesting information back to Monte Cassino. He decided he needed more eyes down there, and within an hour, several birds were winging their way south with instructions.

Two hours later, he was outside the impressive old stone house of Signora Di Monsi. In the older part of the city, it was closer to the port but with high walls and heavy wooden gates, leading to a large courtyard that must have originally been Roman. There was an impressive, ancient Roman mosaic on one wall, from which a dolphin fountain spouted water. Plants and flowers filled the courtyard with several pleasant seating areas in the shade.

A tall, imposing, Nubian servant led him through blue painted, double wooden doors, up a stone staircase, to a large airy entrance atrium lit from an open roof above. Ornately carved doors stood open to an impressive chamber with a wide, stone balcony. The Signora was waiting, and she rose to welcome him, smiling uncertainly, clearly wondering why he was here. He took her hand and slowly but gently kissed her fingers. A shiver went through her. She was unused to a man's touch. Although she had taken the odd lover, they had been brief affairs several years previously. She couldn't deny that something about this man truly excited her.

Instead of taking the chair proffered, he came to sit beside her on a long, low, padded divan, richly covered in silken cloth. Chatillon remembered Bianca having similar new style furniture. As he gazed around his surroundings, everything about the chamber, its furnishings, the beautiful Venetian glassware on the tray, and the silk tapestries spoke of wealth and good taste. Chatillon brought his eyes back to the Signora, who poured him a glass of wine, as he stretched his long legs out and crossed one booted ankle over the other, as if he were a regular visitor.

'Signora, to business. I believe you own several warehouses on the wharves?' She inclined her head, wondering where this was going and what he wanted, more significantly, what the Pope wanted.

She regarded him warily. He was an exceptionally attractive man, but there wasn't only a darkness about his looks—power and ruthlessness also emanated from him. She knew she was strongly attracted to him, but she feared him, which tinged everything with apprehension and excitement.

'I have taken possession of several large estates in the Genoese hinterlands, prime grain-producing land, which will be harvested in a few months. I will need storage for the grain and other products, that my Factor will be selling to the merchants in Rome. Would we be able to do business for the right price?'

She smiled with relief that his request was not more demanding or sinister. As her face lit up, Chatillon knew without a doubt that he had met her before.

He smiled back at her. 'Is it not a lonely life as a widowed merchant in Genoa, especially for such a beautiful woman?' he said, leaning over and picking up her hand again. He stroked it and gently turned it over, lowering his lips to her wrist. His tongue moved gently over her skin, and a shiver of delight coursed through her body. He raised his head and gently cupped her chin. She found his dark eyes mesmerising. 'You know I have wanted to make love to you since I first saw you,' he said, bringing her mouth to his while his hands moved up to caress her breasts.

She raised her hands and placed them on his chest to push him away but found it ineffectual as he pushed her back onto the divan, and she suddenly found that she did not want to stop him. He slowly unlaced the front of her gown, his eyes never leaving hers, and his lips descended onto her breasts. She lay back, eyes closed in pleasure, as he knelt up to unfasten his braies. She felt him lifting her gown, and his hands ran up her legs. She did not object as his hands moved her legs apart, and his fingers stroked her—she lay, just murmuring softly with pleasure. She wanted him. She wanted the feel of a man inside her again, especially this man. She opened her eyes to find him waiting but gazing intently down at her. She found herself saying, 'Yes.'

He laughed, his dark eyes flashing as he entered and drove into her. She arched her body to meet him, her hands kneading his shoulders and caressing his neck, her fingers weaving themselves into his dark, wavy hair. His mouth descended on hers, and she was lost in a sea of passion and forgotten emotions. Afterwards, they lay sated, still entwined together. 'Are you sure we have not done this before?' he asked, grinning down into her smouldering grey eyes and stroking her cheek.

She laughed and then kept giggling as he looked puzzled. 'No Monseigneur Chatillon. Lovemaking such as that I would have remembered,' she said coyly, 'There is so much of you. A woman never forgets that.'

He burst out laughing. 'Yes, certainly not huge, but I have had no complaints. Nevertheless, I know you from somewhere; I would never forget such beautiful eyes,' he said, smiling down at her.

She suddenly remembered the danger she was in and dropped her eyes. Taking the hint, he extracted himself from her entwined legs. 'I think we should do that again very soon, Signora Di Monsi,' he said, refastening his braies. He stood and straightened his clothes. Making for the door, he turned and bowed. 'I will call tomorrow afternoon to finalise our business arrangements. Let us begin a liaison where we enjoy each other without unnecessary strings.'

She began to make excuses, but he cut her off. 'Make sure you're here, Signora, as I intend to see far more of that lovely body of yours.' With that announcement, he was gone, leaving her uncertain about what had just happened, excited but apprehensive. What was she doing? She knew she wanted him to do that to her again. In fact, there were several other things she wanted him to do, but she knew she was playing with fire. He could never find out who she was, or he would denounce her and her life, and that of her daughter Marietta would be in danger.

Chapter Thirteen

With Edvard heading for Marseilles, Chatillon wore his sword that evening to visit the Embriaco Palazzo. He took three of his men with him. He arrived slightly earlier than planned—the family were not yet down in the Great Hall, although other relatives had arrived. The large wooden shutters stood open, on the balconies, to welcome a cool evening breeze. The heat in the city could be stifling in the summer months as the city faced south, nestling at the foot of the steeply rising Apennine mountain range. Chatillon bowed towards the small groups of assembled guests but made his way out onto the balcony.

To his right rose the impressive Embriaco tower. He decided that he would like to see the view from the top. He made his way down the hall to a door that led up some steps to the crenellated battlements. Another door led into the tower, which stood open. He expected the steep spiral staircase, and he began to make his way up when he heard raised voices. Someone was arguing above him. He continued upwards until he emerged onto a half landing with arrow slits on three sides. He paused and glanced down at the harbour below.

The voices above were now clearer. A woman's distraught voice seemed to be belabouring a man for being cowardly and weak-willed. 'You must call him out!' she demanded. 'You have to stop this, Alfredo!' she yelled.

At last, the man responded. 'As usual, Isabella, you have no idea of what you speak. Do you not understand who he is? I believe one of the most powerful diplomats in Europe and a master swordsman.'

'He is an old man, Alfredo. He is my father's age, if not older—a grey-haired cleric. He won't be a match for a fit young swordsman like you. You could at least hold me and tell me how much you love me,' she said in a disappointed tone. It went quiet for a while, and Chatillon continued upwards.

'I must go, Isabella. My father waits below. He is delighted to be invited to this family gathering finally. Your father usually forgets that he is a distant cousin.'

'Go running off to your family and leave me to my fate in the hands of this greybeard!' she spat at him.

The young man gave an exasperated sigh. 'Isabella, there is nothing I can do. Let us meet in the old windmill tomorrow and talk further.'

Isabella snorted with disgust. 'We don't usually talk when we are there, Alfredo, which will probably have to cease now. I may as well throw myself off this tower as face life with an ageing lothario, who complains of his aching joints and can't get his flaccid cock to rise to the occasion.'

Just then, Chatillon emerged out onto the tower's roof. Both of the young people looked alarmed. Chatillon smiled to disarm them. 'I'm sorry, am I interrupting? I just wanted to see the view before the honoured guests arrived below.'

Alfredo bowed and quickly disappeared down the stairs. Isabella turned away and gazed at the sea. Chatillon leant on the wall. 'A lovers tiff?' he asked. She just grimaced. 'It's nothing really. It's just that he has no backbone.'

Chatillon gave a soft laugh. 'Well, my lady, I think you're far too beautiful to throw yourself off the tower because of an arranged marriage. Men need beautiful women like you to enliven their lives, and what a loss it would be when your body smacked onto the cobbles below,' he said, emphasising the word 'smacked' and leaning over and looking down.

Isabella looked with interest at the dark, handsome stranger. He seemed to be complimenting her but making fun of her at the same time. His expensive clothes and gold chain denoted a man of worth and wealth. Now, he wasn't even looking at her, his attention elsewhere as he rested his arms on the stonework and gazed along the coast of Northern Italy. The mountains dominated the skyline as they swept down to the sea. 'I see there is a summer storm coming in, a nasty little squall. It's moving quite quickly. Look at the late-catch fishing boats scurrying towards the harbour,' he said.

Intrigued, she moved over to join him. She rarely took time to look at the view, but with the angry, purple, squall clouds gathering in front of an orange sunset, it was quite breath-taking. They stood in silence, watching the dark clouds sweep towards them, and then he turned and, raising her hand, kissed it before turning to descend the stairs. He halted at the top. 'You could always stay up here in the rain, develop a summer chill on the lungs and die a heroic death, with your parents lamenting how they treated you while kneeling at your bedside.' He grinned at her, his dark eyes flashing with humour as the first drops began to fall, and she found herself shaking with laughter as she followed him down the stairs.

The Signori's small intimate family dinner consisted of about thirty-five people. Embriaco evidently wanted to show off the catch he had found for his daughter. As usual, Chatillon found he felt like a wolf in a flock of sheep. As he crossed the room with his long but measured stride towards his host, the family parted like waves before him. He met Senora Embriaco, still a very beautiful woman, from whom Isabella inherited her looks. A sea of family faces was introduced, including the unfortunate Alfredo, who bowed but coloured up immediately as he recognised him. Chatillon took his arm in greeting and quickly whispered in his ear. 'Touch her again, and I will chop both of your hands off.' Alfredo stepped back, alarmed at what he saw in the dark, glittering eyes looking down at him. Shortly afterwards, he made an excuse of illness to his father and left.

Embriaco looked impatiently around for his daughter, who had not yet appeared. He sent his wife to fetch her. They returned almost immediately.

Isabella was now in a green silk overgown with green ribbons woven into her long honey-coloured hair. She inclined her head gracefully to the assorted family members, but there was a petulant obstinate set to her lips as she was led to her father's side. He was hoping she would be obedient and pleasant. She heard her father's words, 'Monseigneur Chatillon, my daughter, Isabella Embriaco.'

She dropped into a low curtsey, raised her eyes to look up at the older man she was about to marry and met the cynically amused gaze of the handsome stranger from the roof of the tower. She blinked in surprise and even looked around him to see if there was an older man behind. Then realisation dawned, and she was mortified—he must have heard everything she said as he mounted the stairs. Her cheeks coloured up in embarrassment, and then they blanched, for he also knew that she had a lover. Would he denounce or refuse to take her if she did not come to his bed as a virgin? She would be ruined in Genoa or even in the whole of Northern Italy.

Chatillon watched the emotions chase each other across her face. He knew exactly what she was thinking, and he was quietly pleased, for she had unwittingly given him a hold over her. He bowed over her hand and stepped back to look at her, as she lowered her eyes, and her father gushed the usual platitudes. He was pleased with what he saw. She was beautiful: honey blonde but with her father's dark brown eyes and unusual darker eyebrows that framed her eyes; a good height but with a lovely figure. He smiled, for he knew he would enjoy having her in his bed and by his side. Other men would desire her, which was what he wanted.

The dinner seemed interminable to Isabella sitting beside Chatillon. He was pleasant and attentive, picking the choicest pieces of meat for her plate and signalling for her glass to be filled. She glanced nervously up at him. He was a very handsome man, entertaining and confident, completely in control. This wasn't a man that she could manipulate, and he was certainly not the husband she had expected and dreaded.

Embriaco had never seen his daughter so subdued; she was obviously awed by the man he had chosen for her. He signalled for everyone's goblets to be filled, and he stood to raise a toast to the betrothal of his daughter to Piers De Chatillon. Isabella heard the chatter and acclaim break out around her as they applauded what a catch she had made and the implications, for the family, of such a powerful alliance.

As they rose from the tables and moved around the room to accept their congratulations, she sensed wariness and even fear when he approached them, her arm firmly tucked in his. *This is power,* she thought, *when people fear you like this.* She shyly glanced up at her future husband's face. He was a polished courtier. He gave the appearance of listening with interest to all of the conversations and even asked pointed questions, while smiling down at her regularly, his long fingers caressing her hand on his arm.

Finally, he led her out into the coolness of one of the large balconies. The rain had stopped, and the dark sky cleared as he turned her to face him. 'Well, Isabella Embriaco, are you not disappointed that I am not a dribbling old greybeard? Someone who would leave you alone with your much younger lovers once you had given him a child?' He laughed aloud at her expression and pulled her firmly against his hard body. Her mouth dropped slightly open, but she had no idea what to say to him, so she took her bottom lip in her teeth.

'We will be married in two months. I am impatient to get you into bed and hear you squeal with pleasure.' Her cheeks coloured up again. 'Ah, are you worried that you're no longer a virgin? I assure you that I am not. I usually find virgins a dead bore in bed.' With that, he took her hand and led Isabella back into the Great Hall, her mind in turmoil.

Chapter Fourteen

Luc De Malvais and Gerard were in the paddock bringing the young two and three-year-old stallions on in their training when Mathew the Steward appeared at the fence waving to get Luc's attention. 'Benedot, take over and get that grey under control,' he shouted, making his way to his old retainer. 'What is it, Mathew?'

'A message, Sire, from Monseigneur Chatillon. I decoded it and knew you would want to see it immediately.'

Luc took the small piece of vellum, scanning it quickly. He turned and shouted to Gerard, who was riding a feisty young black stallion. He trotted the Destrier over to the fence. Mathew stepped back a pace; he had been caught several times in the past by the snapping teeth of a youngster. Luc handed the message to Gerard, whose face lit up at the news. 'I presume that we leave immediately?'

'We do. I will go and tell Merewyn the news and ensure that a message goes to Morvan,' he said, making his way to the castle beside the Steward. Luc thanked Mathew and sent him on his way with instructions to pack them supplies for a week-long journey.

Meanwhile, Gerard dismounted and handed the young horse to Benedot. He felt a pang at leaving Marie, now his wife, but this was the first real lead they had in nearly two years. They had to go to Marseilles. He found Marie in the new garden he had made for her. Apparently, she had always wanted a rose garden, having seen one once in Paris. So he had surprised her by creating this small, sunny garden behind the kitchen garden and herb beds. He had planted several wood roses and had climbers brought from France. They were still small, but he knew they would grow in this sheltered spot away from the wild, salty Atlantic winds. She had been delighted, and they often came and sat here in the summer evenings, contentedly holding hands and talking through their day.

He leant on the archway he had built and watched her on her knees, weeding and planting some new carnations a village woman had given her. She smiled up at him in a way that melted his heart as he took her hands and pulled her to her feet. He couldn't resist pulling her into his arms and kissing her. She laughed playfully, slapping him away. 'You smell of horses, my love.'

Gerard laughed. 'We are living on what has become a horse farm and stud; we all smell of horses.' She took his face in her hands. She hadn't expected to find love like this in later life, but it had grown from the companionship they had always had.

'What is it? You look pleased. You have news?'

He pulled her to sit down on the bench he had made for them. 'Well, it is bittersweet, my love, for I must leave you for several weeks, if not a month at least. We have a new lead on Conn. Chatillon's men have finally found a mariner who remembers the horseman. This could be the one that points us in the right direction. We need to find out where he took them in his boat.'

Marie rested her head on his shoulder. 'Then, you must go. I depend on you to keep Luc out of trouble.'

Gerard barked with laughter and pulled her to her feet. He held her at arm's length and grinned back at her. 'I do my best, Marie, but I think miracles are beyond me. If Luc does not start or find trouble, it usually finds him.'

An hour later, they galloped out of the main gates of Morlaix on their way to Marseilles. It would take them at least four to five days of hard riding to get there, so they each had a spare riding horse for their packs. On the keep's ramparts, the three women, Marie, Merewyn and Ette, watched them ride along the main road in a dust cloud before disappearing into the trees.

Ette sighed. 'It's ever the same. The men ride out to war and into travail while we wait at home with the children, praying for their safe return. That is if they return.'

Marie turned swiftly to Ette with a frown and placed a finger on her lips. 'Never say that again, Ette. You're tempting fate. Morvan is riding into battle in the north as we speak and God only knows what Luc and Gerard will ride into if they find Conn. My husband did not return from the Battle of Hastings, but my sons have always returned. Gerard has made sure of that.'

In Northern Italy, Conn and the boys gathered barefoot in the dark courtyard of the large stone Hermitage, which clung to the steep cliffs. He had not been outside the gates since he arrived nearly seven years before. This austere, bleak monastery had been his home and his life. Now he was apprehensive and afraid, yet the adrenalin coursing through his veins also delivered a feeling of excitement. They were going out in the night to attack and kill grown, armed men—bandits.

The boys were divided into pairs, a larger, stronger and faster boy with a younger or smaller one. Conn was pleased he was with his friend Georgio. They had trained in pairs for weeks with blunted, heavy, wooden swords that made their arms ache. Parry, thrust, slash, dip under, upward stab. One boy would jump on the man's back, knife to his throat, while the other aimed for his legs, groin or tried to hamstring him. They had become a lethal fighting unit that belied their age. They looked like children until you saw into their eyes reflected the suffering and pain they had borne during their short lives in the Hermitage, along with their burning anger. Scaravaggi could see it, and he wanted to unleash that anger on the bandits in the hills.

Conn shifted from foot to foot as he listened to the final instructions. He stretched his back; the final scabs on the huge tattoo were finally falling off. His back had been sore and itchy for weeks, but they were threatened with a beating if they scratched, as they could make it bleed and ruin the design. So they all suffered, even though Father Franco had given them a herbal balm, which helped.

Finally, with the help of a younger monk, Father Bruno lifted the two heavy wooden bars and opened the huge wooden gates. They filed out in silence after Scaravaggi and the five other Warrior Monks. Stealth, silence, signals and speed were drummed into them. It became their mantra as they attacked and disembowelled the dummies in the training yard. Conn knew that they had at least a league's walk to climb over the rocky slopes before reaching the valley that hid the bandits' camp.

The sky was clear with only a slice of the moon out when Scaravaggi raised his hand to halt. They had just crested a hill, staying close to the ground to avoid detection. They crouched amongst the rocks and looked down on the bandits' camp on the valley floor below. They had set up beside a small stream. Conn could see the faint embers of several fires with dark, sleeping shapes around them. There also seemed to be a wooden structure in the bushes on the slope. As they moved further down the slope, Conn could hear the shuffle of hooves and the odd gentle whinny from their horses. The seventh boy, Verachio, now left them, a small sack on his shoulder. He crept to the south across the moving scree to cross the stream. He had the job of feeding the horses apples to quieten them. He would then untie the hobbles, and when the attack started, he would shout and drive them away down the valley. Scaravaggi wasn't taking the chance of letting even one of the bandits escape.

They slowly descended towards the sleeping men. The mountain stream felt ice cold on their feet as they crossed. Each pair of boys knew which part of the camp they would attack, and each pair had a warrior monk to lead them. After the initial attack, Scaravaggi and the other two monks would attack the makeshift wooden hut further back, where the Turkish leaders would be with the captured women and girls.

A single sentry was nodding over his fire. Scaravaggi quietly cut his throat and gently lowered him to the ground as they took up their positions around the sleeping men. All of the boys stood tensely in the shadows, some apprehensive, some afraid, waiting for the signal—the raised white fist of Scaravaggi.

At last, it came, and they attacked with blood-curdling yells and roars. They were outnumbered nearly two to one, but they had the element of surprise. Scaravaggi went through the bandits with his long, curved blade like a scythe cutting corn as the men struggled to their knees, scrabbling for weapons. He beheaded the first three without a backward glance and then raced for the hut kicking the door open. The men inside now had some warning, and half a dozen stood ready—naked but armed with long, serrated, curved, Saracen blades. The fighting was fierce, women and girls screaming and cowering until they managed to flee naked through the doorway.

Conn and Georgio were feeling triumphant. They had quickly despatched their first two victims, both plunging their blades into the chests of the just-waking men. The third man was more challenging, a huge brute of a man already on his knees, sword in hand. Conn looked around for Father Franco, but he was fighting two men on the opposite side of the fire. The bandit looked in astonishment at the two boys facing him and laughed aloud. This was his undoing.

Conn knew they had to get him before he got to his feet, where he could rain powerful blows down on them from above. He gave the signal for Georgio to go behind, and in an instant, the boy was on the bandit's back, arms around his throat. The man had stopped laughing and was trying to shake Georgio off when Conn rushed at him. Using both hands, he smashed his sword down onto the hilt of the bandit's sword, hoping to make him drop it. Unfortunately, it did not work, and the bandit, roaring, pushed himself to his feet.

Georgio now had his thumbs in the man's eyes as he was taught, but the man swiftly jerked his head and shoulders forward, catapulting Georgio over his head and straight onto Conn, knocking him to the ground. Both boys ended up winded and in a tangle, their weapons gone. The huge bandit stood over them in seconds, glowering down as he raised his blade in both hands to stab downward. Conn froze—he would die here on this bleak hillside. He closed his eyes and hoped it was quick.

Suddenly he heard a grunt as the man's sword clattered to the ground beside them. The boys quickly rolled to the side as he fell to the ground, Father Franco's sword protruding from the middle of his back, the upward thrust into the heart that they had been taught. Conn looked at the prone body. This was all so real. No amount of training prepared you for this. The blood splattered on his tunic, his hands covered in it up to his wrists, the smell as dying men voided their bowels or the burnt flesh of those who fell into the glowing embers.

The monk calmly put his foot on the bandit's back and pulled. The sword came out with a sucking sound and a gush of blood as the boys stood wide-eyed, surprised they were still alive. The monk marked their cheeks with the bandit's blood and whispered, 'You have taken your vengeance on the bandits that were raiding the villages, but there are always some enemy men, or warriors, who may need three or more attackers to take them down. You just met one of them, a bear of a man, but you both showed your bravery.' He bent down and wiped his sword on the man's blanket, and then he ruffled their hair—the first sign of affection that Conn had received in all of his time at the Hermitage. He turned away as the gesture brought tears to his eyes that he had to brush away.

The fighting was almost over; a small group surrendered and were on their knees. One of the monks took cloaks from the dead bodies and handed them to the shivering women and girls. Scaravaggi emerged from the large hut carrying the heads of the leaders. He handed them to one of the younger monks. 'Ride to the surrounding villages. Show these heads to the village leader. The raiders will bother them no more. Father Franco, take two boys, round up the loose horses, and bring them back to the Hermitage. We will sell them.'

It was daylight by the time they had found and gathered the horses. The monk explained that they would ride back slowly; he knew they had never ridden, but he explained the basics. Conn, however, found that he could remember everything, the smell and feel of the horse's coat under his hands, the way they moved, the feel of the reins between his fingers. He suddenly remembered sitting on a huge, dappled black horse. *Was that with my father?* he wondered, as they walked the horses back over the rocky landscape while leading the others. As they reached the crest of the final hill, the horse's name came to him.

'Father Franco, what does Espirit Noir mean? Is it Latin?'

The younger monk looked at him in surprise. 'It means black or dark spirit. Why?'

Conn shook his head to clear it. 'I have a memory as a child of sitting in front of a man on a huge warhorse, and I think that was its name.'

Father Franco knew nothing of Conn's background. He was a dark, good-looking, tall boy who looked about three years older than his age. Conn's question was, however, disturbing, for most of the knights and warriors of Europe knew that horse and its rider. Even as monks, they followed and recorded his exploits and battles across Europe. The horse that Conn mentioned belonged to the greatest swordsman he had ever seen, Luc De Malvais. How had this boy come across the famous Horse Warrior, he wondered. He decided not to mention it to Scaravaggi. The boys were taught never to mention their past lives. The present and the future as part of the Brotherhood of Seven were the only things that mattered. But Father Franco was now even more intrigued by Conn.

Chapter Fifteen

Robert and his forces had been established at La Roche-Guyan for several weeks. The old fortress was in a prime, impregnable, position on a large bluff overlooking one of the few crossings on the River Seine. From here, he had successfully raided the Norman Vexin, attacking villages, burning crops in the fields and driving off livestock. He felt the odd qualm about attacking his own people, but overall, he knew it was essential as a strategy to draw his father's forces north to attack and possibly lay siege to La Roche. They had spent hours poring over maps, and he knew that his father had to cross here if he wanted to retaliate by attacking the French Vexin. Robert had learnt a lot from the tactics and strategies of men like Morvan De Malvais, and he would be here at La Roche waiting for them.

Robert Curthose stood with his entourage and followers in the large upper chamber in the fortified keep when the Steward came in. 'Sire, the Seneschal of France has arrived below.'

'Bring him up. We will show him how well prepared we are,' addressing the assembled nobles around the table. Robert rubbed his hands together, hoping Gervais had brought more money and men from the King of France.

Gervais de la Ferte surveyed the deployment of the troops at La Roche with an experienced eye. 'You have done well, Robert. These tactics should work if we can get him to cross the Seine here, but William is a wily fox. He'll have half a dozen spies here, and he'll know exactly where you are and what you have waiting for him. So why should he come into such an obvious trap? What stops him from riding further up to Vernon and crossing the Seine there? Then he could come down and attack from behind at the weakest point of the fortress,' he said, sweeping his arm to the North.

Robert smiled. 'You think I have not thought of that, Gervais? I know my father; one of his weaknesses is impatience, especially if he is angry. If he rides up to Vernon, it'll add four or five days to his route. More raids will be like wasp stings, and he'll want to deal with this now and end it.'

Gervais narrowed his eyes and regarded the young man. Robert seemed awake to these possibilities. Still, William was the most successful warrior King in Europe for the past thirty years. He revelled in speed, ferocity and the unexpected. 'Where is he now?' he asked.

'I have scouts tracking them and a few spies in his camp who are getting messages out to me when they can. The King's forces left Caen later than planned. The force isn't as big as expected, seven or eight hundred. We have nearly doubled that with the French forces you have brought today.'

Gervais agreed, but he had a prickle of unease, which increased as he sat down to dine with Robert that evening, and he considered why William had brought such a small force.

The next morning Robert was surprised to find the Seneschal already up and standing at the map table staring intently at the River Seine. 'Good morrow, Gervais, have you broken your fast?'

The Seneschal nodded. 'I return to Paris today. Tell me Robert, do you have men at other crossings on the Seine?'

Robert traced the river with his finger. 'Yes, I have patrols and cavalry from here to here. I tell you, a man can't cross without me knowing.'

Gervais frowned. 'Yes, but we are dealing with a wolf, Robert, a dangerous angry wolf who is out for vengeance against you and against King Philip. Just make sure you consider every eventuality. Your friends and followers won't ask you this question, but I will. What will you do if he defeats you? He may even capture and imprison you, which would not end well—he has a history of maiming and blinding traitors and rebels, and you have rebelled against him twice.'

Robert raised troubled eyes to Gervais. 'You think that is a possibility, don't you?' he said in an accusing voice.

'I must admit, I didn't until you told me how small his force is. King William isn't bringing an army to lay siege to La Roche. He learnt his lesson with you at the siege of Gerberoi in a similar fortress. He is bringing an attack force, Robert. I won't be surprised to learn that his force is mainly mounted. This has Morvan De Malvais written all over it. Don't underestimate them, Robert. Now I must go. King Philip demands my presence.' He smiled and clasped arms with Robert before striding out of the hall, leaving a troubled rebel prince behind him, who, for the first time, felt apprehensive as he stared down at the map.

King William's forces were in western Normandy at Evreux. They had been there for several days, resting and then training the horses and men. Morvan rode out on patrol several times a day. He had seen Robert's scouts, he even recognised one of the Captains who had been in Scotland with them, and he raised a fist in greeting. The armies always tracked and watched each other; it was de rigueur.

As usual, he could smell the camp long before he rode into it. You could not put so many men and horses together in close quarters without the strong stench of the latrines and horse manure. There was also the smell of hundreds of cooking fires, men heating pottage or roasting rabbits. Morvan realised he was hungry. He leapt out of the saddle, handed Shadow to his squire and grabbed some bread and cheese before heading for William's double pavilion.

The usual entourage was evident, as William sat in his ornately carved camp chair and regarded the maps on the table. He greeted Morvan, as he entered, and bowed his head to the assembled company. 'Well met, Malvais. Is it quiet out there? Come and look at this.'

Morvan nodded and moved to stand beside him. 'I have decided to move out to somewhere much closer to the border in the morning. There are three possibilities; what do you think?'

Using small wooden flags, the King had marked three villages. Morvan spent a long time looking at the map, running his finger back and forth along rivers. He called one or two nobles over to the map who knew the area and asked them about the terrain, forests, hills, marshes etc. Then he stood back. William, not usually known for his patience, watched and waited.

At last, Morvan picked up a flag and to the surprise and alarm of the assembled nobles, he placed it on a different spot that the King had not considered. 'This is where you should be, Sire Pacy-Sur-Eure.'

There was a deadly silence for several moments, and then Morvan continued. 'It's a small village sitting on the River Eure with a wide ford, shallow in the summer. There are extensive meadows for grazing on the western side and for us to set up camp, with easy access to water for the horses. It's about two leagues from here to our target. We cross the border and stay on the south side of the River Seine.'

So far, there had been no mention of the attack on Mantes; only a chosen few in the tent were privy to the plan to attack France. The nobles gathered round, and there were nods of agreement. Hugh De Grandesmil and his son Aubrey were the only sceptics.

'Target? I presume you mean La Roche. This means we come up from the south in French territory. Is that not risky, Sire?' asked Aubrey.

'No, as we are to attack Mantes in a different direction.' announced William.

Morvan had known Aubrey Grandesmil for almost ten years; he had always been in one of the groups surrounding Robert Curthose. So Morvan had been surprised to find him here in William's train. Undoubtedly, his father was putting pressure on him to show his loyalty to the King. Hugh De Grandesmil was a wealthy and powerful Lord, the Sheriff of Leicestershire, who had ridden beside William at the Battle of Hastings; he wouldn't want both sons involved in Roberts's rebellion. His eldest son Yves had already defied him and embarrassingly was with Robert's traitorous forces in the

Vexin.

Morvan was close enough to hear Aubrey mutter, 'Mantes?' with a frown as if not believing that William would attack France.

There were always tables with wine, cold meats, cheese and bread on one side of the King's Pavilion. Morvan helped himself to more food while the King considered his suggestion. However, he felt uneasy about Aubrey. He glanced over and watched the younger knight suddenly excuse himself to his father, after which he quickly left the pavilion. Gut instinct kicked in, and Morvan followed him while staying out of sight behind the smaller tents.

He watched as Aubrey accosted a thickset soldier, eating beside his fire, and gave him orders. Within minutes, the man was on his feet, buckling on his sword. He bowed to Aubrey and made for the horse lines. Morvan couldn't leave the King, so he glanced frantically around, and his eyes lit on Garrett Eymer. He caught his attention and waved him over.

'God's bones, Morvan. Why are you hiding behind the tents with a piece of bread in your hand,' he laughed.

Morvan smiled. 'In all seriousness, I need your help. A man is about to ride out of the camp. I need you to follow him. If, as I suspect, he knows our plans, then he is riding to Robert Curthose at La Roche. I need you to kill him before he gets there.'

Garrett, now grim-faced, nodded. 'I will go at once.'

Morvan stood thoughtful for a few moments finishing the bread and cheese. Part of him hoped he was wrong. He had always liked young Aubrey Grandesmil, and William would kill him without a second thought if he found out he was betraying him. He returned to the pavilion to find the discussion continuing. 'Malvais, how wide is the ford at this village? Do we know?' asked the King.

Morvan pinned Aubrey, who had returned to his father's side, with a piercing stare. 'Aubrey, you know this village. Would you say we can get four or five abreast in the summer flow?'

Aubrey was startled and finding his mouth had gone dry, he just nodded. But Morvan did not drop his direct gaze, and Aubrey felt the first fingers of fear. Had he been found out?

William announced that he liked the plan and that they would leave early in the morning for Pacy-Sur-Eure.

As the others filed out, Morvan hovered for a while. 'Sire, may I suggest we spread alternative information about our plan around the camp? We spotted a man galloping towards La Roche. He was one of ours and probably carried information that might have been useful to Robert.'

Morvan was unsure what the King's reaction would be, but he smiled. 'It's an astute plan. I can see why Chatillon finds you so useful. Unfortunately, campaigns always have their spies, the planted and the opportunists. Hopefully, we will move so swiftly that we will still have the element of surprise.'

Morvan bowed and left him to his thoughts. He glanced back and saw that William had leant forward, his face in his hands. Morvan felt a pang of sympathy for the King, always on his guard, always alone, especially since the death of Queen Matilda. The weight of responsibility for the whole of the Anglo-Norman Empire was on his shoulders, with trouble on almost every border. There was, again, betrayal by his son Robert and from his brother, Odo, whom he had imprisoned. As he walked back to his men, Morvan prayed that his plan would work, to send both a shock and a message to Philip of

France, that William would take no more. Listening to the King, this could be the first of several attacks in a campaign to put the French King back in his place.

It was a weary Gerard who trotted after Luc into the cobbled yard of the large inn on the outskirts of Marseilles. 'That was a punishing pace you set today, Luc, for the horses and for me.'

Luc just grinned at him. 'Well, you have a day or so out of the saddle now.'

Gerard dismounted with several groans and leaned his head against the horse's flank. He was an exceptionally fit warrior for a man in his early fifties, but four days of hard riding would take it out of anyone. He handed the reins gratefully to the stable boys as Luc gave them detailed instructions for their care and feed.

The innkeeper greeted them effusively and showed them to their room to wash, and wait for Edvard to arrive. Gerard lay on the bed to rest his aching body, and he was asleep in seconds. Luc smiled; he envied Gerard's ability to catnap anywhere. His own mind was always active, and he was a light sleeper.

An hour later, a knock on the door came, and Edvard appeared. Gerard was instantly awake and refreshed from his rest, and he greeted him with enthusiasm. 'So where is he, this mariner of yours? You do still have him?'

'Yes, he is waiting downstairs. Restless, suspicious and a

taciturn individual, but he wants the silver we promised, so he has stayed in Marseilles and waited.'

Both men followed Edvard down to the taproom, where three of Chatillon's men ensured that no one else came in. Luc saw a greying, grizzled man with a scarred, lived-in face sitting against the wall. The man's eyes opened wide to see the tall Horse Warriors, and he nervously glanced at Edvard, who nodded at him encouragingly. He looked like many men who plied their illegal trade in dangerous Mediterranean waters.

'This is Master Mariner Derechi, who has some information for you. He is the owner of several boats, particularly the Mermaid, a large trading cog that travels back and forth between the Mediterranean ports, sometimes with legal cargo and sometimes not.'

Luc and Gerard, their crossed swords on their backs, would be imposing in any room. Their tall muscled physiques gave away their trade. They needed information from this man, so Luc, aware they could be intimidating, pulled up a stool to put himself on a level with the trader and indicated that Gerard should do the same. 'First of all, thank you for waiting so long for myself and Sir Gerard to arrive. I'm aware that you're losing trade and you'll be well recompensed for your trouble.'

Derechi looked somewhat mollified by this, thumbing at Edvard standing by the fireplace. 'He has promised me silver.'

'You shall certainly have that as long as you tell us the truth. We need facts. We do not need any embellishments that you think will get you more money. They won't, but it may get you my displeasure.'

The man looked slightly abashed and nodded. Luc waited while the innkeeper served them drinks that Derechi quaffed noisily. 'Now I know you told him you remembered the tattooed horseman, but I need you to go back to when he first approached you and tell me everything.'

The man took another draft of ale. 'It was late in the season. We should have gone home, back to Italy, but we needed to repair the sail that was damaged in a squall. They came on the evening of the last day, the man and an attractive woman carrying a small, dark-haired boy. I thought it odd because the horseman was one of those red-haired men from the far west, and she had long fair hair. He did not look like their child. They wanted passage across the Mediterranean to Italy. I told them I was making a one-way trip only before the Mermaid was beached and caulked. They were happy with that.

'At first, I did not notice the tattoos because it was dark, and he wore a large, dark cloak with a hood. He paid us well, more than I expected, in silver, and they spread out their beds on the deck in the prow. We were sailing early on the morning tide before the Mistral winds arrived. We were cutting it close, so it was all bustle while the dawn rose.'

The man paused again for another draught of ale and indicated to Edvard that he wanted it filling again. 'As we edged out of the harbour, the horseman took off his cloak. He was wearing a sleeveless leather jerkin, and his arms and body seemed to be covered in blue tattoos, swirls, and linked designs. One of my men began muttering and crossed himself; he said it was a bad omen to have one of those druids on board. The horseman laughed and promised him he wasn't a druid but said they had captured him as a child.

'Once in the open sea and the wind in our sail, I talked to them. He said he was a horse handler going to a good job on an estate in the north of Italy. She said little, but the child prattled on; he talked of horses and going to live in the mountains. A brave young lad, laughing at the waves with his father when it got a bit rough and they washed over the gunwale.'

He stopped, and Gerard jumped in. 'So Derechi, where did you take them?'

'I took them to my home town, Genoa. That is where I lay my boats up for the winter months,' he said.

'Is there anything else you can think of, Derechi? No mention of where this estate was?' asked Gerard.

The mariner shook his head, but his next sentence showed that he had worked out that the child was stolen. 'They did not talk much after that, but they cared for the little boy. They treated him well.' Luc thanked the man, and Edvard took him to one side to pay him.

'So that was them. The descriptions were perfect, and they went to Italy,' mused Gerard.

Luc stood up. 'We leave the horses stabled here and arrange for them to return to Morlaix. We take a ship to Genoa, and we can buy or hire riding horses there.'

Edvard came to join them. 'Get a message to Morvan. Tell him what we have found and that he is to meet us in Genoa if he can. Then find us a passage on a boat for tomorrow. The trail may be several years old, but this horseman is distinctive—people will remember him. There will be those in Genoa—Innkeepers, horse traders—who will have dealt with him.' Gerard could hear the enthusiasm and hope in Luc's voice, and he prayed he was right.

'I will send a message to my master, Chatillon, in Genoa. He can begin sending his men out to question the locals and the people on the docks.'

Luc turned a surprised glance on Edvard. 'Chatillon is in

Genoa? Why?' he asked.

'Yes, Sire. He inherited a raft of properties and land from Bianca Da Landriano. He has the Palazzo Castello on the cliffs. He will be married from there in two months to Isabella Embriaco.'

Gerard smiled; the papal assassin was an enigma. You never knew where he was or what he would do next. 'I am glad for him. That is a very powerful family. I heard from Morvan that the death of Bianca hit him very hard.' Edvard inclined his head in agreement but added nothing else. He would never give away any private details of his master's life.

Chapter Sixteen

Morvan was checking the horse lines in the dark when a tired Garrett rode back in and dismounted. He walked his horse over to the horse lines and started taking the tack off the steaming horse. As he walked towards him, Morvan knew by his face it wasn't good news. He quickly glanced around to ensure they were alone. 'What happened?'

Garrett sighed while twisting a large wisp of straw to wipe his horse down. Morvan picked up another handful to help him.

'You were right, Malvais. He headed north and crossed the River Epte making for La Roche Guyan. I had to gallop ahead across the fields and ambush him in the forest. While on his knees, he admitted that he was taking a message to Robert Curthose. I asked him where the message was, but he said he had to repeat the information—young Grandesmil had not written it down. We stared at each other for some time, realising what that meant, and then he begged me for his life. He has a wife and children back home in Normandy. He was a good man who formerly fought with Robert in Scotland. I have seen him often helping the armourer, always laughing. However, he isn't laughing now. I couldn't take the risk of him passing the message on, so I quickly cut his throat and left him there in the trees. I brought his horse back and left it to wander near the troop lines. They will think he was thrown or even that the enemy scouts killed him.'

Morvan placed a hand on his shoulder and thanked him. 'You did the right thing, Garrett. He knew about the attack on Mantes. He would have given us away, and you had no choice. I admit that I am disappointed that I was right, which leaves me with a far tougher problem. I now need to deal with the nobleman who gave him that information—one of William's inner circle.'

There was only one way to handle this if he had any chance of saving Aubrey's life. He made his way over to the Grandesmil pavilion. The young man had clearly been influenced by his older brother, Yves, fighting alongside Robert. Morvan was pleased that Aubrey's father, Hugh De Grandesmil, was alone in his pavilion, which was fortunate.

Initially, he was pleased to see Morvan, and he plied him with a good red wine that he had brought on campaign. However, his face darkened as he listened to what the Horse Warrior had to say. Before long, purple-faced, he was striding up and down the tent, cursing, fists clenched. He stopped suddenly and turned to Morvan. He lowered his voice. 'William will kill him, or worse, maim him for life. I have watched him emasculate men for less, and you know that.'

Morvan stood up and put a hand on his shoulder. 'This is why I have come straight to you. Aubrey was a friend. We fought together at Gerberoi. I know his older brother, Yves, is with Robert Curthose, but I thought Aubrey had more sense than to betray the King.'

Hugh stood, brow furrowed. 'Leave it with me. I will deal with it.'

Morvan rose to go. 'I am sorry to bring this upon you, but I had to do this. Robert Curthose can't know that we intend to move east and attack the French town of Mantes.'

Hugh nodded while calling for his Steward, who arrived quickly. 'Find and bring my son to me now—no excuses—wherever he may be or whatever doxy he is with tonight. Drag him here in ropes if you have to.'

An hour later, Aubrey was bound and gagged in the back of a wagon escorted by three of his father's retainers. He would be kept, as a virtual prisoner, until the conflict in the Vexin was resolved. He was returning to his father's house in Caen, where his young wife waited.

The next morning, the King's forces left for Pacy-Sur-Eure. The weather was hot and sultry, with dark summer storm clouds gathering. 'I think we may be in for a soaking, Malvais,' said King William pulling his big bay horse alongside Morvan's stallion.

'Let us hope that it'll be brief but useful, Sire. It'll settle the dust.'

The King laughed. 'Yes, I did notice that your Horse Warriors did the sensible thing and put the dust covers on the noses of their Destriers.'

Morvan smiled. 'A necessity in the summer, Sire. As you know, horses do not do well in the heat, with lungs full of dust thrown up by the troops in front.'

William considered the man riding beside him. He always seemed to think of all eventualities. 'What of the other matter we spoke of, our possible spy? Did you resolve it to our satisfaction?' he asked, turning to spear Morvan with his piercing gaze.

'Yes, Sire. Garrett Eymer removed the problem last night.

We intercepted a senior retainer. He was Robert's man, and he is with us no more.'

William was no fool. He watched, listened, and had his own spies to tell him what was going on around him, as his next sentence showed. 'I believe Aubrey De Grandesmil left us last night, some tale about his new young wife and a difficult pregnancy.'

Morvan adopted a surprised expression as he could truthfully reply, 'I had not heard that story, Sire, or realised that he wasn't with us today.'

Neither man was fooled, but William was grateful to Morvan that he wouldn't have to brutally punish, or kill, the son of one of his friends. He had a reputation to keep for always delivering swift vengeance for betrayal.

Shortly afterwards, they set up camp in the broad meadows on the banks of the Eure. As hundreds of Normans rode in on their huge horses and settled in their grazing meadows, the locals watched in alarm. However, as William always insisted on paying his own people generously for the supplies they took, they began to look more kindly at the camp.

Morvan stood on the banks of the wide but fast-flowing river. The location was perfect for their basecamp. In front of him was a long but high, rocky island in the middle of the river Eure called the Ile Des Moulins. The locals said it was named for the old, but working, water mill on the far side. There was a solid, wide, wooden bridge to the island, and on the far side, another longer wooden bridge led over a deeper, wider ravine to the village of Pacy Sur Eure. He put men to camp, securing the island, and he placed sentries on the bridge.

Garrett appeared alongside him. 'A lovely spot, Morvan. It reminds me of Ravensworth. Your brother built a mill race and mill for the villages in the Holme valley.'

Morvan laughed. 'Luc would; he always has ideas for projects and ideas to improve the estates. Listen, Garrett, I expect us to be pursued when we attack Mantes. We will have the element of surprise for a while, but before long, I imagine that Robert's forces will be streaming out of La Roche-Guyan to catch us while we are still in France, on the wrong side of the border. I want your troop of Horse Warriors to hold a rear guard. I need you to use the tactics you have been taught of 'retraite en echiquier', charge and retreat, and again until you reach the far bridge in front of us. I will have men waiting there with axes. They will have sabotaged the central supports of the bridge. You must cross swiftly and take the ropes they give you. The Destriers will pull the damaged supports away, and the bridge will collapse. It's at least ten miles to the next crossing. You will then follow us on the road to Rouen.'

Garrett grinned in acknowledgement. It was a good plan, and he revelled in being at the heart of the action. Morvan returned to the camp as heavy rain began to fall. He made for the King's large double pavilion, where he found William in good spirits, surrounded by his nobles.

'Sire, despite the downpour, I have ordered another hundred campfires to be built on the outskirts of the camp as soon as it lessens. We will look a much larger force, from a distance, to Robert's scouts. Also, I agree with the strategy you mentioned, which worked so well in Scotland. We should move out quickly and quietly at night, the campfires will still be lit, and our younger squires, servants, and hangers-on will sit around the fires tending them. I imagine you'll want to hit Mantes in the dawn light, while most citizens are still abed, and its guards are nodding with sleep? Luckily, if all goes well,

Robert's scouts to the north will not know that we have left.'

William smiled and agreed. He appreciated how Morvan made it sound as if it was his plan. He turned to his entourage. 'Go and share this plan with your captains. Get their men to roll their blankets up to look like sleeping men. We move out when the moon is high.'

Morvan held up a hand as they made for the doors. 'Make sure the horses' hooves are all muffled; a thin piece of cloth will suffice as it's only for when we cross the wooden bridges.' With that, they were gone to make ready, and Morvan was left with William and a few servants.

William sat back down in his camp chair. 'We will send this French King a message he can't ignore. We have not attacked France for over fifteen years; he'll not expect this. Let us hope this torrential storm stops soon, or the going will be hard.'

Morvan grinned. 'You'll certainly do so, Sire, and I think the sky is clearing from the east for us.'

The King dismissed him, and he spent time checking on his men and horses. He found Garrett holding a message when he returned tired and wet to his pavilion. 'This came for you earlier this evening, brought by a very wet, bedraggled bird to the nearest town and brought by a priest to the camp. I don't pretend to understand how they find us, but I'm glad they do. Let us hope it's good news.'

Morvan sat down and quickly scanned the message. 'It's from Luc. Chatillon has found the mariner that took Brian and my son across the Mediterranean Sea. They are leaving for Marseilles immediately and want me to join them there as soon as possible.' He raised eyes full of hope to Garrett, 'This is the first lead they have had for years, and here I am about to do battle in Northern France, a hundred leagues away from them.'

He laughed bitterly but then stood up and shrugged. *Duty comes first*, as his brother Luc would have said. 'Let us ready the men to leave. We need to take this town swiftly, and then, if I live, I will take leave from the King and head south.'

Several hours later, as silently as possible, the camp emptied of men. Blankets and spare saddles were left to look like sleeping forms around the fires. The storm had finally broken and moved on; the fires had been lit. It was a good two leagues to the town of Mantes, but it was cool in the night air.

They now had a moonlit sky to help them on their way. As they crossed the wooden bridges over the Eure, the river below had turned into a raging torrent that pleased Morvan, and he hoped that the River Seine would be the same, preventing some of the crossings from being used. The King had insisted on absolute silence, so only the odd whinny gave them away, as they cantered towards the sleeping French town of Mantes, on the banks of the Seine.

Robert Curthose and his followers gathered in the upper chamber of the Donjon at La Roche. The scouts had reported that the King's force was camped at a village on the Eure, watering and resting the horses. As they discussed this, a further message arrived to say that the force was far bigger than they had been led to believe. The scouts were now estimating well over a thousand men, maybe as many as fifteen hundred.

Robert chewed his lip as he studied the map. William's scouts were seen as far north as Gasny on the River Epte, so there seemed to be no doubt that he was coming north to defeat Robert's forces. However, this meant that he might now cross the River Seine further west, possibly at Bemecort, where a large, low, accessible island was in the centre of the river.

Yves De Grandesmil leaned over with a concerned frown as they looked at the map. 'This means that he may not come to cross at La Roche and has decided not to risk attacking us here. We all know how the King likes a fast-moving mobile war.'

Robert had a sudden misgiving that he was in the wrong place. He had invested heavily in establishing himself here in this strong fortress, recreating the situation when he had defeated his father at Gerberoi. It looked as if his father wasn't taking the bait. He turned back to Yves. 'What then do we do?' he asked, shrugging his shoulders in frustration. 'Where is the information from Aubrey?'

Yves peered again at the map. It seems as if he is avoiding La Roche-Guyan. 'The last report from Aubrey told us they were coming north to cross the Seine. Therefore, we must send contingents of troops to watch all the crossings to the west. We need to be mobile, Robert, and we should attack them as they are crossing the river, especially after this rain. If they get over the River Seine, God help us, as our forces won't have a chance in the open against his Horse Warriors.'

Robert was dismayed. He had been so sure that he would defeat his father again and seize the Dukedom of Normandy. Now, his plans had gone awry. *What would Morvan De Malvais do?* he wondered, covering his eyes with a hand.

The noblemen stood in silence around the table, waiting for his response, concerned expressions on many faces. Some of them had been pardoned and managed to get their lands back after the last rebellion against the King at Gerberoi. They knew he wouldn't be as forgiving a second time. They had to defeat him.

Robert dropped his hand and scanned the group. 'We ride at once; we can stop him. Yves, leave a small force here with half of the Genoese crossbowmen on the walls just in case we are wrong and my father splits his forces. The rest of them can march quickly to meet us at Bemecort. If we make haste, we can be waiting for them on that island in the Seine. We can take them by surprise. They won't expect us to be there.'

Chapter Seventeen

In the east, the opposite direction to the one taken by Robert. Morvan, Earl De Clare and King William looked down on the sleeping town of Mantes in the dawn light. 'I have never seen so many church towers in a town,' said De Clare.

'Yes, over half a dozen, by the look. There is also a sizeable monastery there, now recently changed into a Benedictine order, I believe,' added Morvan.

William snorted in disgust. 'What has happened to The Church? Pope Gregory spread these monasteries across Europe like a plague: corruption, power, and control by stealth. The Abbots control and tax the local populations with their strict Benedictine rules. Pope Gregory has gone to join his maker, but we will send a message to his successor, Pope Victor III. We will teach him a lesson and pay him back for sending hundreds of Genoese crossbowmen to my son to use against me.'

The assembled nobles looked at William in alarm. They could see his face was white with anger. The King had always been a very religious man and had built several cathedrals, but this attack could lead to excommunication from the church. 'Sire, we don't usually sack and burn the churches...' began De Clare, but William cut him off while pulling his horse savagely round.

'I want that town in flames. I want a clear message to go to Philip of France and the Holy See in Rome.' With that, he rode back to the rest of his followers to watch from the slight hill.

The early dawn light sparkled on the River Seine, which was full of trading barges and boats plying their trade between Paris and the coast. Morvan sat for a while longer, looking down on the prosperous town. He could understand William's anger and desire for vengeance, but he couldn't condone his actions this time. Morvan thought such a sacrilegious attack would stir up a hornet's nest of ire and possible counterattacks from all sides in Normandy. He sighed as he went to find his men. He had seen the King's face, and there would be no dissuading him from this decision. Only one person could have done that, Queen Matilda, and she was dead.

He went in search of vedettes, men to ride through the town and over the bridge to the other side of the river. If Robert's scouts had seen and heard them move out, which was possible, then they needed warning of Robert's troops approaching on the north bank of the Seine.

Less than an hour later, over six hundred men were riding down into an unsuspecting town. The watchmen had only just unbarred the great town gates, for the market stallholders, when the first wave of Norman cavalry galloped into the streets. They scattered early risers and livestock alike. The watchmen jumped back with shock—one brave soul tried to push the gate closed but got a sword slashed across his throat for his trouble.

Shortly afterwards, the town guard rallied from the keep and tried to put up a defence, but to no avail against the numbers of mounted troops that had entered the city. Soon the streets were littered with their bodies.

William's troops followed instructions to set fires in all wooden buildings. They threw flaming torches onto the thatched rooves, resulting in plumes of smoke from the damp straw.

The French lord and his family were not in residence in the fortified keep, but the town leaders and the Abbot came to plead with Morvan as he sat directing his men in the large square. He had ridden through the town, telling the people to get out as the town was to be burnt to the ground. However, too many went back to get belongings and became trapped in the burning buildings. Or they came face to face with William's soldiers looking for vengeance on the French.

Morvan listened stony-faced to the town leaders. He told them that King William was outside the walls. He was burning the town in vengeance and retribution for the dozens of attacks on the Norman Vexin. As he and his men galloped through the burning town to the far bridge, Morvan saw several women and girls dragged screaming into stables by Norman troops. Unfortunately, that was the price of war; the men saw this as their loot, and he couldn't interfere.

The Abbot and several of his monks made their way outside to remonstrate with the King, but to no avail, as William glared down at them. As he left to go and save the gold plate and precious reliquaries from the monastery, the Abbot turned and shouted at William, 'God will curse you for this act, William of Normandy!'

Hugh De Grandesmil, who sat beside the King, drew his sword to strike the man down, but the King stopped him and shouted, 'Let the old hypocrite go back and bag up his gold;

we do not kill priests, Hugh.'

An hour later, the whole town was ablaze as people still fled for their lives down the narrow cobbled streets. Morvan ordered all troops to leave the town, which they did, some running out of the smoke, coughing but carrying their assembled loot with them. One soldier even had a kicking, screaming woman on the front of his horse, to the amusement of his comrades, as they galloped up the hill.

Morvan, still coughing from the smoke, returned to the rise outside the town. The flames now leapt high. Smoke from several other fires along the wharves and riverside joined the huge plume of smoke from the tanning yards, where the tallow oils from the pelts went up in smoke. Apart from the sudden downpour, it had been a very dry summer, and the wooden houses were like tinder.

Morvan could see dozens of people streaming across the burning bridge out of the city, away from the conflagration. William rode up beside him. 'The walls and houses to the east appear not to be burning. Why is that?'

Morvan tried to peer through the thick black smoke that kept obliterating the town. 'I am not sure, Sire, but I think it'll soon spread to that area. The wind is helping.'

William wasn't satisfied with that. 'Come, bring some of your men. We will ride around the walls of the town.' Morvan galloped after the big bay horse through smoke, sparks and burning debris blown into the air by the breeze. On reaching the town, they descended into a wide, steep ditch full of broken timber and old vegetation, which they had to descend into and then hop across. This would probably have been a defensive ditch, or vallum, going back to the town in Roman times, thought Morvan as they crested the other side and came out under the walls.

On the eastern side, the walls were old Roman stone, and the keep and monastery alike were built into them. William ordered Morvan's men to throw burning torches up onto the rooves of these buildings as they were covered in wooden shingles.

Morvan could see two of his vedettes from the north galloping towards him. He wiped his streaming eyes while waiting for them. The town had been on fire for several hours now, and he was sure the townspeople would have sent for help from neighbouring towns and possibly to La Roche. The plume of black smoke was now so high that it would be seen leagues away on this clear day.

A vedette skidded to a halt in front of Morvan. 'Sire, there is a small force approaching from the west. We think it is about forty strong.'

King William laughed. 'Shall we face them down, Malvais, and send them packing, their tails between their legs.'

Morvan smiled. 'We might be outnumbered, Sire, with only seven of us.'

The King laughed. 'I never had you down as someone who could resist a challenge.'

For a second, Morvan wondered if William was serious. 'I think we should go, Sire. We need to be away and back across the River Eure before Robert's forces arrive.'

Reluctantly William agreed, and they turned back along the walls to join their forces on the hill. As they cantered back, Morvan noticed that the wide ditch they had crossed earlier was now alight; years of branches and debris were now in flames. They sat and stared at it for a few moments in the rising heat and smoke. The flames were now a man's height, so they couldn't descend into the burning debris and jump.

'We need to jump the whole ditch,' said the King, turning his bay to get a run at it. Morvan was dubious; it was a wide ditch full of flames. However, they had no choice with forces about to gallop up behind them—they had to get across the ditch to re-join their own men. Morvan reached across to touch the King's arm, the roaring from the fire and flames in the town were now deafening.

'Let my men go first, Sire, to ensure we can get across. If not, we will gallop further and look for an alternative.' The King nodded, and the vedettes and the Horse Warriors galloped one after the other at the ditch, only just clearing it.

Morvan eyed the King's big bay gelding. It was a well-built, capable horse in its prime. It should clear the ditch even when carrying William, a big man who had become somewhat portly over the last few years. The King was riding with his usual padded saddle, which had a high pommel at the front and a similarly high wooden back support, so Morvan felt confident that the King would stay in place if, by chance, the horse refused. Also, he knew that William was an exceptionally good horseman, he had spent his life in the saddle.

He watched with apprehension as the King galloped past him at speed, his mouth grim with determination but with excitement in his eyes. Morvan's worst fear was that the horse would baulk at the high flames. It was showing the whites of its eyes in fear, but with relief, he heard the take-off followed by a scrabbled landing above the roar of the flames, then there were several loud cries. The noise and smoke were disorientating, making it difficult to hear where they came from. Were Robert Curthose's forces upon them, he wondered. He could see nothing. His throat burned. They had to get out of here, he thought.

Morvan glanced around, coughing loudly. He could see or hear nothing on the other side of the ditch through the billowing smoke. He had complete confidence in Shadow as the big stallion galloped at the flames. He landed easily on the other side to see, with horror, that the King was unhorsed on the ground crying out in pain.

Chapter Eighteen

Gerard and Luc stepped off the gangplank and onto the quayside at Genoa. Both had been here many years ago in very different circumstances. They had fought as mercenaries in the wars against Lombardy. Luc had just lost his father at Hastings and then his wife and child; he was looking for an escape from Brittany, young and full of anger at what fate had handed him. Marie sent Gerard along as his companion to try to keep him safe.

A different Luc today stood and looked around him. The town they knew back then, twenty years before, had now become a growing city-state with a busy, bustling port. There were barges, masts and spars as far as the eye could see.

Gerard noticed Edvard waving at them, and they wended their way through the dock wallopers moving sacks and boxes on and off ships. The noise was almost deafening as dozens of men shouted at each other and threw sacks onto carts. Edvard indicated they should follow him. The Horse Warriors were trying to keep a low profile, and so their swords were wrapped and carried on top of their large leather saddle packs.

They made their way across the harbour and up a steep path towards the Palazzo Castello, an unusual fortified house, built to perch upon a large rocky ledge, looking down into the city and harbour. It was surrounded by a high-walled garden, stables and outbuildings running down almost to the water. Luc and Gerard stopped to look up at it. 'A very impressive house, I have not seen one completely covered in that cream stucco plaster before, and the marble and stone pillars must have cost a fortune,' said Gerard.

Luc commented on the high stone balconies that faced the sea and would get both rising and setting sun. Gerard gazed up at them; they were substantial. 'Could we build something like that at Morlaix, Luc? Marie and Merewyn would love them,' Gerard mused as they went through the gates.

Luc laughed. 'I think the wild, cold, Brittany weather, straight off the Atlantic, would make them unusable for most of the year, Gerard.'

Chatillon was waiting for them in a large airy chamber above, and he greeted them effusively. It had raised all of their spirits, having a definite lead after so many years with little useful information. 'I have men out with pockets full of coins asking questions along the wharves, in the inns and lodging houses. If they stayed here for any time before moving on, someone must have seen them. The horseman was so distinctive, even here in Genoa, which has a variety of races.'

'As I see it, the problem lies in that we don't know where they were going, or which direction they took from here. Did they mean to land in Genoa? Or, was it that it was one of the last boats leaving the harbour before winter, and they suspected we were close behind them?' asked Luc running his hands through his dark hair in frustration.

Chatillon waved him to a carved cedar wood chair. 'Patience, my friend, this is a good lead. You're right, several roads lead from here, north to Milan and south towards Rome.

As Edvard tells me that the boy talked about mountains, I think we could consider north first. Although I have another lead to Monte Cassino, I'm unsure how accurate that is, and I am waiting for more information. I have sent men out on the road to Milan to call at all the inns to see if anyone remembers them.

Nonetheless, we need to be realistic; it was seven years ago. People die and move on from these places.' Luc and Gerard reluctantly agreed.

'Let me tell you what has happened since last we spoke.' Chatillon told them about his visit to Rome and the following attacks on him in Genoa.

'I think that our friend Dauferio must be running scared if he is trying to kill one of his own envoys and assassins,' growled Gerard.

Chatillon inclined his head in agreement. 'Well, he admitted to me he was involved in taking the boy and was holding him. He probably regretted telling me that before I was out of the room. He has become more cautious since he became Pope. He has changed—still just as ambitious, but my man tells me that he is often confused due to a debilitating illness he has contracted. I talked to my friend, the Archbishop of Genoa, Conrades De Mezzarello. He agrees with me that the boy is probably still alive at present. We think he may be in the hands of a sect of Warrior Monks.'

Gerard shot to his feet. 'At present? Do you think that they will kill him?'

Chatillon raised his hands in a calming gesture and frowned at him to take his seat again. 'We know that a message was sent from Rome to that effect, but my man in the Lateran Palace couldn't discover who it went to—the name was indecipherable—or where. I do not think they will kill him; he is King William's grandson and far too valuable.'

Luc agreed. He knew that they had to be satisfied with that for now; it was a waiting game. 'Get some rest. You have been travelling for over a week. Make the palazzo your home. I have other matters to attend to today.'

Chatillon had enough business to keep him occupied that week. He made time to visit and make love to the Signora Di Monsi most afternoons. She was witty, seemed carefree and made him laugh with scandalous stories about the families of Genoa. He found he was developing a real affection for her. He met her daughter Marietta on several occasions, now she had returned from the country, and found her an intelligent and astute child.

In the evenings, he paid court to Isabella, his wife to be, and was happy with their developing friendship. He did not touch her sexually, just a chaste kiss when he left. He also saw in her eyes that this tantalised her. She wanted more—but not yet. It would be on *his* terms when he took things further.

He invited Luc and Gerard to ride out with him, finding some good horseflesh to enjoy a good gallop. He took them out to the large estates he had inherited from Bianca in the city's verdant hinterland slopes and pastures. They stayed overnight and talked about farming and horse breeding like three old men, which made him smile given their backgrounds. At first, the two Horse Warriors kept a very low profile in the city and turned down any invitations that arrived. Still, Genoa was like a large village, and Luc De Malvais was easily recognisable to those who had seen him before. It went around like wildfire that they were staying with the Papal Envoy. Therefore, they finally agreed to go to an evening reception at the Embriaco household, ostensibly to meet Chatillon's future wife but also for other guests, who had arrived, to make trading deals with the new maritime republic.

Signora Di Monsi was a very private person. She occasionally attended the more significant events, usually linked to her business activities. A prominent Roman merchant had arrived in Genoa, and he would be at the event tonight, so she decided to attend. Chatillon had not mentioned that he had guests staying with him. Their liaison was very much about their exciting physical relationship. Neither wanted more involvement. She was blissfully unaware as she arrived at the Embriaco residence that her world was about to be rocked.

She was sitting quietly with acquaintances at the far side of the hall when Chatillon appeared with his two guests.

There was an instant hum of excitement; this was the famous Luc De Malvais, the most feared warrior and horseman in Europe. An older, handsome, distinguished knight with grey, swept-back hair accompanied him. Malvais was everything the women in Genoa wanted and expected: tall, dark, very handsome with flashing, steel-grey eyes. Under the fashionable, shorter velvet tunic, there was a lithe but muscled physique, broad shoulders and powerful thighs. There was much giggling and lip-smacking behind hands and fans as they watched him stride confidently across the floor to meet their host.

The new arrivals were hidden from sight for a while as a crowd of socialites went to greet them. Signora Di Monsi, however, froze in fear. She would have recognised Luc De Malvais anywhere; he still haunted her dreams and worst nightmares. She knew that she had to get out of there immediately without them seeing her, for they would recognise her instantly, and she was convinced that Luc De Malvais would kill her. Knowing him as she did, he would calmly cut her throat in front of the assembled guests. Everything she had worked for and established here was now at risk, including the future of her daughter Marietta who she had to protect.

She waited until the new guests were occupied and then made an excuse to her friends that she was unwell. She took her leave, head down. She walked swiftly behind the marble pillars that supported the high roof, making her way towards her distinctive Nubian manservant standing near the entrance.

They did not see her leave, but Edvard saw her whilst standing in his usual place, and he thought her behaviour odd. She looked afraid, hands clutching her cloak. It wasn't until the next day that he mentioned it to Chatillon, who admitted he did not know she would attend that evening.

He pondered it for a while. *Was it because the Signora did not want to see him with Isabella?* Then he dismissed that thought; she loved the pleasure he could give her each afternoon, but he knew that her heart was not engaged. He made her laugh. She liked him, but she was not in love, and she wasn't jealous. So if Edvard was right, he wondered what had scared her off. He determined to find out. It was a bright, clear early morning as he walked across the city. He was alone for a change and so preoccupied he did not notice he was being followed to her house. They had watched him visit her every afternoon. They had found out who she was.

When he reached her residence, to his surprise, the large gates to the street stood open, and a carriage was being loaded with chests and leather bags—men were stacking and tying them on the roof. He cut through the bustle to the entrance just to see her emerging from the covered stone staircase in travelling clothes.

She smiled at him and held out her hands in greeting, but the smile did not reach her large, grey eyes. She seemed agitated and anxious. 'Ah, Piers, you have saved me a note when I am in a hurry. I am leaving. Marietta is ill, a summer chill, they think. I must take her away from the city immediately. I do not know when I may return. If she is well enough to travel, I might go further south with her to our house in Rome, where it'll be warmer.' She found it difficult to raise her eyes to meet that puzzled, piercing gaze, but she stroked his cheek.

Taking her hand, he kissed her fingertips. 'I will miss you,' she whispered as she mounted into the carriage.

He stepped back. 'I hope that Marietta recovers soon so that you can return to us in Genoa. Bon voyage Signora.' With that, the horses leapt forward, and she was gone out of the gates.

He walked and watched the carriage travel briskly up the steep hill where it would wind its way out and into the countryside. He stood for a few moments outside the gates, pondering what he had seen. There had been an inordinate amount of luggage on the back and roof of that carriage. Something was amiss here. He realised that she did not intend to come back, certainly not for a long time. He intended to find out why.

The Signora sat in the bouncing carriage, trying to hold back the tears but not succeeding. She was crying for the danger she was in, for her daughter, for the relationship with the exciting Piers De Chatillon, the best lover she had ever had, and for her life and friends in Genoa that she could lose.

For the wolves were closing in, and she had to run. First, she would go to their villa and plan how to consolidate her wealth and where to go next.

Chatillon returned to the Palazzo Castello to find a buzz of excitement that pushed the Signora out of his mind. Gerard was striding impatiently up and down the large chamber. He greeted his guests but then turned. 'Do sit down, Sir Gerard. I find I'm exhausted just watching you.'

Luc laughed at the disgruntled expression on his friend's face. 'Leave him, Chatillon. We have news. Edvard tells us that your men have found a woman who rents rooms in the lower, older part of the city. She remembers them. She says she rented them a room for a few weeks. She is downstairs.'

Chatillon whirled to look at his manservant, leaning on the doorjamb, who smiled and nodded. 'Bring her up then. Let us see what information we can get out of her.'

The woman who arrived was clearly overawed and frightened to be brought into a house like this, and then expected to speak to what were quite intimidating lords. She had convinced herself that she had done something wrong and would be expected to pay for it.

Gerard seeing all this and listening to her whispered concerns stepped forward and smiled. Taking her hand, he led her to a chair, reassuring her that they just needed her help finding a child.

Chatillon stood impatiently, eyebrows raised. 'Tell us about the man you rented the room to seven years ago if you can remember, the one with blue markings on his body. If you're helpful and can remember any details, you may get a silver coin for your trouble.'

The woman's eyes widened, and she nodded. 'I remember

them well. They stayed in a room I rented out when times were tough. They arrived just before the winter, and they were waiting for better weather because they were going north. They were here for several weeks, almost a month, and he paid well. He was a handsome man, charming, and he clearly cared for his wife and child, but he said very little. She was different. She came from better stock, almost genteel but light-hearted and happy to chat—a lovely girl with beautiful grey eyes and a happy little boy. Always laughing, the boy was, and talking about big horses and mountains.'

Gerard felt his eyes becoming wet, but he nodded encouragement and handed her a tankard of breakfast ale, which she gulped noisily. 'Did they say where they were going?

She nodded. 'She told me that he had a job on a huge estate outside of Milan somewhere, one of those places where they breed lots of horses to sell. The man seemed to be very wealthy. I went in one day to find him with bags of silver, and he shouted at me to get out. That is all I know.'

Luc and Gerard looked at one another; that estate should be easy to find. Gerard thanked her and took her towards the door where Edvard paid her. Luc's eyes were alight, hoping that they would find them, and then the woman stopped at the door and turned.

'A strange thing happened. My neighbour who works on the quayside told me that he had seen the woman, that she had come back to Genoa—he said her man had died—but I have never seen, her if she did.'

Edvard showed the woman out and down the stairs, and there was silence in the room. They could hear her chatting happily about what she would buy with the silver.

'Surely your men would have found her if she was here

162

in Genoa, Chatillon?' asked Luc. The envoy nodded almost absentmindedly, preoccupied with what he had just heard. But then Edvard appeared, a shocked expression on his face. He held out a message to his master.

'It's from Morvan,' said Chatillon scanning its contents. Then his face blanched.

'What is it?' whispered Luc, thinking of his family back in Morlaix or of Morvan fighting battles in the Vexin. Chatillon did not answer at first.

'Morvan is on his way. He expects to be here in just over a week. He says the King was badly injured in the attack on Mantes. He says William is dying.'

Chapter Nineteen

It was almost a week since the burning of Mantes, and Robert Curthose was back in the fortress of La Roche-Guyan. He fumed with anger and frustration as he walked up and down the chamber. His father had made a fool of him. He had been fully prepared for a battle at the fortress on the River Seine. His father had tricked him into thinking he had a far bigger force, and they were moving north to attack him.

Instead, King William had not ridden into the Norman Vexin at all; he had attacked France and burnt a prosperous trading town to the ground. He burnt not only the town but also six churches and a Benedictine monastery. By the time he had ridden to their aid, even the wooden bridge was alight, and there was nowhere for him to cross to pursue the attackers.

The door opened, and the French Seneschal, Gervais la Ferte, strode in. Robert gave a cynical smile. 'Bad news travels fast. It has certainly brought you hotfoot from Paris to my side. No doubt you bring the condemnation of King Philip for my abysmal failure to stop my father from burning Mantes.'

Gervais looked at him in surprise. 'Yes, you're right. Philip isn't happy at losing the town of Mantes; the Cardinal of Paris is demanding retribution and reparation for the loss of the monastery and churches. Nonetheless, I'm puzzled to find you here. I expected you to be in Rouen at your father's side, despite your differences.'

Robert gave a sort of disdain. 'He wouldn't want me there. He dislikes me as much as I dislike him.'

Gervais frowned. 'Your brothers are there. Henry is kneeling at his side, trying to persuade him to give him the Duchy instead of you. William Rufus sailed from England when he heard your father was dying.'

Robert looked alarmed at this news. 'He is injured is all; he will recover. My father, the King, the Conqueror, the Bastard Duke of Normandy, is immortal. I assure you he will recover just to spite me.'

Gervais studied the young man in front of him. Robert was now in his thirty-sixth year, and they had to ensure that he, not his brothers, inherited Normandy. They had to stop them from stealing the Duchy from under his nose. 'He isn't just injured Robert; he is dying. They say he'll not last the week.'

Robert frowned. 'I do not believe it. I think it's a ruse to get me there so that he can capture and imprison me. I refuse to go!'

Gervais shrugged. 'We can't force you, but I will take command of the forces and order the captains to mass them on the border of Normandy, to show the support you have from France. Also, as Seneschal of France, I will ride to Rouen as King Philip's representative. I will aim to gain the support of your brother, William Rufus, and ensure that Henry does not steal Normandy from you. But you should be there, Robert. What would your mother, Matilda, say to see you and your father still so estranged at this moment while he is on his death bed?'

Robert flushed with embarrassment, but he turned away, and Gervais, his mouth a thin line of disapproval, turned on his heel and left. His anger grew as he rode for Rouen. If Henry had stolen Normandy, all their efforts and money on Robert would have been wasted. Gervais could only imagine King Philip's anger if that happened.

Morvan was standing on the boat's prow as it entered Genoa's wide but sheltered harbour. He did not remember it, but he was a young, callow youth who had run away to join Gerard and his brother, in the Lombard wars, when he last arrived here. Gerard had severely boxed his ears and tried to send him home, but Luc intervened and allowed him to stay.

The city seemed to rise from the sea and climb up the steep slopes of the mountains behind it. Staunch sea walls had been built along the coast, and it was a hive of activity on the long wooden wharves. They sailed in close to the northern cliffs, and Morvan noticed several men and women carrying bundles of wood up the steep path and onto the rocky promontory. 'What are they doing?' he asked the master mariner who stood beside him.

'They are building the bonfire on Capo di Faro. A fishing fleet will come in later, and the bonfire guides them away from the rocks like dragon's teeth. They have talked about building a lantern up there for years, but nothing happens. However, now we have a city republic, and with the Signori Embriaco, we may see some progress.'

The city looked beautiful in the setting sun, the light reflecting on the gaily-painted houses and hundreds of ships moored, waiting for the morning tide, as the little trading cog nudged its way through the ships towards the wharves.

The journey across the Mediterranean had given Morvan time to sit and ponder the last few weeks' events. He thought back to what had happened in Normandy. The King's fall had been tragic and was proving to be fatal. King William still used the older type of saddle, on his bay gelding, that he had used at the Battle of Hastings. It was built to be more secure as the knights dropped the reins and swung their swords, two-handed, at the enemy. The saddle had a very high, rigid front pommel with a similar high piece of wood at the back. When William's horse had jumped the fire-filled ditch, it had made it to the other side but then stumbled to its knees. The King had been thrown violently forward onto the high pommel, inflicting serious internal injuries. He had then fallen sideways to the ground clutching his middle. Morvan and Earl De Clare had managed to get him to his feet and back on his horse. They had to get him away, although they could see that he was in considerable pain. By the time they crossed the River Eure and Garret had destroyed the bridges, the King was ashen-faced and sweating. A wagon was brought and filled with pallet beds to cushion the journey. A physician gave him juice of the poppy and then travelled with him and a priest in the wagon.

Morvan had spent the next hours breaking camp and ensuring that any wounded were seen to, while his mind was on the King. Every soldier knew that internal ruptures were never good, and he feared the worst. He couldn't imagine life in Normandy without the King. It seemed to take days until the King was finally in Rouen, where it became increasingly obvious that this wasn't an injury he would survive. The Earl De Clare had already sent messengers to the Conqueror's children, but only two appeared, Henry and William. The Duke of Brittany, Alan Fergant, did not even share the news with Constance that her father was dying.

The King was surrounded by his sons, nobles, physicians and priests, so Morvan had only managed to see him once when William had asked for him.

Morvan was shocked by what he saw. William was a tall, well-made man with a huge presence and a booming voice. The grey-faced man propped up on the bed was a shadow of his former self, even after such a short time. The King had shooed the others away and had reached out to take Morvan's arm. 'I have paid, Malvais. I have paid for the churches and monasteries I burnt in Mantes, and God has punished me.'

Unsure what to say, Morvan had been silent as the King continued. 'I have paid reparation; I have sent money to the Archbishop to rebuild them all.' He dropped his head back on the bolster, exhausted. There was a sheen of sweat on his face, and his eyes had an unnatural glitter. He had seemed to have trouble focussing as he closed his eyes.

He had been silent for some moments, and Morvan could see the assembled nobles and priests hovering at the far side of the chamber. Then William had whispered, 'Tell me the truth, Malvais, I only have days left. Is it indeed true that my daughter Constance had your child?' Morvan's eyes widened. This may be a dying King, but he was always vengeful.

William had grimaced a smile. 'Do not fear. I have known for some time. Matilda told me on her death bed. She begged my forgiveness for not telling me, but she made me promise not to punish you or Constance.'

Morvan had nodded and then dropped his eyes. 'His name is Conn, and he has her blue eyes. I have never even seen him—he has been kidnapped, taken by Pope Victor because he is your grandchild.'

Williams's brow furrowed in anger, and he signed that he wanted some more of the heavily drugged wine and brandy. Morvan held the goblet up to his dry lips, and he drank deeply. 'I thank and reward you for your service, Morvan De Malvais, but I now release you to return to your home in Brittany,' he said in a loud voice to be heard by those in the room. Then he whispered, 'Find him, Morvan. Go and find my grandson. You don't need to be here. I have had my day, and now it's yours.'

Morvan gestured that he understood but then quietly added before he left, 'Chatillon is using poison to ensure we will have our vengeance on this Pope.' William had smiled, and then, closing his eyes, he had dropped his head back while wearily waving Morvan away.

When he reached the door, a scribe had handed him a bulky leather pouch and made him sign a document on the table in the hall. Looking inside, he had discovered the title deeds to several manors on the borders of Normandy and Brittany. There was also a bag of gold. The scribe sanded the ink and rolled the sheet. 'For services rendered, Sire, the King's wish.'

Morvan bowed. He found his eyes were wet with tears as he left the building. He had ridden to Caen and handed over the command of the Horse Warriors in Normandy to Garret Eymer, who was sad to see him go but understood and wished them well on their quest. He had then left at a gallop on the road south to Marseilles. A message had been waiting for him in Marseilles to find a boat to take him to Genoa.

Now, at last, he was here, and Gerard sat waiting for him on the harbour wall. They clasped arms, and Gerard held him at arm's length. 'You look as if you have been to hell and back,' he said, looking at the thinner grim-faced young man whom he had brought up like a son. 'Nothing, some decent food and a few decent nights' sleep won't put right, Gerard,' he replied, smiling.

'Come, I will take you to Chatillon's house. We can talk there and tell you what we have discovered.'

Morvan laughed. 'Why does it not surprise me that Chatillon is here and has a house.'

Gerard smiled back. 'It was Bianca's house, and it's very impressive and beautiful but not as secure as I would like. It isn't a real donjon.'

Luc greeted his brother with a smile and a bear hug, the first one since they had fallen out so tragically eight years before. Morvan smiled; it was good to be back with his family. 'I just hope you don't expect me to call you Papa since you married our mother,' he joked. Gerard grinned; he loved these two young men as if they were his own. He couldn't begin to explain his happiness when he looked to a future life at Morlaix with the woman he loved by his side and his two adopted sons and their families.

Luc gestured him to a chair. 'Come, sit down, and we will tell you what we know. You must be impatient for news, but we have come further in the last two weeks than we have in the last two years.'

'Where is Chatillon?' asked Morvan, glancing around the large airy chamber with its expensive furniture and wide sunny balcony.

Edvard, who was serving them wine, replied. 'He was called away to see a friend in the countryside—something urgent he had to deal with—and he'll return later.'

Chatillon galloped up the tree-lined track to the large estate in the hills. One of his servants knew the way, and as the Warrior Monks were known to be still somewhere in Genoa, he took four of his men as an escort. It only took an hour to reach the fortified manor house, and again Chatillon could see the Roman influence as he walked through the large doors into a cool square courtyard. The Nubian servant took him into a large room with floor to ceiling shutters standing open to let in the afternoon breeze.

Signora Di Monsi knew as soon as she heard the sound of hooves galloping up the drive that she was discovered. She was surprised to see the Papal Envoy alone; she expected Luc De Malvais to be with him.

'This is a welcome surprise, Piers. I thought you would be too busy with your guests,' she said in a light, carefree tone that did not reflect the turmoil inside. He had risen from his seat, and now he slowly walked towards her, his dark eyes never leaving hers as he took her hand, kissing her fingertips. He was a very good-looking man in a dark satanic sort of way. You never knew what he was thinking or what he planned, but he was exciting.

He held her chin and looked down into her large clear grey eyes. 'Can we dispense with the pretence now? I know who you are or who you were.'

She found it impossible to keep looking into those accusing eyes, despite the smile that played around his lips. 'How did you find out?' she asked, resigned to her fate and sitting down on a long carved settle.

He sat beside her, still holding her hand in his. 'The widow who returned to Genoa at just the right time, with long fair hair and large grey eyes—hardly Italian colouring, is it Signora?'

She smiled. 'I get those from my Norman grandfather, a knight in Maine, but he was murdered by Anjou troops, leaving the family penniless.'

'I must admit, your daughter had me confused for some time; I presume she is the daughter of Brian Ap Gwyfd, and he never saw her.'

She nodded, and tears ran down her cheeks. 'Brian never came back. He rode off with Conn for two days, and I never saw them again. We were so happy and planned to buy a large manor and farm in Ynys Mon to breed horses, but he left me a wealthy woman with the bags of silver he had accumulated. I waited for him for weeks on the farm, hoping they would appear. Then a local farmer told us they had found his horse. They searched the area again to see if he was injured, but they found nothing.'

Chatillon pulled her close and held her in his arms for a few minutes. Then he held her at arm's length. 'Now tell me again. Every detail, no matter how small. We think that Conn is still alive, but I fear he'll not be for long. We must find him!'

She opened her eyes wide. 'Alive? So is Brian alive as well?'

Chatillon shook his head. 'No, I am sure that Warrior Monks killed him. He was paid to bring Conn here and then hand him over, but something went wrong, and they decided to get rid of the evidence, or any links to the child. He clearly never told them about you, Hildebrand, or you would also be dead.'

She told him everything twice and then ordered her servant to bring some maps, and she showed him where she thought the farm was and which direction they had ridden.

She sat back and looked at Chatillon, a quizzical but concerned expression on her face. 'What are you going to do, Piers? Are you going to expose that I have been living a lie here in Genoa?'

He regarded her solemnly for a moment. 'You knew that it was wrong to take the child, but you were unaware that Brian was kidnapping him to order?'

She shook her head, throwing back her long fair hair. 'I loved Conn, Piers, as if he was my own. I could see that having Luc's bastard by blow there would cause problems for Merewyn and the other children. It was only much later that I found out it was his brother's child, and he was banished from Brittany, so he would never see Conn. I believed Brian when he said he would take us to the west and that we would be a true family together.'

'His father is here, Hildebrand. He arrived in Genoa today to join Luc in searching for the child. The Malvais family have searched for nearly seven years for this child, as have I; we have never given up hope.'

Hildebrand put a hand to her mouth in shock. 'They must hate me.'

Chatillon sat silently for a while, not saying a word, and then he stood to go. 'I must return to Genoa, but I will talk to them. I will try and persuade them that you were duped as well. Today, stay up here on the estate, out of the way. Return tomorrow night.'

For the first time, hope appeared on her drawn face. They walked across the courtyard, and Marietta came running over. She had large grey eyes like her mother but with auburn hair and freckles. Chatillon had met her a few times before, but he couldn't prevent a smile. A part of the horseman, Brian Ap Gwyfd, lived on in Marietta.

It was very late when he returned. His men pointed out that they had been followed, and even now, two horsemen were in the trees behind them. They raced down the road and then halted in a rocky pass, to ambush them, but surprisingly they did not appear.

Chatillon found that his guests had retired, but Edvard, as usual, waited up for him. He invited his manservant and companion to sit, and he found himself relating the tale of Hildebrand. Chatillon was now sure that the boy was somewhere in Northern Italy. He had to see Bishop Conrades—he may well know the area she described, in the foothills of the Alps.

'What are you going to do about the Signora?' asked Edvard, his head on one side.

Chatillon took some moments to answer. 'I will try and protect her. She is my mistress, and I am fond of her. She has a razor-sharp mind for business and will prove very useful. I just need to convince the Malvais brothers not to expose her or kill her.'

Edvard shook his head in disbelief with a snort of cynical laughter. 'I wish you well with that. When you tell them, I may find that I have important business out of the house.'

Chatillon rose to retire when they heard a scraping sound

from the balcony. Both men drew their daggers and advanced with silent stealth towards the large shutters that stood open onto the balcony. They paused. Edvard met his master's eyes and nodded, and they burst onto the wide stone balcony. It was empty.

They both stood and scanned the gardens and walls below, but nothing moved in the shadows. Chatillon told Edvard of the two monks who had followed him today.

'They are still here in Genoa. We need to be vigilant, Edvard.'

The manservant nodded, and pulling the shutters closed, he barred them securely.

Outside, underneath the stone balcony, the leader of the Warrior Monks was clinging to the stonework, with pure determination. He had been on the balcony in the shadows, but he swung himself onto the balustrade, having heard enough. Unfortunately, his sword scabbard scraped the stone. In a flash, he swung underneath, his fingers clinging to the narrow stone ledge and one foot on the carved support.

When he heard the shutters close, he dropped to the ground in a roll and came up onto his feet. He had no chance to kill the envoy, but what he heard and now intended to do would please Scaravaggi. He was satisfied with the night's work.

Chapter Twenty

Early next morning, Chatillon sent Edvard hotfoot to Bishop Conrades to ask him to call. Edvard returned sooner than expected. 'The Bishop is called away to Milan, but they expect him to return for mass, in the Basilica of St Syrus, on Sunday.' Chatillon had to be content with that, which meant Hildebrand's fate had to wait.

He sent a message to that effect, to reassure her, before heading to break his fast with his guests. Morvan was pleased to see him and greeted him warmly, roasting him about his forthcoming wedding to a young, beautiful Italian wife.

They spent an hour or two discussing the new information that they had. Luc asked if they had possibly moved the child—was he now down in Monte Cassino close to Dauferio?

Chatillon shook his head. 'Initially, I suspected that might be the case, but now I do not doubt that the child went north and is still there. I'm waiting for Bishop Conrades to return as he is bringing me more information on the whereabouts of Scaravaggi, the Master of the Warrior Monks that I believe are holding Conn.'

They sat in companionable silence for a while, each with their thoughts, and then Chatillon told them that he had found Hildebrand.

He watched the shocked expressions appear, and then Gerard jumped to his feet. 'Where is she? I will throttle the truth out of her with my bare hands. She stole Conn from us.'

Chatillon was ready for this, and he calmed Gerard and told him to sit. However, Morvan was on the edge of his chair, staring at Chatillon, tight-lipped, while Luc's knuckles were white as he gripped the arms of the chair, his steel-blue eyes narrowed in anger. He told them what he knew, the story she had told him yesterday. They listened raptly, various emotions crossing their faces.

'Did you believe her Chatillon, or was she trying to save her own skin?' asked Luc in an ice-cold voice.

'I believed her absolutely. She has too much to lose; she has a daughter, Brian's child. She truly loved him and believed what he told her. She had no idea that she was stealing the child to order. I am willing to take one of you to talk to her so that you can hear it and judge it yourself.'

It went quiet for some time as the three men considered what they had heard. 'It can't be me; I find that I'm still too angry,' said Gerard.

Chatillon was relieved. 'She is returning to the city tonight. I will take one of you there tomorrow morning,' he said, looking at Luc and Morvan.

'No, you will not, Chatillon. Both Morvan, as Conn's father, and I will accompany you because she was my servant.' Chatillon sighed; he had to be happy with that. At that moment, Edvard entered with a message. His face was solemn as he handed it to his master. He thanked Edvard, who did not move.

Chatillon stood and, raising a glass, indicated that the others should do the same. 'My friends, King William is dead, and

Robert Curthose is now Duke of Normandy. William Rufus is King of England, and Prince Henry is now a very wealthy young man.' Even though it was expected after what Morvan had told them, the shock on Chatillon's face was reflected on their own. King William had influenced all of their lives for the last twenty-two years, and now, one of the greatest warrior kings in Europe was dead.

They raised their glasses in several toasts, and the previous plans for the day were forgotten as they recalled their exploits riding with, and for, William. 'It's the end of an era, and I must send messages immediately on behalf of myself and the Pope to congratulate the new rulers,' said Chatillon as he rose and left the two brothers and Gerard to their thoughts.

'You probably spent more time with him than most, Morvan. How did you find him?' asked Gerard.

Morvan regarded them both for a moment. 'He was a giant in his time. Now that I have met several other European rulers and kings, I would say that William was a level above them, decisive, driven, and loyal to those who were loyal to him. Quick in his thoughts and actions and, above all, fearless—laughing in the face of death. Yet, there was the soldier side of William. A man who had the common touch, a man who would walk around the camp, sit at the campfires with his men, and jest with them. They loved him for it and would follow him anywhere.'

'That is a good assessment, and I'm glad that you overcame your hatred of him for marrying Constance to Alan Fergant.' added Luc.

Morvan shrugged. 'I was young and naïve. She was a royal princess who would always marry for political advantage, but we were so in love that we thought we could escape that. I still love her, Luc,' he said with an almost defiant glance at his brother.

The next morning they left the Palazzo Castello to meet with Hildebrand. Chatillon was rarely ever apprehensive, but as they walked across the city and up to the gates of the Signora Di Monsi's townhouse, he felt uncertain about what the Malvais brothers would do or say to her. He glanced across at them; they were in full Horse Warrior regalia with the laced leather doublets and the crossed swords on their backs. Luc's face was stony and unreadable. Morvan was tight-lipped but with an air of expectancy. It would be difficult for him to meet the woman who took his son, the son he had never seen.

When they walked up the old cobbled street, Chatillon was surprised to see that one of the big wooden gates to the courtyard and stables was slightly ajar. Usually, you would have to ring a bell for a servant. He pushed it open, and there wasn't a servant in sight. Had she decided to stay in the countryside, after all, he wondered, or that she was unable to face them? He crossed the large courtyard to the covered tunnel-like staircase that ascended to the chambers above. Luc and Morvan followed, glancing around and behind them as they sensed his uneasiness. He held up a hand for them to stop and stay there.

It was dark and cooler in the shadows of the steep entrance, but the sharp metallic smell was unmistakable, and he could feel the stickiness on the stairs as he mounted the steps. Halfway up the stairs, it was even darker, as the heavy door at the top was closed, and the only light came from below and behind him. He almost fell over the sprawled leg and body of the Signora's Nubian servant, a mountain of a man lying prone with his throat cut, his scimitar lying on the step below.

Chatillon glanced up at the door above and drew his sword. Turning to the Malvais brothers, who had not yet seen the body, he put his finger on his lips and indicated they should wait. Stepping over the dead man, he made his way slowly up the staircase alone. He pushed the door open and emerged, sword in hand, onto the wide landing, while glancing quickly around. There was no sound, and the sun shone from the balcony across the chamber and onto the landing. He moved forward to stand in the centre of the entrance hall, hearing a slight sound as Luc and Morvan moved up the stairs. Again, he raised a hand for them to stop at the top of the stairs.

There were two dark passageways from the landing and a double window, almost floor to ceiling with closed wooden shutters, the entrance to the big chamber and another room with the door closed. Chatillon moved lightly and silently into the large chamber. A maid lay sprawled behind the door in a pool of dark blood.

He stopped, his eyes searching every nook and cranny for hidden assailants. The room appeared empty, but then he saw her as he made his way toward the large balcony. She was in the corner propped up against the stone balustrade, her blue embroidered overgown soaked in blood. One hand clutched her chest, and blood oozed between her fingers. She raised a hand feebly to Chatillon, but it dropped back by her side.

There was so much blood he knew that she could not possibly live. He took her hand and knelt beside her, pushing her bloodstained hair back from her face. 'Marietta?' he whispered.

'In the country, still. Look after my daughter, Piers,' she pleaded hoarsely. Then alarm filled her eyes, and her hand clenched him as she whispered in a broken voice. 'They are still here, the monks, still here....' She looked up, and Chatillon followed her gaze. Above the balcony on the next floor was a window, and the tattooed monk that Chatillon had seen sitting on his garden wall was sitting, sword in hand, on the ledge above.

The man dropped lithely to the balcony as Chatillon yelled, 'To me!' The monk smiled. He expected Chatillon's large protector and maybe only a servant or two, as he gave a signal that brought two more Warrior Monks running from the dark passageways.

Luc and Morvan had followed Chatillon's orders reluctantly, and they had remained out of sight on the tunnel-like staircase. Both men had drawn a sword as they had seen Chatillon do the same, and they knew that something was amiss as soon as they saw the body of the Nubian. They heard the muffled sound of conversation, but then there was the sound of running bare feet and the war cry from Chatillon. They burst out of the staircase to see two Warrior Monks, swords raised, racing towards the Papal Envoy, who was engaged in a sword fight with a larger monk.

The two monks whirled, their eyes wide at the sight of two Horse Warriors, now with a sword in each hand. Their leader fighting on the balcony was finding it much harder than he expected; Scaravaggi had omitted to tell him that the Papal Envoy was a master swordsman. Chatillon was tall and fit. His upper body was muscular from the weekly sessions with Edvard with both sword and staff. The tattooed monk found that every stroke and slash was parried and returned. They were standing face to face, blade to blade when the Horse Warriors burst into the chamber.

Chatillon saw the sudden fear and apprehension in his

opponent's eyes, as the man nervously glanced left into the chamber. He brought his knee up and slammed it into the monk's groin. The man fell back, doubled in pain but with his sword still in his hand. Chatillon raised his sword and slashed downward as the monk, his back pressed against the balustrade, weakly fended him off, the blades grating together. Chatillon, with gritted teeth, growled into his face, Don't worry, I am not going to kill you. I will skin you alive to get every piece of information from you.'

The monk's mouth set into a grim line. He pushed Chatillon back using all of his strength. The monk looked across into the chamber, panting with exertion. He then glanced down behind him. Before Chatillon could stop him, he flipped downwards over the balustrade, slamming face down into the cobbled street some distance below.

Chatillon clutched the stone mantle and swore loudly. He had chosen to take his own life rather than give information. He could see the dark pool of blood spreading from the monk's head as some locals gathered around.

He turned and made his way into the chamber. One monk was wounded on the floor, Morvan's foot on his throat. Luc De Malvais was engaged with the older monk, who was very good but not good enough, as Malvais thrust his sword through the man's chest. He dropped to his knees and fell face down on the floor, his sword spinning and clattering away.

'Keep him alive,' he shouted at Morvan as he turned back to the balcony. He moved to Hildebrand's side, but he could see that she was gone. He heard a movement behind him, and Luc was there.

'She has hardly changed since I found her in a burnt and ruined manor house on the borders of Maine. Her husband

and grandfather were dead, only twenty-one years old, and she had just lost her baby.

Chatillon straightened up. 'She was a remarkable woman. She built a well-respected trading empire in Genoa. You changed her life by taking her to Morlaix. She asked the local priest in Morlaix to help her improve her reading and writing when she found that the druid priests had educated Brian.'

Chatillon gently closed Hildebrand's eyes. 'I will get Edvard to deal with the bodies, and the female servants can see to their mistress. The city authorities must be notified, and I will arrange the funeral with the Bishop on his return tomorrow.' They left her and moved back into the chamber.

'Why did they kill her?' asked Morvan.

Chatillon rubbed his eyes before he spoke. 'I imagine that she was being used as a trap for me, but she refused to go along with their plans. I found a dagger on the floor beside her; she fought back.'

Morvan pulled the injured monk to his feet and tied his hands behind him. He had a nasty wound on his leg, and Morvan bound it with strips cut from his robe. Several hours later, the monk was chained in the cellar at Chatillon's house. Hildebrand's body had been washed and dressed by the servants, anointed by the priest and laid on a bier in the hall of her house. There were many tears both for her, as she was much loved by her servants and neighbours, and for her murdered servants.

Chatillon stood looking down at her. Would he bring death to all of the women he loved or felt affection for, he wondered. She looked as if she were sleeping. He kissed his fingers and placed them on her cold lips in farewell. Tomorrow or the next day, he would have to ride out to her estate and break it to her daughter Marietta that her mother would not be coming home again.

He would have to decide what to do with the child. Her mother wouldn't want her to be hidden away in a convent. When she reached her majority at twenty-five, she would be a very wealthy young woman. However, he would be her guardian until then, which brought a smile to his face. It wasn't a role that he was comfortable with, or suited to, with his reputation and past. He decided to consult Isabella about it; she knew Signora Di Monsi and may have thoughts about what should happen to the girl.

He shook himself and laughed aloud as he walked out into the early autumn sunshine. At this rate, he would be unrecognisable. He now had himself a 'ward' he was responsible for, and a future wife that he was consulting about what to do with her. Edvard would think that he had run mad!

Chapter Twenty-one

The whole of Genoese society was shocked by the murder of Signora Di Monsi. None more so than Bishop Conrades Mezzarello when he returned to the city. He came immediately to see Chatillon, and he was somewhat taken aback to find three Horse Warriors waiting for him as well.

He recognised Luc De Malvais and Gerard instantly from their days as mercenaries in Lombardy. In fact, Sir Gerard had actually saved his life when he was a lowly priest fleeing from the war. He doubted that the tall, stately warrior with the grey sweptback hair would remember that. Conrades was certainly aware of Luc's reputation, and he eyed him more warily. Although he regarded Chatillon as a friend, he had often thought it was like sitting down with a snake. You never knew when it would strike. Now he felt as if he was in a pit of snakes, as he gratefully accepted a goblet of wine from Edvard and settled himself into a high back chair facing the room.

'I was shocked to hear of events in my absence. Do we know who was responsible?' he asked, frowning at Chatillon.

Instead, Luc answered for him. 'We think the Warrior Monks were trying to kidnap her to set up a trap for Chatillon. She was courageous; she fought back, so they killed her and the servants who tried to defend her.'

185

Bishop Conrades lifted his eyes in surprise to Chatillon. 'Dauferio must really want you dead, my friend, and Scaravaggi is the weapon he is using. He must be mad even to contemplate doing this so openly.'

Chatillon nodded. 'I think there is no doubt that he is losing his mind. He is not making rational decisions, and he is leaving too many trails that lead back to him as Pope. I think you need to let the enclave in Rome know this. They need to act before he brings disgrace on the Holy See.'

The Bishop nodded in agreement. 'Have you heard any more about the Pope's condition? I believe he is now very ill, is that true?'

Chatillon smiled and met Morvan's eyes. 'They say that he could go any day now or last a week, a month even. He is in God's hands.'

Morvan sat forward. He did not care what happened to Pope Victor. 'Have you found him? Have you found Scaravaggi? Do we know where he is hiding?' he asked the Bishop.

Conrades nodded and steepled his fingers. 'I called in many favours, and the name of one place kept coming up. As to whether he is there, that is debatable. As we know, he moves around, and with the Pope's deteriorating health, it's expected that he'll be at Monte Cassino soon.'

Luc's impatience got the better of him. 'What is the name of this place you have found, and where is it?' he demanded.

'It's a large Hermitage, a monastery cunningly built into the side of a mountain, almost hanging over the valley. I spent a week there as a young novice, a bleak place high in the foothills of the Italian Alps. It's run by a strict military order of Warrior Monks. It's impossible to get inside or attack it because of its position; it only has one steep, narrow entrance along a cliff path. It's called the Hermitage of San Colombano.'

Chatillon stood and crossed to a table at the side of the room, he had marked the farm, where Brian left Hildebrand, on the map. He moved the table into the light from the balcony and called his friend over. 'Show us where you think it is, Conrades. This is a rough map, but it'll give us an idea.'

The Horse Warriors gathered beside him as the Bishop followed a valley north with his finger along the side of a large lake. He then moved east along a range of mountains and north again. 'Here,' he announced. 'I am sure it is here; there are two distinct peaks behind it.'

Gerard slapped him on the back and smiled, 'We leave tomorrow, we go to find Conn, and we bring him home.'

The Bishop turned and looked at the triumphant faces of the Horse Warriors. So the stolen boy belonged to one of the Malvais brothers. He thought at that moment that Master Scaravaggi might have bitten off more than he could chew. Did he have any idea whose child he had in the Hermitage, or what would happen when they tracked him down? He decided that he was better off not knowing anymore, and he took his leave of them, to go and prepare for the funeral of the Signora.

Meanwhile, Chatillon, for once, was advocating caution, much to Gerard's annoyance. 'It may be that the Hermitage is where the child was delivered but is he there now? It's quite a journey to fight your way into an inhospitable building full of Warrior Monks and then find that the boy has gone to Monte Cassino.' He could see by their faces that they saw the sense of what he was saying, but it did not mean that they liked it.

'We have a captive downstairs; let us find out what he knows,' said Gerard. Chatillon stood and indicated that

Edvard should follow him. Morvan moved forward as well. Chatillon put a hand on his arm.

'What I am about to do may not be for those of a more sensitive stomach. He may break with little persuasion for being young, but he has also been indoctrinated. He watched his leader fling himself to his death rather than tell us anything.'

Morvan nodded his mouth, a thin line. 'They have my son Chatillon. I need to be there. I need to hear where Conn is and if he is alive.'

Chatillon paused for a second but then said, 'Very well,' and indicated that he should follow them.

Gerard and Luc sat with their wine, pulling chairs out onto the balcony to watch the bustling harbour below. They sent messages back to Morlaix, so that the wives waiting there knew that they were in Genoa, had a strong lead on Conn's whereabouts and would be going to find him. Even through the thick walls of the Palazzo, the odd scream penetrated to interrupt their reverie, but they had both seen and done worse in the past, so it did not affect them. This was war, a war against the Pope and his minions, a war they intended to win by any means.

An hour later, a white-faced Morvan appeared. Gerard did not comment on the blood spots splashed on his doublet and face. He came out onto the balcony and rested his hands on the stone balustrade, looking at but not seeing the normal harbour scene below. He poured himself a large wine, with a hand that wasn't completely steady, and gulped it down.

'Conn is at the Hermitage. He is still alive. He is one of the seven chosen Knights of God. He has been there with Scaravaggi and the monks for nearly seven years. Will, there be anything left of the boy you raised, Luc?' he said, his voice breaking with emotion.

Gerard stood and grasped him by the shoulders. 'He is a Malvais, Morvan. Always remember that he is the grandson of King William. His parents are some of the bravest people I know. He will be strong, have character, and have fought to survive. And now we go and get him back.'

Morvan saw the tears in Gerard's eyes, this man who had been as a father to him for most of his life, and he pulled him into a bear hug. Gerard responded and then held him at arm's length. 'Now go and get washed and changed. Let us have dinner. We have a lot to plan as we leave tomorrow.'

Chatillon heard them as he crossed to his room, wiping the blood from his hands on a cloth. The young monk had tried to hold out, but the pain and the threats had been too much, and he had finally broken as they removed the third finger, gasping out the truth. Chatillon instructed Edvard to cut his throat as he mounted the stairs. After all, he was an assassin, sent to kill both him and the people that he had cared for in Genoa. For a few moments, he could see the large, beautiful eyes of Hildebrand smiling into his, and he made a decision. He sat and wrote a coded message to his man in Monte Cassino.

The day is nigh.

He then wrapped it and placed it in a tiny tube, ready to be attached to a bird's leg. He smiled; the devious Pope Victor III, known as Dauferio, was to breathe his last. He would no longer meddle in the affairs of Europe, or snuff out innocent lives as if they were of no account.

He sent the same message to his uncle, the Cardinal, in Rome. He knew that Odo De Chatillon had gathered his allies, and within days of the Pope's death, the infighting and bribery would begin in earnest to select the next Pope. Chatillon was confident that his uncle, the powerful Cardinal and Prior of Cluny, would win. He had even selected his name—he would be Pope Urban II—and it would be Chatillon's mission to spread his uncle's influence and extend his power in Europe.

First, however, he had to solve the problem of Master Scaravaggi. He changed his clothes and headed back to join the three Horse Warriors, who were still poring over the map and the position of San Colombano. Edvard served dinner as they discussed the route, and Chatillon took over.

'The Hermitage is in an area called Trembileno. You'll go directly north of Genoa. It'll be hard going, but hopefully, the weather will be good. When you reach Piacenza on the River Po, you turn east, following the river to cross at Cremona. Then you go northeast to the shores of Lake Garda. You'll need to replenish your supplies as you go north into the mountains, following the River Adige in the Vallagarina valley. The next days will be the hardest as you climb and cross the high jagged hills of Trentino. The terrain there is inhospitable, with few villages before you drop slightly south and reach the Hermitage.

Chatillon paused and looked at the faces around him. He noted the frowns of concentration as they realised how arduous this would be.

'You can see how they could easily dispose of Brian's body. There is nothing in this area but bears and wolves,' said Luc, following the route with a finger.

'Little is known of this area; most people avoid it due to the bands of roaming bandits and deserters.' added Chatillon.

Gerard grinned. 'You're making this journey sound more

attractive all the time, Chatillon.' They all laughed, which broke the tension somewhat.

'I will have Edvard create a smaller version of the map onto a sheet of vellum that you can fold and take with you. I have arranged for sturdy riding and pack horses. It will take you four or five days to get there, and then several more for scouting the territory and finding a way to get into the Hermitage.'

Luc stood and stretched. 'Come, let us pack and assess what supplies we need. I would imagine that we will need rope of some description.'

Chatillon nodded. 'Edvard has laid out what he thinks you will need on the benches outside the stables.'

Gerard set off to check, but Morvan and Luc lingered to thank the Papal assassin who had become a friend. 'I'm so pleased that I did not slit your throat eight years ago in that dark alleyway in Ghent, Chatillon. Who knew that you would become so useful to us?'

Chatillon put his head back and roared with laughter as they headed down to join Gerard. 'Indeed, Morvan. I am so pleased that I did not slide my second knife between your ribs and into your heart. Think of the excitement and intrigue we would have missed.'

Luc, walking behind them, shook his head in disbelief. He never ceased to be amazed at the friendship that had developed between Europe's most dangerous assassin and his brother.

Chapter Twenty-two

While the Horse Warriors prepared for their journey to the Hermitage, Chatillon had an unpleasant task ahead. He had decided to enlist the support of his future bride Isabella Embriaco. Their relationship had developed into a growing friendship with pleasant banter and amusement. Chatillon found that the girl had hidden depths but had been held back by the attitude of her father and older brothers. Hence her demands for attention and her stubborn behaviour. However, under Chatillon's tutelage, she began to blossom, for suddenly, she had a man who asked for and seemed to value her opinion on matters. He found that she was a quick learner, with a ready wit, and an excellent memory, that he thought may be useful in the future. He certainly had plans for the beautiful Isabella, of which she was blissfully unaware.

As for Isabella, she found Chatillon fascinating. She had learned far more about him and now understood her father's immense pleasure, and her brother's awe, at the match. Chatillon not only had wealth, but he also had influence. She listened to the amusing, and sometimes shocking, tales that he told her of the happenings of the courts of Europe, and she was mesmerised by it. This was now to be her life, travelling the courts and cities of Europe, an escape from Genoa's small, enclosed society. They were to be married in two months, and Bishop Mezzarello was to officiate in the basilica of St Syrus. Part of her could not wait. Despite this, she felt some apprehension at being in the power of such a man, who had dozens of mistresses and had been about to marry the stunningly beautiful Bianca Da Landriano before she was murdered. Chatillon had hardly touched her since that first night. He seemed to regard her with amused affection, but now and again, she caught a glint in those dark eyes that told her he desired her.

This morning he was taking her riding, so she had dressed with care. It was September, but the days were still warm. He arrived promptly and helped her mount, running his hand lightly up her booted foot to caress her calf and the soft area behind her knee. She felt a shiver of excitement that she had never experienced in her short liaison with Alfredo—but he was a mere boy. She knew that Chatillon was an experienced lover.

It was still cool as they rode out of Genoa up into the hills, before dropping down onto the fields of the plain. He had not shared where they were going, just that it would take an hour or so. They chatted pleasantly but broke into a canter once down in the meadows. They reached a tree-lined track that led to the soft slopes of the hill in front of them. It led to a large, old, walled manor house with a red-tiled roof. It faced south, and laden fruit orchards, and olive trees, lined the sunlit slopes. She noticed that over a dozen men up ladders were picking the fruit, and she wondered if this was one of his many estates. They rode to the large wooden doors of the manor and dismounted. He lifted her down and walked towards a small group of women spreading plums on large sheets, checking them for wasp damage before being stored, or preserved, in large stone pots. Looking at the stains around the mouths of the laughing children, they were also testing the quality, and Isabella smiled.

Chatillon stopped a short distance away and then called, 'Marietta'. A young girl with braided auburn hair looked up and waved. The older woman, who seemed to be supervising the group, shielded her eyes to look at the visitors and recognised him. She came and bowed to him and Isabella but then looked beyond them. 'Is the Signora not with you, Monseigneur?' she asked.

In a low tone, he told her what had happened in the house in Genoa. She covered her mouth with her hand, the tears falling unashamedly. 'Everyone loved her,' she said to Isabella, who now realised where she was and whose daughter was sitting oblivious under the plum trees.

She looked questioningly at Chatillon, who, understanding that look, smiled and shook his head. 'No, Marietta isn't mine; she is the daughter of a man from the far west who died before she was born. I promised her dying mother that I would make sure she was taken care of.'

Isabella looked at the carefree child under the trees. 'Will you tell her today?' He nodded as the tearful servant gently pulled Marietta to her feet and took her back into the house.

She returned the young girl to them, washed and dressed. They were sitting in the room where Chatillon had recently discovered that the Signora was Hildebrand as he suspected. The shutters were open, and it was flooded with light. The servant led Marietta to sit on the divan beside Isabella, who looked down with sympathy at the girl's huge, grey eyes. Chatillon took a deep breath and started to explain what had happened, but Isabella stopped him. In a low voice, she explained to the girl her mother had been such a good person that the angels had decided to take her away to heaven.

Chatillon sat and watched. This was a side of Isabella that he had never seen, compassion and empathy with the child as she kept explaining. He had to look away as the young girl sobbed on Isabella's shoulder, her arms around her waist. He rose and left them there, walking outside, to sit in the shade. After a while, Isabella joined him. 'What will happen to her, Piers? Does she have another family who will take her in?'

He shook his head. 'She'll become my ward. She is a very wealthy young woman, and I have not yet decided where she'll go. A convent was my first thought, convenient for me, but I can't think that it was what her mother would want for her.'

Isabella shuddered at the thought. 'They would crush her character and spirit. No, Piers. She'll come to us. She'll be no trouble with her own servants, who clearly love her, and she'll keep me entertained and occupied when you're away, for I believe you'll still be travelling a lot.'

Chatillon looked at her and smiled. She had passed the test, and taking her chin in his hand, he leaned forward and kissed her deeply, leaving her breathless. 'Everyone warned me that I shouldn't even think of marrying you, Isabella. *A spoilt termagant* was one of the nicer things they said about you, but I think you might have just proved them all wrong. Let us go and make arrangements, as the child shouldn't be left on her own to brood and grieve.'

They stood, but then, emboldened, Isabella put a hand on his arm. 'One thing. The Signora Di Monsi, was she your lover?' she demanded. She noticed that his eyes suddenly seemed darker, and harder, as he turned and firmly took her wrist to remove her hand.

'Yes, she was, and I had some affection for her. But we won't speak of this again. I assure you that there will undoubtedly be more mistresses, but they won't be any concern of yours,' he said in an ice-cold tone. He moved ahead of her through the large shutters into the room, and she stood there for a few seconds, blinking. For a few minutes, she had seen a softer side to the Papal Envoy, but in an instant, that had gone. Instead, she faced a man she wouldn't want to challenge; she felt her stomach knot.

When he returned to the Castello, he found that the three Horse Warriors were ready to depart. He explained where he had been and the arrangements for his newly acquired ward, Marietta. 'If she is anything like her parents, she'll lead you a merry dance when she is older,' laughed Gerard.

Morvan just smiled; he had seen the other side of Chatillon on a few occasions now. He clasped arms with the Papal assassin, who was fast becoming a friend. 'If you're not careful, Piers, your reputation will be in tatters at this rate. Chatillon the merciful, Chatillon, the philanthropist. These descriptions do not instil the same fear as Chatillon, the arch manipulator, the spy and assassin.' They all laughed and mounted their horses.

Luc had just picked up the reins when Edvard came running. 'A message, Sire. A message from Monte Cassino.' The Horse Warriors looked alarmed. Did this mean that Conn was in the south after all?' However, Morvan caught the fleeting satisfied smile on Chatillon's face as he turned to look up at them, and he knew immediately what the news was.

'I'm afraid that the Holy See has lost its father. Pope Victor III is dead.' Cardinal Dauferio, who had meddled in their lives and hundreds of others, even after he became Pope, was gone. There was silence in the stable yard for several minutes as they absorbed the information.

Morvan felt a wave of anger for the man who had used him, to undermine King William, and had then taken Conn for his own ends. He found that he was pleased Chatillon had poisoned him. At the very least, the man had deserved the pain and discomfort he had suffered, from a severe bloody flux, for several years. He even hoped that it had not been an easy death. He would undoubtedly do penance for these thoughts at another time, but he would revel in it now for a while.

His eyes met the dark, glittering ones of Chatillon, and he smiled. 'Thank you.'

Chatillon smiled back and bowed in return. Gerard looked at them with a puzzled expression. Even Luc gave him an enigmatic smile. Gerard knew that he had missed something here, but he would find out what it was.

Within three hours, Genoa and the province of Liguria were left behind them as they headed north to the River Po and Piacenza. They knew it would take them almost a week, but Morvan could hardly contain the feeling of hope that surged through his veins. They were going to find his son, Conn. They would rescue him and exact vengeance on those who had taken and mistreated him. Dauferio was dead; he had paid the price. Now Scaravaggi and his warrior sect would pay with their lives

Scaravaggi stood by the window of the tower. His knuckles were white as he grasped the rough stone lintel and tried to manage the emotions raging inside him. The pigeon had just arrived, and he had read the message. He had howled with rage that sent a bolt of fear through boys and monks alike. He pulled the bird from father Bruno's hands, snapped its neck and threw it from the tower window, to bounce forlornly on the jagged rocks below.

Dauferio, Pope Victor III, was dead. His mentor and master had supported and guided him almost his whole life. They had made such plans together, and now he was gone. He felt hollow; there was an emptiness inside, almost a loss of direction. He knew that now he had to step up. He must take over the other groups and stay focused and motivated. He was also concerned that he had heard nothing from his men in Milan—a group sent to kill Chatillon, but none had returned as yet.

He had been suspicious about the Pope's illness for some time; it did not seem natural. It came and went, leaving him weaker and more exhausted each time. Although he could see no poisoning symptoms, he knew it had Chatillon's mark all over it. *Who would gain from the death of Pope Victor III?* he asked himself... *Why, Chatillon's uncle, of course.* He howled in rage again and beat his fists against the stone walls until they bled. If Chatillon were still alive, he would find him and kill him. He would exact vengeance for his friend, Pope Victor.

Chapter Twenty-three

Luc hoped they would make it to Piacenza in a day if they set a good pace, but he had not considered the steep inclines, which lasted for nearly nine leagues. The steep twists and turns and the gullies on the road were exhausting for the horses. They encountered several swift-flowing torrents, but fortunately, there were bridges, as this was the road to Milan. Luc finally called a halt outside a large roadside village called Tortona, as they had only covered half of what they expected. There was a welcome inn with beds and stabling for the horses, and they all appreciated the hot cooked food and rich red wine provided by the innkeeper's buxom wife.

Their entry had caused quite a stir, but they loudly mentioned going to Milan. Morvan deflected interest by asking them if they knew about the Pope's death. The innkeeper immediately sent for the local priest, who had not heard. Goblets and tankards were raised for the Holy Father. Gerard was happy as they did not pay for anything that night, and the innkeeper's wife, who was very taken with Gerard, packed them huge rounds of fresh bread and tasty cheeses, wrapped in oiled linen, for the journey the next day.

Once they were out of sight of the inn, Luc unfolded the map and spread it on a rock. He knew that the road would divide shortly and that they would travel east. They would drop down into the valley of the River Po, which would take them directly to Piacenza. The two Malvais brothers teased Gerard about his conquest at the inn and swore they wouldn't tell their mother, which triggered much laughter.

The fields near the river were cultivated, and livestock grazed on the lush grasses of the river meadows, but the sides were steep and mountainous and gave a taste of things to come. They made good time galloping through the meadows.

As they rode into the bustling town of Piacenza, Luc realised that this was a much bigger place than they had imagined. He was unhappy about the amount of attention they were garnering; three Horse Warriors in laced leather doublets, and double swords on their backs, stood out in a rural market town. They rode through as swiftly as possible, but many eyes followed them.

Gerard guided them to an inn on a busy crossroads on the eastern outskirts. It was a huge stone building. This had been a thriving Roman town, and the townsfolk had cleverly preserved and used the Roman buildings and stone instead of destroying them, as he had seen done in France and Spain.

Gerard's eyes darted from left to right as they dismounted, looking for any trouble. He was unhappy with the amount of Milanese troops he had seen in the town. Having fought in several wars in Lombardy against them, he did not want to attract their attention. While the brothers saw to the horses, Gerard walked back to the street to check that no one had been interested enough to follow. He leaned against a post and scanned the long street for five minutes, but a few peasants, dogs, and a priest who turned up a side street were all he saw.

However, his fears were realised shortly afterwards. Just as the sun was setting, they heard the sound of hooves. Morvan's eyes met Luc's, and they slowly moved the wooden tables out, so there was more room if they had to draw their swords quickly. Half a dozen troopers entered the inn—Lombard cavalry by their crests. Their leader was a huge, older, grizzled individual with a weathered, lived-in face. They stared for a while at the Horse Warriors, who had smaller tables in the corner, by the fire. Then they studiously ignored them as they flirted and groped the two serving girls, who squealed in mock dismay, as they served ale in the busy hostelry.

Luc, however, noticed that the innkeeper leaning on the kitchen doorpost was nervously eyeing the men. Seeing the leader, he stepped forward. 'Comandante Danton, it has been too long since you graced my poor establishment.'

The man gave a booming laugh. 'We did pay for all of the damage last time, Benito!' The innkeeper gave a thin smile as the troopers moved to take over a large table at the back of the room, ejecting the two customers who were eating. Their leader, however, stood at the counter and, leaning on it, he surveyed the three Horse Warriors.

'You seem to be far from home for mercenaries, or is it that you're lost?' he asked, indicating their dress.

Luc and Gerard had their backs to him and did not move, but Morvan sat back and smiled. 'We have business in Parma. I have inherited an estate there, and we go to visit the Bailiff.'

The Comandante regarded them in silence for several moments. 'You're Normans? I hear your King William is dead—and not before time.'

Morvan curled his hands into fists beneath the table. Luc and Gerard still said nothing and did not move as Morvan answered. 'No, we are certainly not Normans. We are from a

201

port in Brittany, much further south, almost near Spain. Are you on patrol?' he asked, still smiling and indicating the men, who had stopped talking and listened intently to the exchange with grins.

The Comandante nodded. 'The area is plagued with bandits, strangers from outside who come in and steal livestock and horses. The six in the stables—are those horses all yours?' he asked.

Morvan gave a light laugh again. 'Yes, they were bought and paid for in Genoa.'

The man straightened up. 'Can you prove that? We don't take well to horse thieves around here. We hang them,' he chortled, and his men joined in.

'We didn't think we would have to prove it,' said Morvan, his hands out and palms up in a disarming gesture. Their journey to find Conn was too important to be caught up in a brawl with this Milanese. For a few moments, there was silence as the leader drank his wine. Then he left the bar and came to stand closer to the fire, blocking the heat and towering over the seated Horse Warriors.

'Your two friends are very quiet,' he said to Morvan.

Luc looked at Gerard and sighed, and then he turned and stood almost face to face with the Milanese Comandante. The man's eyes opened wide in shock, and he dropped his wine. 'Malvais,' he spat, his hand going for his sword.

He had hardly grasped the hilt when the tip of Luc's blade was at his throat. Gerard was also on his feet, and the man's face suffused with anger as he recognised him from his past as well. 'This can go one of two ways, Danton: we can sheath our weapons and sit back down to finish our meal, or this can become a bloodbath where we slaughter you and all of your men.'

The rest of the troopers were now on their feet, swords drawn. The customers and serving maids were all cowering against the walls. The innkeeper stood with his hands clutching his scanty hair in dismay.

'You killed my brother,' the man shouted at Luc.'

'It was war, and men die in war, you know that,' retorted Gerard while keeping a wary eye on the men behind him.

'There was no way those men could have fought back against the Horse Warriors. You slaughtered them all,' he said, his voice breaking.

'Danton, Luc and Morvan Malvais were only boys themselves. That was twenty years ago. It is the past, let it remain there. We are leaving in the morning. We do not want trouble. What say you?' asked Gerard.

The fight seemed to go out of the man, and his arms dropped to his sides. Luc warily stepped back a pace. The leader dropped his eyes and then muttered through gritted teeth, 'Boy or not, the name of Malvais brought fear, even then, as he gave no quarter. Few could stand against him. But I'm making a stand for them now!'

He drew his blade and whirled around. Instead of engaging, however, he punched Luc forcefully backwards. Luc felt his legs connect with the stool, then he was toppling onto the table, and Danton was on top of him. Luc had managed to bring his sword up as he fell, and now the two blades scraped together in front of his face. He could feel the hot, stinking breath of Danton on his face, as he scrabbled with his feet on the floor to get any purchase.

With a heave and straining every muscle, he shoved the man to one side and used the dagger in his left hand. He plunged it upwards into the man's heart. The Comandante groaned and slid down to his knees before rolling onto the floor, blood pooling beneath him.

Morvan and Gerard had taken on the other men but now stood leaning on their swords. Only two troopers remained, and they stood in fear at the back, looking at the bodies around them.

'Go!' shouted Gerard as he stepped towards them, a sword in each hand. They fled, leaving a scene of carnage behind them.

Gerard walked over and slapped Luc on the shoulder. 'As I said to your mother, trouble comes looking for you, Malvais.'

Luc smiled, but part of him wondered how long this would go on. He found that the name 'Malvais' was greeted with either raised fists and cheers or with a shudder of fear and a drawn blade. He had fought in many wars, killed many people, and had accumulated many enemies. They moved to the table vacated by the troopers; the dice still lay upon the board.

'It occurs to me that there may be more troopers in Piacenza who will be alerted to the death of their comrades. We need to leave in the early hours; we can't risk staying here all night. I will take the first watch.' said Morvan.

None of them slept, however, and they left the inn while the moon provided enough light, to take the road north to Cremona, where they would cross the River Po. From there, they would head up the shores of Lake Garda.

Conn felt as if he had spent weeks either on his knees or lying prone in front of the altar while the monks intoned prayers and psalms for the departed soul of Pope Victor III. Almost all other activities, classes, or training had stopped at the Hermitage. Instead, there were two—often three—masses a day. They had to sit in silent contemplation and prayer the rest of the time. Combined with this was the enforced fasting each day for the first week. They were told they had to be pure in mind and body to participate in the Requiem Mass that would take place this Sunday. Conn hoped and prayed that things would return to normal following this.

The attack on the bandits had been a huge success, and the boys had returned, bursting full of adrenalin. Scaravaggi had praised them for their courage in adversity, particularly Conn and Georgio, who had not hesitated to take on a warrior nearly three times their size. Extra rations were issued for a week, and they ate like kings until the bird arrived from Monte Cassino. As he sat in silence in their dormitory, two things returned to Conn's mind. The feeling of freedom he experienced as they ran barefoot over the starlit slopes towards the camp. And secondly, the conversation that had taken place with Father Franco when they were riding back. The monk appeared startled at the name 'Espirit Noir', and Conn felt that the man knew more about it, but he had no way of finding out.

For the first time, Conn contemplated escaping from the Hermitage. In the dark hours of the night, he would envisage opening the big barred gates and running, fleet as a wolf, down the track into the valley and away from Scaravaggi and his knotted rope. He lay there and fantasised about what he would need for the journey. Definitely, a dagger or knife; he thought he could steal one from the kitchens and some food. He knew that he would need a winter cloak or blanket as it would soon snow in the mountains.

He took Georgio into his confidence and swore him to secrecy, but the boy was dismayed. 'Don't leave me here, Conn. Please take me with you. It'll be better with two of us to protect each other.' Conn reluctantly agreed.

The other problem they faced was where to go. Georgio was Italian and spoke fluent Latin and several Italian dialects. Conn was also fairly fluent in Latin, but other words kept coming into his head—his home language, he thought—but none of the other boys recognised the Breton words. Thanks to Father Franco, the boys now knew far more about the outside world, and they decided that they would become famous warriors, mercenaries who would hire their swords out to the highest bidder.

Scaravaggi, oblivious to the boys' plans, found himself to be somewhat lost. At first, with the death of Dauferio, he had been inspired to take the mission of the Seven forward. He had contacted the other groups, and the Masters would meet in Milan in a few months under his leadership. Since then, he had learned that Chatillon had killed all of his men in Genoa. He also found that the Malvais brothers were in Genoa; Bishop Conrades had been helping them, and they were leaving soon to travel north to look for the boy. They were closing in on him. He decided to move the boys, and it had to be soon.

He had been impressed by Conn's behaviour on the raid; he was a natural leader, and tomorrow, he would make him the Captain of the Seven. A few days later, they would move. He could not work with Cardinal Odo De Chatillon, the man who would become the new Pope of Rome. Therefore, he would take the boys and his plans to Pope Clement. The other antipope was chosen personally by Henry IV, the Holy Roman Emperor, in retaliation to Pope Gregory excommunicating him. They would go to Avignon, and they could hide on the outskirts of the bustling but dangerous city. Chatillon and the Malvais brothers would never find the Seven there, and their training could continue under the patronage of Pope Clement.

Chapter Twenty-four

Luc sat and looked back on Lake Garda. He had never been this far east in northern Italy, and the lake framed by the mountains was a beautiful sight in the early morning mist as the sun emerged behind them. Morvan and Gerard pulled their horses alongside. They had clung to the wide shores of the lake as they had headed north and so made better time. Now they climbed up through the mountain pass, and to the east, they could see the River Adige sparkling in the sun. Luc rubbed his hands, the mountain air was cold on his fingers as he unfolded the map. 'We follow the river north and then turn east again before dropping down into the valleys where the Hermitage is supposed to be.'

'I believe we have only one more full day if we make good time, and then we will be there.' said Morvan as he followed the rough guide with his finger. 'It'll be like trying to find a needle in a haystack in these mountains if it's built into the cliffs, as they say.' Grumbled Gerard, whose tired bones and muscles were beginning to ache in the colder air. 'We know it faces south, and we will find it even if we have to spend a week looking. We are so close I can feel it.' Said Morvan lifting their spirits and bringing a smile to even Gerard's face. It did not last for long as the going became much tougher that day, especially when it began to rain heavily. Long ago, any sign of a road had deteriorated into a narrow stony track that ran with water and proved to be treacherous underfoot, which slowed them considerably.

It was a wet and bedraggled group of men and horses who finally stopped to make camp in the dusk. The skies had finally cleared, and Gerard, an old hand at this, unwrapped the bundle of dry kindling he always strapped to the back of his pack. Before long, it was ablaze, and they added some of the drier undergrowth from beneath the waist-high bushes that covered the slopes. It was damp and smoked at first, but it finally caught as they kept feeding it. Morvan unhooked the wineskin, and taking their tin cups, he placed them full of wine in the wooden embers to warm. He then unrolled the food pack and laid its contents out in the light of the fire. 'A feast fit for a king,' He declared, unwrapping the cheese and sliced meat. They ate in silence, washing the food down with the warm spiced wine while their clothes steamed in the heat of the blazing fire.

'If we find the Hermitage tomorrow, our plan must be foolproof. There are too many unknowns. We know the building is unassailable, even with ropes. We have no idea how many Warrior Monks are there. We could be seriously outnumbered, and we know they are well trained. Chatillon said that Scaravaggi is one of the best swordsmen he has ever faced, and he has trained the monks. We think there may be a group of boys there. If like Conn, they have been there for years and are indoctrinated, they may attack us.' Gerard burst out laughing, 'You make it all sound so easy, Luc. I agree that there is no way that brute force will work here. We are outnumbered and at a disadvantage as we have no idea of the layout.' The two brothers agreed with him, and they sat in silence around the crackling fire as they mulled over various options.

'We either do a stealth raid at night, all three of us over the walls and try to catch them napping, but it's risky. Again, we could find ourselves cornered, trying to snatch a boy who does not recognise or remember us. Alternatively, we infiltrate the Hermitage, where do they buy their food, cheese and meat. They must buy it from local farmers, as Bishop Mezzarello said. There is no space to grow food. It's on a cliff face.' As Gerard finished, Morvan gave him a sceptical look, 'Are you saying that we pretend to be a farmer or peasant delivering food? Surely they will know all the local people by name!' Gerard reluctantly grunted in agreement.

'I may have a better idea. These places never usually turn away a penitent or supplicant, someone who comes for succour, who has fallen on hard times or to join them. It's the basic tenet of their order, even for Warrior Monks. We brought the two monk's robes with us in the pack. I will shave my head and go to the gates.' said Luc. Both men looked at him in astonishment, and then Gerard crowed with laughter. 'Luc De Malvais, I have never seen anyone look less like a needy monk than you. There isn't a penitent bone in your body! Just your stance would give you away. If anyone does it, it has to be me, an older monk who has fallen on hard times and has come to do penance for broken vows. One of us has to go in and discover the layout or even if the boy is there.'

The brothers were silent for a while as they thought it through. It was a dangerous option, but what other alternative did they have? 'Sharpen your dagger on that rock over there, Luc, and let's get rid of this,' he said, running his hands through his thick collar length head of hair. Luc smiled, and an hour later, a shaven-headed Gerard, his long steel grey locks at his feet, let Morvan wipe the blood from the nicks on his scalp. 'You were supposed to take the hair, not the skin, off. I only pray that it grows back before I return to Marie.' He growled. Morvan stood back and looked at him. It makes you look younger,' he laughed. 'Ah well, maybe I will stay like this,' he said in such a serious tone of voice that Morvan thought he was serious before he playfully pushed him away. As they climbed into their damp blankets around the fire, Morvan was determined to have the last laugh. 'I have heard that it grows back pure white if you shave your head at your age.' The alarm on Gerard's face had both brothers laughing as they curled up to get some sleep.

It took them three days to find the Hermitage. They sat and stared in silence at the long, imposing building built high up on the cliff face. 'God's bones, look at it, how did they manage to build that up there, the bones from how man labourers or monks lie amongst the jagged rocks in that steep ravine, I can't even see the bottom.' said Gerard.

Luc sat and assessed the building he had heard so much about recently. It surprised him that it had several stories and a squat square tower at one end. It was much bigger and longer than he had imagined, and it could easily house over a hundred monks. He knew from the bishop that numerous rooms, dormitories and even a chapel had been built into the cliff. It would be like a maze inside. He had to admit he had some doubts about infiltrating, but they had no choice now, having seen the Hermitage. It was the only method they had to find out if Conn was here. It was pointless risking their lives in an attack if he wasn't here.

'We will wait until dark, and then we will scout the route to the entrance, come back and get you into your robe. We will set up camp now in the other lee of this crest. I noticed a deep overhang there, which will shelter the horses and us. No one will see our fires under there, and there is a stream at the bottom.

The next morning, a barefooted and bareheaded Gerard, with only a staff and an old leather pack on his shoulders, set off to cross the valley and climb the steep, narrow path to the Hermitage. Luc and Morvan crouched in the scrub bushes on the high bluff opposite to watch his progress. For the first time, Luc felt apprehensive, he loved Gerard like a father. They lived in constant warfare, which meant that they often lived with the chance of death. They were not immune to it or nonchalant, but it was fate if God willed that they die that day. His Celtic roots told him that you tried not to tempt fate, but sometimes it was unavoidable. He felt a shiver go through him and a sense of foreboding, as Gerard's distant figure reached the gates.

Gerard approached the gates with apprehension, he certainly looked the part, sleeping rough, and several weeks of hard travelling and little sleep had taken its toll. His skin had a weathered tired look as he walked towards the high solid forbidding gates. He could sense the remoteness and isolation before pulling the heavy chain to ring the bell. He rang the bell again and walked to the track's edge. He looked down the precipice onto the cruel jagged rocks below. He stepped back as he wasn't fond of heights such as these and waited for some time, but nobody came. He wondered if anyone was there, in the eerie silence, before vigorously ringing it again.

Finally, a thin door set into the main door opened, and an

old monk appeared. As Gerard assessed him, he felt relief. If the monks here were this old, they wouldn't have a problem. He stepped forward, 'In Nomine Patris, et Filii, et Spiritus Sancti,' he intoned while bowing his head. He then held out a hand, which shook slightly to Father Bruno, who regarded him warily. 'I appeal for succour, Brother. I have walked here from Verona,' said Gerard in a breaking voice. 'Stay here. I will fetch the Master, as he is the only one who can decide to give you entry.

Again Gerard waited for some time, then there was the sound of a bar lifting, and one of the large gates pulled back to reveal the old monk and a much younger man. This was obviously Scaravaggi from Chatillon's description, and he was indeed an imposing figure. Gerard dropped his eyes and swayed from exhaustion. Finally, the Master spoke, 'Father Bruno tells me you demand succour. Are you a penitent or a pilgrim?' Gerard looked up but kept his expression hopeful. 'I have broken my vows several times, and I have come to do penance. I climbed the hills and found water, but I have been out of food, for several days, as it was much further than I thought.' At this point, he swayed further and dropped to his knees. Scaravaggi narrowed his eyes and stepped outside, ignoring Gerard, and scanned the hills and cliffs. From years at the Hermitage, he knew every tree and bush and could see the slightest disturbance by a goat or wolf. Gerard sank back on his heels, hands on his thighs and head hanging. Finally, Scaravaggi seemed satisfied and signed to Father Bruno. 'Bring him in, search him thoroughly and feed him. Keep him isolated until I have time to question him.'

Gerard was pulled to his feet, and he shuffled after the old monk, leaning on the wall and darting glances around, as the monk dropped the bar back into place. As he followed Bruno through stone arches, tunnels and long corridors, he realised that it was indeed a maze. They entered a large room full of tables and benches. Bruno explained that this was the refectory where he would always eat. Gerard nodded in understanding and smiled as a full plate of goat stew was put in front of him with a large chunk of fresh bread. Gerard did not have to pretend as he wolfed the hot food down. Father Bruno gave a small smile of satisfaction, as Gerard mopped up every drop with the bread, before handing him a tankard of barley ale to wash it down. The man was obviously starving. He then led Gerard further through the building to a cell at the base of the tower stairs. It had no window, just a narrow arrow slit to let in some light and the cold breeze. He indicated the narrow pallet bed and blanket. 'Rest. The Master will wish to question you this evening.' Gerard nodded and stretched out, dropping almost immediately into a deep sleep.

On the hillside opposite, Luc and Morvan crept back through the bushes. They had both seen the tall, well-built monk come out and scan the hills, so they had dropped face down for some time. When they raised their heads again, they had gone. 'Well, he is in, let us hope he finds Conn quickly in that nest of vipers and sends us the signal.' Morvan sat down cross-legged, feeding branches into the fire. 'Let us hope he can do so safely.' he said, snapping a branch with more violence than was necessary. Both men remained quiet and pensive for some time. Both of them felt uneasy with Gerard now being inside the Hermitage on his own.

Chapter Twenty-five

Ette leant her arms on the weathered stone of the high castle walls at Morlaix. She realised that she was cold, it was late September, and she had not brought a cloak. She was on the western wall, and the sun was setting over the Atlantic Ocean.

It was nearly six months since Morvan had ridden to join King William. Since then, the messages had been few and far between. The campaign in northern France and Normandy had succeeded, but they knew that William had been badly injured. He had sent his love to her but then told her that he wasn't returning to Morlaix. He was going to Marseilles and taking a ship to Genoa to join Luc and Gerard.

She couldn't fault Marie and Merewyn. They had welcomed her and the children with open arms, and the castle was beginning to feel like home. But Ette was the wife of a Horse Warrior. Since they had married, she had been at his side. She had ridden into battle for him, wounded and killed the enemy Scots and would do so again. For Merewyn, it was different, for she was now the Chatelaine of Morlaix, as Marie had been before her. This position meant that she managed it all. She ran the castle with its home farm and met with the Bailiffs and Stewards of the estates, if Luc or Gerard were not there. Even Benedot, the Captain of the Breton Horse

215

Warriors, came to her with questions. Ette accepted that Morlaix was the Malvais family home, but she still wanted their own home, whereas the children galloped around the corridors and meadows as if they had been born there.

Then the message arrived from Chatillon in Genoa that they had found Hildebrand, but Warrior Monks had brutally murdered her. They thought they knew where Conn had been taken, but it would take at least a month to get there and back. This further delay was too much for Ette as there was shocking information but no detail. Were Morvan and Luc unharmed after these attacks? So she had made a decision, she was going to Genoa. She wasn't going to sit here waiting for news. No matter where he was, she would be by his side. So she packed her saddlebags with clothes and money and put them in the corner of the tack room. She wrote a note to Merewyn explaining what she was doing and why.

She glanced at the sky and wondered if Morvan was watching the same sunset, wherever he was. Then she made her way down to her rooms. Ette slipped into the children's room, kissed them goodnight and told them that she was going away for a week or two. She told them to be very good to their aunt and grandmother. Marie looked at her wide-eyed. 'You are coming back, Maman?' she asked. 'Yes, Marie, hopefully with your Papa and your new brother Conn.' Marie looked at her younger brother, Gervais, and wrinkled her nose in disgust, 'Another boy,' she muttered. Ette laughed. 'I promise there will come a day when you don't think like that. Ette then lay down to get a few hours' sleep. She planned to leave in the early hours, just before dawn. She was heading to Marseilles, where she would take a boat for Genoa. Five hours later, dressed in men's clothes with a thick woollen cloak, she galloped west to find Morvan, her Horse Warrior.

Scaravaggi stood at the door to the cell, staring down at the penitent monk. He was naturally suspicious about anyone who turned up unannounced at the Hermitage. Father Bruno said he had devoured the food as if he had not eaten for a week, and the man certainly did not look or sound like one of Chatillon's creatures. However, the man looked as if he had been through hardship, his face worn, weathered and covered in grey stubble. More significantly, he was sound asleep. Scaravaggi doubted if an apprehensive spy, planted in the Hermitage, could sleep like this. He turned to the old monk behind him. 'Let him sleep for another hour, then wake him with some food and bring him to me after evening Vespers. We will find out who he is.'

Gerard was shaken awake by Father Bruno and handed a tankard of ale and a large chunk of bread and cheese. He felt refreshed as he followed the old monk up the steep spiral stairs of the tower. He knew he would now have to have his wits about him if he was to escape detection. He felt confident that his back-story was good with just enough truth to sound plausible. The tower room at the top was large, sparsely furnished as befits the tenants of the Warrior Monks. It had two windows with shutters that faced south and west. Scaravaggi stood at the window with his back to them, and Father Bruno gently coughed. Gerard regarded the monk known as the 'Master'. He was certainly a fine physical specimen. Tall, broad-shouldered with a muscular physique, but it was the eyes that struck Gerard. They were the palest of blue, but they shone with ambition and intelligence. As he met that uncompromising stare for the first time, he felt a trickle of unease. He immediately dropped his eyes and bowed his head, in obeisance, as would be expected. Scaravaggi dismissed Father Bruno and waved him to a bench.

'So what is your name, and where are you from, our wandering pilgrim?' he asked, but Gerard could hear the edge in his voice. Fortunately, he had been over and over his story with Luc, and he hoped it would be foolproof. 'I am Father Geradino. I am from a large village in France that you will never have heard of, but I entered the church as a young man, and I was sent as a monk to the Abbey of Saint-Germain-des-Pres. I did well and spent all of my formative years there, but as I got older, I was enticed away by friends into the darker side of life in Paris. I left the order and found a post as a guard, at the palace, on the Isle de Cite. While there, again, I progressed and became a Serjeant and then a Captain, but I have to admit I led a life away from God. I gambled and drank. I went with whores until I finally found a beautiful country girl, and I married her and changed my ways.' Gerard paused and looked away, and the silence hung in the room. 'Go on,' murmured Scaravaggi.

'She was eight months pregnant with my child when she was raped and murdered one night, as she searched the alehouses and stews for me. For I had fallen into disrepute and bad ways, I was easily led astray by other men. I had not been home for two days. I found her body on the street, down an alleyway. They had cut her throat.'

Gerard paused again, eyes downcast and then continued,

'At first, I drank myself into oblivion, then I became angry and looked for those responsible, but it was impossible in the back streets of Paris. Girls die every night. The guilt I felt for what had happened almost destroyed me. I lost my job, my home, the woman I adored, and I wandered for months, hiring my sword out before I found myself back at the Abbey on the Isle one night. I climbed the walls and prostrated myself on the chapel floor. The monks, my former brothers, took me in, and I returned to the fold of God. However, the Abbot refused to let me return to the Abbey. He sent me to Monseigneur Gironde because he needed a servant and a man with sword skills. I stayed with him for several years until the Monseigneur suddenly disappeared just after arriving in Avignon five or so years ago. He had gone there for the Catholic Synod, having received preferment from Cardinal Dauferio.

I admired and respected Gironde, and now he was gone. I began to feel that I was a curse on the people in my life, so I became a monk again and wandered, praying and serving God where I could. However, my guilt still sits on my shoulders. It weighs me down.' He finished and wiped away a tear that was very real, as he thought of his love for Marie, and he prayed he would get them all back to her because this man in front of him was a killer, and a real threat. Gerard could feel the ruthlessness emanating from him.

Scaravaggi sat and studied the man in front of him. He was known for being a good judge of character, but now he was unsure. The story was plausible and poignant, so he decided to probe. 'I myself had dealings with Gironde. Wasn't he a chaplain to some great family?' Gerard nodded enthusiastically, 'Yes, he was attached to Count Hoel of

Brittany for many years, but Cardinal Dauferio offered him a far better post for services rendered, hence the move to Avignon. I stayed behind in Nantes to sort out his affairs and find a tenant for his house. When I arrived in Avignon, he was gone, his clothes and horse were at the inn, but he had just disappeared. The wardens of the city thought he was robbed, and his body dropped in the Rhone. I waited there and searched for three months, but he never returned.'

Scaravaggi was mollified and reassured by this answer. The man seemed genuine. 'You are welcome to repair your soul here for as long as you wish, Father, but you must abide by the strict rules of the brotherhood.' Gerard inclined his head in acceptance, and Scaravaggi dismissed him. However, when Gerard reached the door, he spoke, 'One more thing, what skills have you brought here, Geradino? All of our monks here are useful.' Gerard put his head on one side and looked thoughtful. 'I can read, write, scribe and cipher very well like any monk, but because of my role as a Captain at the palace and a bodyguard for Monseigneur Gironde, I am accounted to be very good with a staff and a sword.'

Scaravaggi smiled. 'I presume you'll want to spend much time in prayer each morning, but please come to the pell yard tomorrow afternoon and show us these skills. You might even find that the monks here are more skilled than the palace captains.' Gerard descended the stairs feeling that he had allayed any suspicions. The next day he spent the morning in the chapel and presented himself that afternoon in the pell yard, where a dozen young monks were training. Scaravaggi was at one side, his foot resting on a stone water trough. He waved Gerard over, and they stood quietly watching the fighting pairs. Gerard had to admit they were good. He now felt justified in their decision not to storm the Hermitage. It would have ended in death. One young monk was exceptionally good, and he commented on this to Scaravaggi. 'Yes, he is, and he leaves us tomorrow to go to Milan with two others to recreate our cell there.'

'Do you want to try your skill with him?' he asked, not expecting Father Geradino to agree, but the newcomer nodded.

He waved the young man over, who bowed deeply to the Master. 'This veteran swordsman thinks he can teach you a few more tricks, but he is more than twice your age, so be gentle with him.' The young man smiled and beckoned Gerard over to a rack of heavy but blunted swords. Choosing and weighing their weapons, they took up their stance and began. Gerard tried to play down his skill, making a few careless mistakes. However, he began to enjoy himself, and he had to admit that his pride got the better of him. The young man was disarmed and on his back within a short time. Scaravaggi had watched with an interest that had sharpened as he realised that he was watching a master. How did a penitent monk get to be this good from a few years in the palace guards? He narrowed his eyes as he watched the young monk hold his hand out to be pulled to his feet for the third time. He was clearly embarrassed. Gerard slapped him on the back and then taught him the unusual disarm that had floored him repeatedly.

Two things occurred to Scaravaggi, he could use him in the training yard. He even wondered if he could take him on and beat him. Surely, he could, the man must be nearing sixty. He would be slower and without the stamina for a prolonged fight. The second was that he needed to know more information about him. 'Very impressive, Father Geradino, and is that what they taught all of the guards at the palace?'Gerard smiled, 'Oh no, Master, Monseigneur Gironde paid for me to go to a master swordsman in Ghent, an Englishman who taught me a lot. I have picked up the rest by watching others and adapting their moves.' Scaravaggi looked at him, his head tilted as he considered what was said. Then he turned to go. 'I'm sure you would like to rest after your ordeal. We will see you at Vespers.' Gerard bowed deeply and returned to his cell.

The chapel at the Hermitage was beautiful. It was carved deep into the rock, but they had also used natural rock pillars. It could easily hold over sixty monks. Gerard, woken by the Vespers bell, slipped quietly into the back. He found the singing of the psalms uplifting as the sound of the soaring voices resonated around the chamber. It was the first time he had seen the whole community together. He counted at least thirty monks of varying ages and sizes, but all of them seemed to have a large tattooed cross on their neck. He leaned his back against one of the pillars and closed his eyes. He mouthed the words silently. The brief prayers and psalms ended, and the monks began filing out. It was then he saw the boys. There were seven of them in white belted tunics. They were hidden at the front by the rows of standing monks.

Gerard's heart was in his mouth as he watched the young boys shepherded towards the arched entrance. They would pass within an arm's span of him. He bowed his head as if in prayer to look sideways at them. Father Bruno and an open-faced young monk were escorting them. Gerard found that his hands were clasping so tightly that they were shaking. He examined each boy in turn while thinking, *What will he look like now?* He need not have worried. The taller dark-haired boy at the back was the image of a young Morvan. He gave a sharp intake of breath, which drew the young monk's attention, so he began coughing. The man stopped, concern on his face. 'Are you well, Father? Do you need some wine or water? It's fresh cold spring water here, very safe.' Gerard waved him away, 'No, it's just too many nights in damp blankets on cold hillsides. I will improve now that I am here.' Conn stopped, waiting for Father Franco, but he looked up when the man spoke. There was something about his voice, a memory. He met the man's grey eyes. He was staring intently at him, and then they continued, leaving the monk behind.

Gerard found that he had to stand for several minutes to catch his breath and pull himself together. He had found Conn here in the Hermitage. He was alive and looked well. He was suddenly filled with joy at the thought of taking him home to Morlaix to Marie, her grandson returned. She had loved him so much. He needed to send the signal to them as soon as possible.

Chapter Twenty-six

A woman on her own, even in disguise, meant that Ette travelled as much as she could at night or early evening and morning. She usually found a copse of thick trees to sleep in during the day. It was now October, and there was a chill in the air at night, so that she could hide her long dark hair in a loose cap. She bought cheese and bread in several small villages. Finally, she rode into Montpellier feeling triumphant but bone tired. She had decided to avoid Marseilles after the stories she heard when she admitted that was where she was going. It was a dangerous place for any young man, never mind a woman travelling on her own. It took her several days to find a boat that agreed to take her across to Genoa. She sold the horses and boarded the rough old cog early the next morning. She had told them that she was a trainee lawyer in Paris summoned to Genoa, where her father had been taken ill. They seemed to accept that, and on the whole, they left the young man to lay out his bed in the corner of the foredeck and wrap himself in his thick cloak.

The journey was rough, as the Mistral rushed down the Rhone valley into the Mediterranean, and the little boat dipped, climbed and shook its tail in the squall. It became so rough that they were all clinging to the gunwale at times. At one point, she had to hold down the sail, while they wrapped it, and her hat lifted, letting her hair drop. She quickly pushed it back under and jammed it firmly on her head, but the mate was watching her when she turned back. It finally calmed and left them clear skies as they crossed the Ligurian Sea. Ette stood on the prow, filled with excitement. It had been so long since she had seen Morvan, nearly six months. They had finally made up after Gerard and Marie's wedding, and those last days together had been wonderful. They had two sweet nights of lovemaking with a hunger to equal their early days. They found pleasure in every kiss and touch as they passed in the Hall. She loved him so much, and then he had gone off to Caen to be with the King.

William's death shocked everyone at Morlaix, but Ette knew it would affect Morvan even more. He had galloped the King to safety at the siege of Dol and saved his life escaping from the French forces. A few years later, he had saved William's life on the battlefield at Gerberoi. He may not have agreed with King William's treatment of his son Robert, but he was loyal to William. He had built the Caen contingent of the Horse Warriors, from scratch, for him, and Ette knew he would have been with the King when he was injured.

Chatillon had kept his word to keep them informed at Morlaix, and she knew that Morvan had joined with Luc and Gerard to travel north, in Italy, to find Conn. Wherever Morvan was, she would find him, and hopefully, they would bring his son home together. They would reach Genoa on the early morning tide, and so she ate the last of the food that she had bought, and wrapped a blanket around her, before curling up on the lumpy pallet mattress. It was a clear starlit night and cold, so it took a while for her to drift off. Fortunately, she was a light sleeper, so she felt the blanket lifting, and she slowly moved her hand to draw the dagger in her belt. She opened her eyes, and she could see the burly shape of the Mate above her. So he had seen, she thought as she tensed her knees, raising them slightly to kick out. Suddenly he clamped a hand over her mouth. 'Make a sound, and I promise I will drop you overboard so quickly that no one will even know you have gone.'

He straddled across her and ran his other hand under her tunic to grab her breasts. 'I knew you were too pretty to be a lad. We will have some sport together, as you pay a bit more for this voyage, and I will relieve you of some more of that silver you seem to be carrying.' He took his filthy calloused hand from her mouth, and she spat at him while trying to throw him off. It proved to be more difficult than she expected. He was a heavy man, and she was still tangled in the blanket. He held her by the throat, 'You need to be nice to me, or I swear that after I have swived you, I will throttle the life out of you and take the whole purse.' He hissed at her. His stinking breath was close to her face, and he covered her mouth, thrusting with his tongue while he moved to try to pull her braies down. Ette now had no choice. The blanket still pinned her upper arms, but she had drawn the dagger, and now she plunged it up through his ribs, twisting it as hard as possible. He gave an astonished grunt and fell off her to the deck.

Ette clambered up, throwing the blanket off as she struggled to her feet. The Mate pulled himself up, and he looked in surprise at the dagger still protruding from his ribs, as he staggered against the gunwale. Ette's mind was racing, the man had attacked her, and he was intent on raping her. He would possibly even have killed her. But would the Captain and crew see it like that? After all, she had travelled under false pretences with them. The man was gasping for breath as she quickly scanned the sleeping forms on the stern deck. No one had stirred, or seemingly heard, a thing during the struggle. She could see that he had tied the tiller, the sail was down, so they were slowly floating in on the tide, but she couldn't see the coast yet.

She knew she had no choice. She ran at him, and using all of her strength, she pushed him back over the side. For one horrible second, he seemed to balance moaning on the gunwale, but then she grabbed his foot and lifted it high, and he slid back into the water with barely a sound. She whirled around, scanning the boat, but no one had moved. The only sound was the loud slapping of the waves on the hull. She found that she was panting as she picked up the blanket. There were several drops of blood on the deck, and she quickly rubbed them away before curling back down on the pallet to pretend to be asleep. A few hours later, she heard a shout of anger from the Captain as he found out that the tiller had been tied up and the mate was nowhere in sight.

'Where is that lazy bastard?' he yelled, waking up the entire boat. He has driven us off course. We should have turned north hours ago. It wasn't a big boat, but it was a sizeable trading cog, and it took several minutes of searching for the Captain to realise that the Mate wasn't on board the boat. No one had seen or heard anything, which perplexed the Captain. The mate, was certainly not a pleasant or popular man, and he knew that several crewmembers had grudges against him.

Nonetheless, he had disappeared, and no one was admitting anything. He hardly glanced at the sleepy young man sitting up, blinking in the early morning light. He was of no account. The Captain decided that someone had settled a score, and after glaring around at the silent crew, he left it at that.

A few hours later than expected, they pulled into the harbour at Genoa. Ette watched as the Captain expertly guided the wide bellied cog through over a hundred boats and ships. She thanked the Captain, who barely nodded at her and jumped lithely down onto the wharf. She looked in wonder at the array of colourful houses and buildings that climbed the cliffs and hills, behind the port. Finding a street boy who could guide her to Monseigneur Chatillon's Palazzo took no time. She pulled the metal chain on the bell at the side of the large wooden gates, and a servant appeared. On hearing that she had business with the master, he showed her into the small antechamber at the bottom of an impressive staircase, where she waited until Edvard appeared. 'I believe you wish to see the Monseigneur?' he asked, regarding the travel-worn, slight young man who carried two large saddlebags over his shoulder.

Ette regarded him with amusement. Edvard had not recognised her. 'Can I ask the nature of your business?' Keeping her voice as deep as possible, she answered, 'You can, but I have information for his ears only, and I believe he can help me.' Edvard stood in thought for a few moments. The young man did not appear to be a threat or armed, so he took him up the stairs to a large entrance atrium and bade him wait. He knocked on the large ornate doors and entered. 'A young man is here who seems to have information. He isn't armed, and I could detect no malice. I believe he has just arrived by boat.'

Chatillon turned from the desk where he was preparing

several messages and raised an eyebrow, 'Show him in Edvard.' Moments later, he regarded the young man standing in front of him with interest. His clothes and boots were high quality but salt-stained, his face was grimy and was that dried blood on his hands? However, it was the eyes that held him. He knew this young man, he knew those eyes...

Ette dropped the saddlebags to the floor with a thump and pulled off the cap to shake down her long hair. 'This isn't the welcome I expected, Piers, but please tell me you'll give me some decent food and wine.' Chatillon stared in astonishment at Minette De Malvais, then he burst out laughing, and even Edvard smiled that she had tricked him. 'Well, you had us both fooled, but what are you doing here?' She grinned, 'I have come to be with Morvan to fight by his side, if I have to.' 'It looks as if you already have,' he said, indicating the stained sleeve and blood caked nails and fingers of her right hand. Ette nodded, 'Yes, I had to kill someone on the boat. I had no choice, he was a pig, and I threw his body overboard. I want to wash now, please, Edvard.' she said calmly.

Chatillon smiled but shook his head in astonishment. He had known her since she was a lively young girl in the court of King Philip. You never knew what scrape she would end in next, she was always a handful. However, he would have to tell her that she couldn't join Morvan. She would have to wait here. When he found her here, he was unsure what the Horse Warrior would think as she had left their children and risked her life to get here.

Chapter Twenty-seven

Gerard made no move for several days. Instead, he secured his position by helping wherever he could, even giving the cook in the kitchens a hand, which the overworked monk appreciated. He bantered with him that it was for extra food. He purposefully showed no interest in the boys. Although when he knew he was unobserved, his eyes moved to Conn immediately. He entered the pell yard early, and the boys were still at practice. He was astonished at what he saw. It must have shown on his face as Scaravaggi strolled over to stand with him. 'I'm pleased with them, they are coming on.' Gerard narrowed his eyes, shading them to watch and then gave a measured answer. 'I have never seen a group of boys this young fight like this, and I own I am amazed, the skill and the ferocity.' Scaravaggi gave a smile of satisfaction. 'I have trained them myself. Imagine what they will be like in another five or six years. They will be unbeatable.' Gerard nodded. His eyes were on Conn. The speed, accuracy and fluidity of movement were astonishing.

They watched for a while longer as Conn easily disarmed his opponents. 'Who will they fight? The Master again gave that thin smile, 'They have already been blooded. Every boy there has killed or helped to kill, a grown man. We wiped out an entire nest of bandits in the hills.' Gerard couldn't conceal the look of concern on his face, 'At this age?' he murmured.

'I need them to feel nothing when they kill. They will be soldiers of Christ fighting the infidels, and hopefully, you'll add your skills to mine to make them truly terrifying.' Gerard swallowed and then assumed an expression of admiration. 'I would be honoured. What a plan. What a vision.' Scaravaggi inclined his head in thanks, 'It's a long term plan, but it'll pay dividends. There are more boys like this all over Europe. They will each take over the training of another seven and that boy there...' he said, pointing at Conn, leaning on his sword and wiping the sweat from his eyes. 'He will be their leader. I'm developing him myself. He now has an extra hour on his own each day with his tutor Father Franco. However, he still needs the disobedience beating out of him every week.' Gerard hid his anger and looked suitably stunned by all of this information carelessly shared. He was immediately wary. Was this a test?

The boys finished and filed out for food. Gerard forced himself to look away, as Conn reached him, when all he wanted was to pull him into his arms and hug him, to reassure him that this nightmare would soon be over. He would try to send the signal tonight, as he had seen the bruises and cuts on Conn's arms and legs. He had managed to find a lantern and secreted it in his cell under the blanket. He would wait until everyone was asleep and then climb the wall near the gates. He prayed that no one would be out there late at night.

Luc and Morvan were by now thoroughly bored and frustrated. They had been in their camp on the hillside for over a week. Each day they hunted for food. They even caught a small hill goat, which gave them a challenge, riding it down as it zigzagged across the hillside. Luc riding over the dangerous terrain without reins, leaned down and grabbed its horns, lifted it over the front of the saddle. Morvan rigged up a spit while Luc skinned it, and they sat and enjoyed the succulent roast meat with some red wine they purchased in a distant village. Luc had to admit he was becoming impatient. The worst part of it wasn't knowing what was happening. Was Gerard still alive? Was Conn even there?

As usual that night, they climbed the hill behind the camp as the sun was setting and descended the far side so that they were facing the hermitage. They could just make out the white walls and red-tiled rooves in the gloaming. Morvan did not like to say the words aloud, but he now thought it had been too long. Gerard must have been discovered and killed. The ruse had not worked. They spread their blankets down in a space between the bushes and settled down for several hours of waiting.

Morvan had dropped to sleep beside him when Luc saw the first flicker of light. He elbowed Morvan, who was instantly awake. They watched in anticipation as a small light was held high and swung from side to side. 'That is Gerard. That is the signal. It means that Conn is there.' Unable to stay on the ground, Morvan leapt to his feet, reaching for the tinderbox to light the small fire they had stacked several days ago. Within moments, it was alight after a week of dry weather, and Luc went to stand in front of it with his cloak. He covered the fire from view and then revealed it several times to let Gerard know they understood. Unfortunately, the breeze caught the flames, and it lit the larger bush beside it. They both started stamping, but it had taken hold until Luc smothered it with his blanket. He held up the charred remains with a rueful grin but slapped his brother on the back. 'We have found him, Brother. We have found him.' They laughed in the euphoria of the moment as they headed back up the hill and over the rocky crest, to return down to their camp.

The arrangement was that Gerard would signal again in two days if he had a plan to get them both out, without help. If not, Luc realised that they would have to go in, probably at night when security seemed lax. He had questioned the local farmers and goat herders who delivered milk and cheese twice a week. They now knew that there were more than twenty monks inside at least. These were trained Warrior Monks so that any attack could be costly.

Scaravaggi rarely slept for more than a few hours, but he was more than restless tonight. He felt uneasy. Perhaps it was knowing that Dauferio's enemies were closing in on him. He stood with his hands resting on the stone sill of the window staring into the night. He had decided that they would leave tomorrow. They would take the northern overland route, which would still be passable at this time of the year. It was only early October, and the valleys would still be snow-free. They would sweep down into Provence to the city of Avignon. He would deliver an army of trained recruits to Pope Clement III. He was turning away when he saw the light. It was near the top of the hill opposite. Then it was gone. He blinked and rubbed his eyes. Had he imagined it? Then it was back, and he realised that someone was signalling the Hermitage but signalling whom? He watched in disbelief, and then he raced down the stairs. As he reached the bottom, he slowed, it could only be one of the monks, and to reach their cell, they would have to traverse the long narrow corridor that led to his tower. He stepped back up a stair so he was out of sight and kept still, for from the entrance to the staircase, he would hear them. He waited and waited, but there was no sound. Impatiently, he took a burning torch from the wall and made his way out to the gates. He searched every nook and cranny, sword in hand, for intruders, but there was no sign. He then opened every cell door to see if the monks were in their beds and asleep.

Gerard had been alarmed at the size of the fire that Luc and Morvan had lit, it stood out in the black of the night, and someone could be awake and see the light flickering on the walls of their cells. He quickly scrambled down the wall, onto the barrel below, and raced with his lantern to his cell. He doused it just as he heard feet pounding down the stairs. He softly closed the heavy cell door and climbed into bed. Scaravaggi seemed to stay just outside the door for a very long time before he heard him moving along the corridor, and the bang of the outside door opening.

Sometime later, he returned. By the pauses, in the footsteps, he realised Scaravaggi was searching every cell. Gerard lay on his bed, his eyes tightly closed as the door opened, and then he stirred slightly and turned over to make it realistic. He heard Scaravaggi step into the cell for a while but then turned and left. Gerard breathed a sigh of relief but then picked up the pungent smell of an extinguished wax candle. He realised that he should have doused the candle earlier, rather than carrying it to his cell. He lay there undecided. Should he make a break for it now? They could easily gather more men, mainly rough mercenaries, and carry out a full-scale attack, or should he try to bluff his way out of the situation? Moments later, it was decided for him as he heard a key grating in the lock.

Chapter Twenty-eight

Chatillon stood with Ette looking down at the maps spread out on the table. She stared in amazement at the route they had taken. 'The Hermitage is so far and inaccessible?' she asked plaintively. Chatillon gave a sad smile. 'This is why we found no trace of them for years, Ette! They killed Brian when he went to hand the boy over. Fortunately, they did not know of Hildebrand's existence or the life she created for herself in Genoa. I led them unwittingly straight to her door, and they murdered her to tie up a loose end and wait for me so they could kill me too.'

'Do we know how many of these Warrior Monks are there?' she asked, in concern at what he described, her finger still on the Hermitage. 'Not exactly, Ette, but I can imagine it'll be more than twenty in a community such as that.' Her eyes widened in dismay, 'I know that Gerard, Morvan and Luc are exceptional fighters and swordsmen, but those odds are surely impossible unless they have help.' Privately Chatillon agreed and had tried to talk them out of it, but he wouldn't share his misgivings with her. Instead, he took her hand and smiled. 'They are the most formidable and resourceful people I know. They will have a plan. Now we need to find you some female attire, so I can take you to meet my future bride, Isabella, and my newly acquired ward, Marietta. They will love you, I'm sure. We will be dining at the Embriaco house tonight, so not a word of what is afoot.' he said, his finger on his lips and eyes narrowed in warning. He knew how impetuous she could be. Ette stood there, torn but frustrated. She had come to find Morvan and help him, but the journey through the mountains would take weeks. Also, it was a huge area, and she had no guarantee that they wouldn't cross in the middle of the night if they were on their way back with Conn. All she could do was wait.

Gerard sat in the cell without food or water for a full day before the key finally turned in the lock, and Father Bruno stood there with two of the younger monks. 'At last, I do not understand why my door was locked. I'm no threat to anyone.' he said plaintively. Father Bruno just beckoned him out, so he swung his legs onto the floor and went without resistance. The two monks flanked him and took him into the high walled pell yard. It was empty, but they took him to the high wooden T cross in the centre, put manacles on his wrists that fed through rings on each end of the structure, and left him alone. This yard was one of the few places in the Hermitage where the sun penetrated, and even in early October, it was hot as it beat down on his shaven head. Also, he had been given no water for over a day.

It was late afternoon before anyone appeared. Gerard looked up to see Scaravaggi striding towards him. 'What have I done to deserve this treatment?' he asked. Scaravaggi did not answer. He regarded him in silence for some time. 'What is your real name, and why are you here?' He demanded. Gerard shook his head, 'I swear to you that my name is indeed Geradino,' he answered in all truth. 'The ruse is over. We know that you were on the walls signalling to someone out there, your compatriots, no doubt. We saw them signalling back to you. So who is it out there? Is it the Malvais brothers? Have they come to try and take the boy from me? If so, they will be disappointed, for I swear I will cut his throat before letting them take him!'

Gerard knew he couldn't prevent the look of anger and fury on his face at those words, so he dropped his head. 'I don't know what you're talking about, Master. I went for some air as I felt unwell. I saw no signal. I have not heard of these people. I am here as a penitent, that is all.' Scaravaggi smiled and waved to Father Bruno, standing in the shadows. 'Bring the boys out and line them up over there,' he said, pointing to the wall where the staves and blunted swords stood in old wine casks. Gerard watched in apprehension as the boys were brought in and several of the young Warrior Monks followed them. The boys stared in surprise at the monk chained to the tall T bar. They had seen a boy die there but had never seen an adult punished.

'Scaravaggi addressed them all. 'We have a traitor amongst us, a spy, a man who came here under false pretences asking for help, but no doubt he planned to murder us all in our beds.' The boys narrowed their eyes at this man, most believing blindly what they were told. Some glared at him. 'He has signalled to more of his men outside where they are waiting to come and attack us at any moment. We need information from this spy, but at the moment, he is lying, refusing to tell us who is outside. I need you to persuade him to talk. Pick up your staves and show him how we treat traitors and spies.' The boys picked up the wooden staves and approached the manacled man with some trepidation. Attacking an unarmed man who couldn't fight back was different, and for Conn, it had an unpleasant feel. The man fixed his eyes on Conn in a mute appeal, and again he felt a jolt of memory about this stranger.

Ever the bully, Gustave attacked, swinging his stave at the man's legs with a cry of 'The Seven'. This triggered an attack by all of them, including Conn, who kept repeating 'He was sent to murder us all' in his head. Gerard gasped with pain as the blows fell, and he heard the crack as his right arm broke. Scaravaggi was pleased by the boys' actions, and he raised a fist and shouted, 'Enough'. The boys stood back, some panting with exertion, some like Gustave, grinning with pleasure, but Conn found it difficult to look up from the ground.

'Well, Geradino, if indeed that is your name, are you ready to tell us of the band of attackers outside? Were you going to open the gates to them at night? Is this their revenge for our attack on their camp?'

Gerard hung in a sea of pain in the chains, his body battered and bloodied. He knew he had to give them something to give Morvan and Luc time to rescue him and Conn. 'No,' he gasped. 'We were not going to murder anyone. We are here for the boy.' All of the boys looked at the beaten monk's face. He could see anger and confusion on their faces. 'Who is out there?' shouted Scaravaggi. Gerard said nothing.

'Attack him again,' he shouted in rage, and the boys rained blows down on him once more. Gerard felt and heard his

239

collar bone crack as he gritted his teeth in agony until he threw his head back and gave a roar. The boys stepped back in surprise. 'You know who is out there, Scaravaggi? It is Malvais and his brother. They are not here to kill the boys. They are here to kill you.' Gerard managed to lift his bleeding head and look at Conn. 'It is your father. He is here to rescue you, Conn. We have been searching for you for years since this man stole you. Don't you remember me? It's me, Gerard.' Conn froze on the spot. He found it difficult to take in what the man was saying. But as he looked into the pleading eyes of the beaten monk, he suddenly remembered a man lifting him onto a small pony. A man called Gerard, who laughed a lot. Was that this man?

Scaravaggi had heard enough, 'Father Bruno, take the boys, prepare them with packs of food for the journey. They will need thick cloaks and weapons. We will leave through the tunnel. Father Franco pick ten younger monks to go with us. The rest will remain and defend the Hermitage. Take your staves with you, and you'll be given long daggers in the dormitory.' Father Bruno ushered the boys towards the archway. Scaravaggi stared at the beaten and bloodied man hanging in the chains. He knew exactly who he was now. No wonder his sword skills were so good. This was Sir Gerard De Chanville, a master swordsman, but he did not say a word as he turned on his heel and headed for the door. He would leave orders with Father Bruno to deal with him. He could not afford to lose the boy. They had to leave now.

One younger monk still stood in the shadows in the far corner of the pell yard. He had followed Scaravaggi's orders and sent ten monks to gather their things. More erudite than the rest, more of a scholar than a warrior, Father Franco had found distasteful what he had just watched. He picked up a ladle of water from the stone trough and walked over to Gerard. Lifting his head, he wet his cracked lips and then poured some down his throat. Gerard spluttered his thanks and whispered, 'Help me,' Father Franco looked down on the beaten man with pity and gave him more water. 'Unfortunately, I can't release you. He would kill me if I did. Is it true what you said? Is Conn the son of Malvais?'

Gerard nodded, 'He is a Malvais, he is Morvan's son, but Luc brought him up for the first few years of his life before he was stolen from us. His mother is Princess Constance. He is King William's grandson. That is why they want him, and they intend to use him as a weapon.' Father Franco took a step back. 'Dear God, what has Scaravaggi got us into here?' He went and refilled the ladle and poured it over Gerard's bloodied head. 'Try to stay alive until they rescue you. We are leaving, so there will only be a smaller number of older monks here.' He turned away as Gerard croaked after him, 'Where? Where is he taking him?' Father Franco quickly scanned the empty yard and doorway. 'Avignon!' he whispered, and then he disappeared.

Gerard tried to stay conscious, but the waves of pain were just too much, and he drifted away into unconsciousness. He was shaken awake to see that it was the beginning of a sunset. The sun was a huge red ball in the sky. Father Bruno and three of the older monks stood there. They undid the manacles, and Gerard screamed as he dropped to the ground. He knew that an arm and his left leg were broken, but it felt as if several ribs had gone as well. 'I can survive this. I can get back to Marie.' He whispered over and over.

'He isn't going anywhere in that state. Let us get the braziers and carry them to the gates.' said Father Bruno leaving Gerard on the ground where he stretched out his unbroken right arm and watched them leave. In the rough grit and sand, he wrote one word and then, in agony, he pulled himself over, leaving a trail of blood. He wrote the word again and then again. Then he put his head down and closed his eyes until they came for him. Father Bruno had exact instructions from Scaravaggi.

Luc and Morvan climbed over the crest of the hill again and positioned themselves in the bushes to wait. It was a beautiful red-tinged dusk. The sun was sinking when suddenly, what looked like a fire was lit on the wall near the gates. 'Look, Gerard plans to get Conn out,' shouted Morvan in excitement. Then a second fire appeared slightly further along the wall, which was unexpected. As the fires took hold, the flames leapt higher and higher, lighting up the walls of the Hermitage. Soon, the brothers could see these were braziers placed on top of the wide walls. Luc narrowed his eyes, his lips tight as he realised that Gerard wouldn't risk this. The flames were lighting the cliffs behind the buildings and would be seen for miles. Suddenly they could see movement in the bright lurid light cast by the flames, and three figures appeared. Two men were holding a third figure up between them. One of the monks shouted, and it echoed across the cliffs of the valley and deep ravines below. 'This is for Dauferio, Malvais, an eye for an eye.' Morvan went cold, for the figure in the middle was Gerard.

Gerard could not stand. His left leg was broken. He was picked up in the pell yard by two monks and dragged up a ladder, to the top of the wall, in agony. Once there, they held him up between two flaming braziers. Gerard surveyed the scene. He always knew he would never die in his bed, not with the life of constant warfare that he led, but he always expected to die on a battlefield. Now he worked out what they would do to him, and he stared across at the dark hillside opposite. The two brothers would be there watching. He could almost imagine their pain and loss. He treated the two warriors as sons, and he felt a sense of incredible sadness for the life he had wanted, and now lost, with Marie and their families. He would never have that now. He sighed, resigned himself to his fate and filled his mind with the happy moments of his life with his boys and the woman he loved. The grip on his arms tightened. He closed his eyes as he was thrown into the darkness.

The two brothers jumped to their feet and watched, in horror, as the monks flung Gerard from the walls to drop steeply onto the sharp, ragged pinnacles of rocks below. The monks stood in the light for a few moments with triumphantly raised fists, then they disappeared, leaving the blazing braziers to light the brutal scene. Luc let out a roar of rage. 'They will die, every last one of them, I swear it.' Morvan stood white-faced in shock before a half sob escaped him. Luc pulled his brother close and held him, while unbidden tears ran silently from his own eyes. Gerard had gone… He had been the mainstay of their lives since they were young boys. Luc closed his eyes tightly as he thought of his mother. She and Gerard loved each other so much and had looked forward to a life together at Morlaix.

The sun finally disappeared, but still, the brothers stood, holding each other in the deepening gloom, reluctant to move apart and face the reality of what they had just watched.

Chapter Twenty-nine

November 1087

Chatillon found himself unusually irritated. Yes, the turbulent and shocking events of the last months had not helped. Now he was here in Avignon in his family's old antiquated mausoleum of a house, which, despite the many roaring fires he insisted were lit in every room, always seemed to be cold and echoing. He should have sold it years ago, but he rarely visited the city if he could avoid it. He sat close to the fire in the impressive manorial hall. It had carved wooden balconies and galleries and an impressive vaulted cedar wood roof, but it was so high that the light from the dozens of candles barely reached it. He pulled the fur coverlet further round his shoulders and then laughed. 'I'm sitting here like an old dotard. What would Isabella think if she saw me now?' he wondered aloud to the echoing hall.

He hoped to have his beautiful bride in his bed by now, settled into his house in Rome. Instead, because of Scaravaggi's escape with Conn, it had been postponed while they hunted him down. Therefore, Isabella was still in Genoa in her father's house, with his ward Marietta, and he was stuck here with Ette, in his least favourite house, in a city that always made him feel uneasy. Avignon was the temporary home of the anti-pope Clement III, elected to the position of rival Pope, by the Holy Roman Emperor, in opposition to the reforms put in place by Pope Gregory.

Avignon had always been a nest of vipers. They said that they would cut your throat for a groat in Marseilles. However, in Avignon, they would cut your throat for pure pleasure. Edvard arrived with a goblet of warm spice wine, which he put in his master's hands. 'Any news, Edvard?' he asked, taking a large sip and rolling the warm wine around his mouth. 'Not a whisper. We have men on every road into the city and on every corner of the streets. We would know if a new beggar arrived, never mind a large group of Warrior Monks and seven boys.' Chatillon nodded in satisfaction. He was sure they had beaten Scaravaggi to the city. If, as Luc and Morvan believed, Scaravaggi and the boys were coming here, then they would be waiting for them.

It had been a month since the news of Gerard's death had reached them in Genoa. He had not spent a great deal of time with the knight, but he certainly knew of his reputation, and he had a great deal of respect for his sharp military mind and fame, as one of Europe's swordmasters. The manner of his death was shocking for the people who loved him. He had been beaten, tortured and thrown from the walls of the Hermitage.

His thoughts were interrupted by the arrival of Ette, who pulled up a chair beside him. She was still in male attire, as she had walked to the Pope's residence and back, unable to stay in the house. 'Could they have got this wrong?' she suddenly asked. 'Surely the monks would have arrived by now, even walking!'

Chatillon placed his wine on the small table and sat forward.

'It wouldn't surprise me if he lost one or more of his group on this forced march. I believe that Scaravaggi has chosen the northern mountainous route across to Grenoble, and with reduced rations in the cold weather, the boys' stamina will only last so long.'

'God's bones, let us hope that one of them isn't Conn. Morvan and Luc would find that difficult to take on top of Gerard's death,' cried Ette just as Chatillon's two greyhounds began to bark, denoting an arrival. Minutes later, a tired and travel-weary Morvan appeared, followed by Luc. They dropped their saddlebags by the door and headed for the fire. Ette had not moved as Chatillon strode across and clasped arms with them. 'I am sorry to hear of Gerard's death. I know how dear he was to you and your family.' Luc thanked him as Edvard handed them a large goblet of wine. Ette looked at Morvan's drawn, pale face. She could see the pain on both of their faces.

Morvan turned to address whoever the other guest was by the fire, and his mouth dropped open in astonishment. 'Ette! How…' he began as she stood and ran into his arms. He dropped his lips to her hair and breathed in her smell. He had missed her so much. She pulled back and looked up into his amber eyes. 'Don't be angry with me. I had to be by your side. I'm not one to sit at home and wait.' He smiled for the first time in over a month and then kissed her thoroughly. 'How and when did you get here?' he asked. She told him of her trip to Genoa and receiving the awful news. 'Chatillon was amazing, he set things into motion all over Europe, and a week later, we were on a boat to Avignon.'

Luc looked on, happy for his brother that Ette was here, although she was incorrigible, as again she had put herself in danger. Then a thought occurred to him. 'Do they know yet? Have you told them back at home in Morlaix?' Ette shook her head. 'We thought it would be for you to let them know, Luc.' He nodded, wondering whether to send a short missive, or wait and tell them when they returned. His mother, Marie, would be heartbroken. Edvard announced dinner, which was a subdued affair. It was afterwards, as they sat mulling over their wine that Chatillon finally broached the question. 'Tell us what happened,' he said softly. The brothers glanced at each other, the anguish still reflected in their faces. Then Morvan took a deep breath and began. He described the long journey to the Hermitage and its impregnable position. Ette raised a smile at the thought of Gerard as a penitent monk with a shaved head. Morvan explained the plan, but his hand sought Ette's hand under the table, holding it tightly. 'He gave us the first signal to tell us that Conn was there, and we waited for the second one a few days later but instead….' At that point, his voice broke with emotion, and Ette pulled her chair closer and put her head on his shoulder.

Luc took up the tale to describe what they saw. There was silence for several minutes, even Chatillon had not known all of it, and they could see that he was affected by the brutality of his death. 'It took us three days to retrieve his broken body from that inaccessible jagged ravine. We enlisted the help of some local men with ropes. Morvan and I washed, straightened, and bound his body with the waxed linen strips the local women supplied. Then we paid for the body to be taken to the small nunnery at Santa Margherita, where he would lie in the chapel, as befitted a knight of his stature. We decided to bury him there, as it would be nigh on impossible to take his body back to Morlaix.'

Morvan had recovered, although his eyes shone with unshed tears. 'We grieved for the rest of that week, but the anger was building within us, so we hired ten mercenaries, and we attacked the Hermitage in the dawn of the following day. The fighting was fierce, but few could stand against Luc. He took five or six down in the first foray through the entrance yard.' Luc gave a reluctant smile, 'I think you should add that although they were Warrior Monks, they were older. They were not the fit young warriors we met in Genoa. As we raced through the long stone corridors and dormitories, we realised that Scaravaggi had taken the boys and gone.'

'How?' asked Chatillon. 'Through a tunnel that came up on the other side of the mountain, it was very clever. However we gathered the few survivors in the training yard, but they refused to talk. Only when I killed them one at a time did the large monk on the end speak out. There were only two left by this time, the well-fed cook and an older narrow-faced man called Father Bruno, who still refused to say a word. The cook was more forthcoming. He told us what had been done to Gerard. The boys and monks attacking him with staves while he was manacled to a post, beaten and broken with no water for days. He had no chance against them. He was a Horse Warrior, a master swordsman, a knight. He should have died with a sword in his hand.' Luc had to stop this time, but Chatillon saw no tears, only cold anger on his face, as he stared away at the fire for a few moments.

Morvan continued, 'The cook told us that Bruno was Scaravaggi's scribe and right-hand man and that he had flung Gerard from the walls. However, no matter what we let the mercenaries do to him, he never said a word. He was loyal to his master to the end as he chanted the same psalm repeatedly.

I could see Luc's frustration mounting as they refused to tell us where they had taken Conn. Suddenly, he drew his blade, whirling in one movement, he took the old monk's head from his shoulders. The cook had soiled himself in fear, and Luc walked away to the T bar where they had hung Gerard. The dark stains of his blood were still there, all around on the ground and on the manacles that still hung there. I saw Luc rest his forehead on the top wooden bar, and I could hear him offering a prayer for Gerard's soul.' Tears ran down Ette's face as she listened. She could picture the scene. Even Chatillon sat there narrow-eyed, his fingers steepled in front of his face as he followed every word.

Morvan took a draught of wine. 'Then Luc called me over. He was staring at the ground, for someone had written 'Avignon' in several places. We knew this had to be Gerard. His last message to us before they dragged him away to his death. We now worked out the route he had taken, but he had a week's start on us, and we had to go to Santa Margherita to bury Gerard. Luc sent a man to Verona, praying that you had a priest there with pigeons, and fortunately, you had, and we could warn you they were heading for Avignon.' Morvan finished and sat back while they sat there with their thoughts, some consumed with sadness for the terrible death of a great knight and much-loved father figure.

Then Ette sat forward, 'How do you do it, Chatillon? How do you have birds which can fly anywhere? I don't pretend to understand how it works.' Chatillon laughed, and the mood lightened slightly. 'It may seem like that, Ette, but the birds have two metal tags on their legs, one to attach the all-important message tube, and the other tag has a number of their home city, town or even castle. Each of my men has a decoding book with a list of numbered destinations. Sometimes it may take three birds, or more, to get a message to the recipient. Your bird from Verona flew to Milan, and then a different bird brought your message to Genoa. It took only three or four days, rather than the weeks it would if you sent a mounted messenger. Within ten days, I had men searching Avignon and watching every road.' Ette clapped her hands in amazement, 'What an amazing system, and you invented it.' Chatillon laughed again, 'No, my dear, the Romans and Greeks used it extensively. I found it mentioned in some old rolls and texts during my days as a scholar at Monte Cassino, and I began setting it up. Twenty years later, we have hundreds of birds.'

Luc pushed his chair back and stretched out his long legs. For the first time in many weeks, they were well fed and warm. The constant journeying and adversity were beginning to show on their tired, strained faces. 'As ever, your hospitality is excellent, Chatillon, and we thank you, but I admit I'm surprised that there has been no sign of Scaravaggi! A group that size can't be invisible.' Chatillon sat forward, 'We are doing everything we can, Luc, but we are dealing with an intelligent and cunning man who will be moving the group at night and living off the land where they can. I assure you that the second we hear anything, you'll be the first to know. I suggest that you go and get some well-earned rest, although Morvan and Ette might have other plans.' Ette felt her colour rise as she glanced shyly up at Morvan. They had been apart for so long that she felt like a young girl again. Morvan grinned and squeezed her hand as they said their goodnights and headed for their chamber.

Luc sat for a while longer with Chatillon, 'You know more

about Scaravaggi. What is his plan, do you think? Why bring the boys here?' Chatillon looked pensive for a few moments. It's obvious when you think about it. He is carrying out the plan and vision of Pope Victor III, who we know as our devious friend, Dauferio, but now he is dead. If Scaravaggi had taken the scheme to my uncle, he would have him killed, and the boys dispersed. Therefore, he brings it to the antipope Clement III who is here for a few months before returning to Ravenna. He'll present Clement with a fait accompli, an army of Christ that Odo De Chatillon has turned down. He'll ask Clement for his support, and more importantly, he'll try to garner the support of the Holy Roman Emperor, Henry IV, who will almost certainly back any idea turned down by the Holy See in Rome, especially an army of Christ trained to fight against the infidels.'

Luc looked thoughtful, 'So we need to stop him and rescue those boys before he reaches Pope Clement.' Chatillon inclined his head. 'I have men inside and outside the Pope's circle. I also have several now working as servants and guards inside the Dominican monastery, where he resides in the new Bishop's episcopal residence. Any sign, message, or request for an audience with the antipope from Scaravaggi and I will know. Our biggest problem is the power and influence that his name carries. As Master, he is the head of over four hundred highly-trained Warrior Monks across Europe. People fear him.' Luc grim-faced nodded in understanding. Chatillon stood and stretched, 'Sleep on it, Malvais. We will make plans tomorrow. I do not doubt that Gerard was right, Scaravaggi will come here to Avignon, where he'll secrete the boys, we don't know, but I promise you we will find out.'

Chapter Thirty

Conn thought he would never be warm again. They had walked barefoot across the Italian and Swiss Alps before dropping down into the long valley near Grenoble. He was so cold that he couldn't sleep, even though they huddled together. The boys had only their belted white tunics that dropped to mid-shin and a thick woollen cloak, but these were of little help in the freezing mountain temperatures of the high passes that Scaravaggi led them through.

The Master refused to light a fire just in case it gave away their position. Scaravaggi constantly looked back across the slopes to check for pursuit. After the first week, they had lost Verruchio. Conn had tried to shake him awake, but his thin hands were white and cold, and his lips were blue. It was the first time he had heard the Master curse and blaspheme as he stamped around in the snow. Two of the boys had frostbite, and Father Franco, bravely defying Scaravaggi's glare, gave the boys torn pieces of a blanket to tie around their feet.

While shivering in the night, Gerard's words went round and round in Conn's head. His father had been searching for him for years since he had been taken and stolen from his family. He was no peasant or miller's son. He was the son of a knight, a famous knight, a Horse Warrior with the name of

Malvais. Conn had seen Father Franco's face at that moment. His mouth had dropped open, the shock clear on his face to confirm what he had only suspected. Conn realised that the Malvais brothers were to be feared, and they were here to kill Scaravaggi and find him to take him home. He determined to try to talk to Father Franco if he got the chance. Scaravaggi was pushing the pace, but the boys on frozen feet and minimal cold rations were capable of only four or five hours walking each day before they collapsed in the icy hills.

Occasionally they were lucky and were given shelter in a barn by a sympathetic farmer. They slept on those nights in a warm bed of hay, and it was here that he found himself beside Father Franco and apart from the others. Most of the boys were asleep. They had feasted on apples, cheese and bread from the farmer. Conn sat beside the younger monk and whispered. 'Tell me about Malvais.' Father Franco glanced around, the other monks were further away, and Scaravaggi had not yet joined them in the barn. 'Luc De Malvais is the greatest Horse Warrior in Europe. He is a master swordsman, the famous leader of the Breton Horse Warriors. That is the most formidable cavalry in Europe, feared everywhere. The Warriors wear distinctive double swords on their backs. Their horses are huge and trained to fight as….'

The large wooden door was suddenly pulled open, and a biting wind blew in as Scaravaggi entered, banging the door closed behind him. Conn dropped his head so that he would not be seen talking to the monk. Scaravaggi strode up and down in the small space cleared of hay and grain bags. He turned to the monks, who had all woken with the cold blast and noise. A storm is blowing in, and we may have to shelter here for a day or two. The relief and joy on the faces of the boys were clear to see, but Scaravaggi scowled at them and retreated to a corner to wrap himself in his cloak. His only consolation was that the storm might slow any pursuit as well.

They spent three days there. The farmer's wife often came to the barn, to Scaravaggi's displeasure, she mothered the boys, bringing goose fat for their feet and extra blankets. The farmer and one of his labourers carried in a large cauldron of mutton stew on the second night. The boys were almost overcome at having hot food and ate it ravenously, licking their bowls clean. The boys had little or no memory or contact with women, and they were taken aback by the unconditional kindness they received. That night Conn yet again dreamed of the face of his angel. Father Mezzi had told them before he left that everyone had a guardian angel, and sometimes they would leave a white feather for you. Conn believed that the green-eyed, silver-haired woman was his guardian angel's face.

The following day the wind dropped, and they set off again. However, it was hard for the boys with another four days of cold sleet before they dropped down into the valleys near Grenoble. Their spirits improved as the temperatures rose, and the frozen ground gave way to greener alpine pasture where animals grazed. Scaravaggi was still cautious, and he kept them away from the roads and tracks, only going to buy supplies of milk, bread and cheese at the smaller villages and homesteads. They were met by astonishment and curiosity until Scaravaggi explained that they undertook a pilgrimage through Avignon to visit and pray at the church at Saintes-Marie's-De-La-Mer on the Mediterranean. In the village where it's said that the three Marys, Mary, the mother of Jesus, Mary Magdalene, and Mary Salome, who wiped the face of

Christ at the crucifixion, landed in a boat fleeing from the Romans in Palestine. This explanation satisfied the villagers and farmers alike.

A few days later, they crested a hill outside the larger village of Sorgues, and the plain of Avignon spread out in front of them. Father Franco gathered the boys together and pointed out the sparkling river Rhone descending to the Mediterranean Sea in the far distance. Conn was excited, they had read so much, studied so many maps, and now the huge sea lay in front of them. Scaravaggi, as usual, sat apart as they sat and ate their bread and cheese. Conn could see the faint outline of the city ahead in the morning mist. They could see the many church towers and the smoke rising from hundreds of breakfast fires as the mist cleared.

'So is this France?' he asked his tutor. Father Franco explained that France was further to the northwest, like Normandy and Brittany. As they broke their fast, Conn sat and stared out over the lands to the west. He was born there and had been stolen by these monks. He had a family there that loved him and wanted him back. He turned and, narrowing his eyes. He glared at Scaravaggi. He could feel the anger and hatred building inside him towards this man. Everyone feared the Master, but it had gone much further in Conn. He did not even hear Giorgio's words or feel the hand on his arm until Father Franco pulled him to his feet, and they set off on their final leg to the west of the city.

It was dark when they entered a large village and headed for a homestead and manor on its outskirts. They could certainly smell it before they got there as they followed a narrow stony cart track across a field. Father Franco lit a lantern for the boys as they followed on behind Scaravaggi, striding ahead.

However, Conn and Georgio stepped back in alarm as the light from the lantern reflected in what seemed to be hundreds of large eyes. The tutor laughed at them and swung the lantern in an arc to show them the goats. It's a goat farm it produces hundreds of cheeses, milk and meat for the city. It's a very lucrative business. The boys laughed and followed him into a large barn with goat pens down one side. The owner held the large barn door open and clasped arms with Scaravaggi. 'They will be safe here. I trust my men, like me, they were men of the cloth who fell by the wayside. There is food, milk and ale here for them. When you have them settled, you can come to the house and tell me what is afoot.'

An hour later, the goat farmer had sent his family to bed, and the two men sat and chatted about earlier days together as former brothers when they had trained at Monte Cassino and in Milan. 'I heard of Dauferio's death. He'll be a loss. I know you were close to him.' Scaravaggi looked away for a moment and then dipped his head in acknowledgement. There were few people that he could talk to like this. 'I'm convinced that Chatillon had him poisoned, Jean, but I have no proof. He was clever in the way that he did it.' Jean spat on the packed earth floor, 'Chatillon that viper, I hated him at Monte Cassino, so clever, so quick, so much better than us with his wealth and his uncle the Cardinal. I will happily stick a knife between his ribs for you.' Scaravaggi smiled at his friend and took a long draft of the rich burgundy wine. 'Don't worry, Jean, I swear I will see my day with him. Now I must get the boys into the west of the city. We can use the underground tombs and chambers in the old deserted episcopal palace. The bishop left the palace years ago. As you know, he refused to support the antipope, so he moved to Rome to support Pope Gregory, and it has fallen into ruin and decay. Pope Clement is staying at the monastery, I believe?'

Jean nodded, 'Yes, but getting you and the boys into the city will be almost impossible. Men are watching every road.' Both men sat with their thoughts for a while as they mulled over various possibilities. 'How often do you take your cheese and milk to Avignon?' he asked his friend. 'The cheese goes by cart three times a week. The herd of nanny goats go every day to our compound where they are milked every morning and then driven back to the pastures in the afternoon.' Scaravaggi thought for a few moments. 'The cheeses are all wrapped in wax cloths?'

'Yes, layers of them on the cart.'

'So we could have one of my men, Father Franco, dressed as a labourer with your driver, and two boys can be hidden between the cheeses. Another two boys and a monk could drive the herd to the city. We just need different clothes for them all. We could have them all in the city by the end of the week.' he said triumphantly, slapping the table in pleasure.

Jean nodded, 'That might work, I will get my wife, Margaret, to sort out the clothes tomorrow, and we can buy more at the market. I presume that money is no problem.' Scaravaggi patted the bulging purse at his belt. 'Of course not, and we will gladly pay for our food and drink.' Jean shook his head, 'I wouldn't hear of it.'

Two days later, Conn, dressed in a tunic and braies with wooden salops on his feet that felt strange, climbed after Georgio into the cavity created in the middle of the cheeses. More waxed cheeses were stacked around them, but there were still several narrow chinks and gaps where they could see the fields and buildings. Father Franco shouted to them to be deathly quiet until they stopped in the compound. The road into the city got busier and busier as it was one of the market days. The boys watched carts, horses and laden pedlars on the road, all new to them after their restricted existence.

As they reached the high sand-coloured city walls, Conn suddenly heard Father Franco say,' God help us, we are undone!' The boys looked at each other in fear in the dim light of their hiding place. However, the cart stopped only for a short while as the driver exchanged abusive insults with the guards at the gates, and then they moved on. Conn looked back and saw two horsemen, warriors with crossed swords on their backs. They waited inside the gates for the carts to come through, but now they cantered out of the city. His breath caught in his throat as he now understood Father Franco's exclamation. They must be the Breton Horse Warriors. Were they searching for him? Was one of them his father? Is this why Scaravaggi was hiding them? He thought for only a second of shouting out to them, but he was too afraid.

The whole party had been hidden in the cold stone tombs beneath the old episcopal palace by the end of the week. They were waiting for Scaravaggi, who was coming over the rooftops at night. He arrived when they were asleep. He was now dressed in a black Benedictine habit, and round his neck was a long string of wooded rosary beads with a wooden cross attached. No ostentatious decoration was allowed for the strict Benedictine orders. Scaravaggi had ordered his monks to let their hair grow during their arduous journey, and he would now shave their heads into the Benedictine tonsure demanded by Pope Gregory. The following day he would attempt to see Pope Gregory close by at the monastery.

Chapter Thirty-one

As they reached the top of the hill a few days later, something had occurred to Morvan. It had been in the back of his mind, and now he realised what it was. A driver, or man, on one of the carts at the gates to the city had reacted in shock, when he saw them, not just surprise at seeing Horse warriors in Avignon. Luc and Morvan were used to the curious glances or stares, but this was white-faced fear. The man had also dropped his eyes immediately, as it occurred to Morvan that it was a good way to get the boys into the city, disguised or hidden in carts. He whirled his horse around and shouted at his surprised brother, 'With me!' Luc galloped after him, and he watched as Morvan flung himself out of the saddle at the gates to the dismay of the guards as he strode towards them. One of them fingered his sword hilt nervously, but Morvan held his hands out in peace. 'There was a cart that came through here a few days ago with two men. Before we rode out, do you know who it belonged to?' The guards looked at one another in disbelief, 'Sire, there are often over a hundred carts a day come backwards and forwards through these gates, more on market days. We don't know them all.'

Luc sat on his horse, listening. He could understand what Morvan thought as he remembered the cart as well. 'This driver swore at you,' said Luc pointing to the fatter of the two guards. 'He called you a useless sweating pig as you took his toll.' The guard stared at the ground for what seemed like an eternity to Morvan before finally saying. 'It might have been the cheese man. He always hates paying the toll. They have a big goat farm in the next valley.' He pointed over the top of the western hill in a direction they had not ridden yet.

The brothers headed west until they crested the hill and rode down the valley. They saw a small stone manor house surrounded by numerous wooden outbuildings with thatched rooves. Slightly apart stood a large wooden barn. In the fields in front of them, there seemed to be hundreds of goats of all shapes and sizes. They cantered through, scattering the animals while a woman shook her fist and shouted, 'Do you want to curdle the milk?' She was an attractive woman in her prime. Her husband, Jean, had chased her out to deal with them when he saw them descending the hill. 'How can I help you, Sire? Do you want some cheese?' she asked, one hand on her hip, the other shading her eyes so she could see their faces. 'We are searching for a group of monks who have stolen seven boys. We believe you may have seen them.' Margaret frowned, 'stolen?' she whispered. Morvan heard her and narrowed his eyes, 'One of them is my son.' She quickly glanced back at the Manor House and then, 'No, we have seen no one.' she said nervously, turning back to the house.

Morvan and Luc looked at each other. 'Is your husband here?' asked Luc, staring intently at the house. 'Yes, but he is busy with the cheese.' she answered, walking briskly across the meadow. Luc ignored the comment and cantered over to the house, followed by Morvan. Dismounting, he ran up the steps into the hall and found the farmer standing in front of the fire. He was a tall, fit, muscled man in his forties. His wife came running in before Jean could even utter a greeting. 'I couldn't stop them,' she panted. 'Shut your mouth, woman, before you say too much.' he growled.

'So the boys were here then,' said Luc in a voice full of menace while stepping forward. The man raised his hands and stepped back, 'Only for a night or two, I swear, they slept in the barn. I know nothing else about them.'

'Do you know where they went?' asked Morvan.

'The one in charge said that it was a pilgrimage to Avignon and St Mary's church.' he replied. Morvan turned to Luc. 'Let us look in the barn. They may have left some clues.' Luc's eyes were still on the farmer, who had dropped his hands and now stood watching them warily. Jean knew all about Horse Warriors. In fact, he was now sure that he had been part of a group that had attacked the younger man, in a wood near Ghent, many years before. They had lost many men and been forced to flee. He prayed that the Horse Warrior did not recognise him.

Just then, a log fell from the fire and rolled out. The man bent down to pick it up and place it back on the fire. As he reached down, Luc suddenly saw it… in seconds, his dagger was out, and he held the man tightly by the throat, forcing him to his knees. He bent him backwards over the large open fire. His wife was screaming while Luc hissed in Jean's face, 'You're one of them. You have the cross tattoo on your neck.' The man was gasping and choking as Luc held the dagger to his eyes, tightening the death grip on his throat even more.

'He left them. He left the order of Warrior Monks for me over fifteen years ago. He has nothing to do with them now,' she shouted. Luc stared into the frightened man's eyes a moment longer, but released his grip slightly so he could talk. 'Where are they?' he growled. 'I just helped them get into the city to my compound. I do not know more than that, although Scaravaggi said he would go to see the Pope.'

Luc suddenly pushed the man backwards, and he landed on the fire. They left him squealing in pain as he tried to push himself out while they headed for the barn. Here they found several monks' habits and the boys' tunics in a pile in the corner of the barn. 'They are in normal clothes,' spat Morvan. Luc put a reassuring hand on his shoulder. 'They are in the city. It isn't that big. We will find them, Morvan. I promise you.'

On arriving back at Chatillon's house, they related what had happened that morning. 'So they are here, close to us in the city.' said Ette clapping her hands in excitement. 'That is good news, no? Surely there can only be so many places they can hide?' she asked. Within minutes, Chatillon was on his feet, shouting for Edvard. 'Find me a plan of the city. We will divide it into four sections to search.' An hour later, messengers ran in every direction to bring in Chatillon's men and mercenaries scattered throughout the city. Edvard gathered them all together in the Great Hall. There must have been over a hundred men. Chatillon mounted the staircase to stand halfway up to see them all. 'Edvard, divide the men into four groups, with a capable leader for each group,' he ordered. That took some time as disagreements ensued about who should be the leaders until punches were thrown. Morvan impatiently paced back and forth at the front until Luc grasped his arm and pulled him to a stop. 'Patience.' he growled.

Chatillon then addressed the four groups and explained the quest, outlining the generous payment they would receive.

He added an eye-watering amount for the man that could bring Conn De Malvais back alive and unharmed. Each of the four, Chatillon, Edvard, Morvan and Luc took a group. There were gasps of pleasure when some realised the Malvais brothers were here and would be with them. Ette insisted on changing into men's clothes again and going with Morvan, who frowned, but she hissed at him. 'You will have to lock me in a room and chain me to a chair if you want to stop me.' He gave in with a rueful smile. Chatillon then explained how the city would be divided among them. They were to work in smaller teams of five and six and move methodically through the city, which may take several days or longer. They had orders to search every house, every church, every yard, and compound. They would find the boys.

Chapter Thirty-two

It was cold and damp in the crypt, down amongst the tombs. There was little light apart from the dozen or so cheap stinking tallow lamps bought in the market. The boys sat huddled together in a group with their blankets around their shoulders. Their spirits were low, their life in the Hermitage may have been a harsh and bleak existence, but it was far better than this. Gustave constantly moaned and paced about to the extent that Scaravaggi stirred himself from his thoughts and walked the full length of the chamber, to deliver a punishing blow that knocked him from his feet. 'Another complaint and I swear I will cut your throat and leave you here. Boys like you, I can find them on the streets outside.' The boys crouched down as Gustave managed to crawl back to his place, his hand on his jaw. The rest of the monks stayed silent, even Father Franco was subdued, and he called a halt to the bible lesson.

Scaravaggi curled back up on his blanket on top of a large flat tomb near the stairs. He had sent his envoy yesterday morning to ask for an urgent audience with Pope Clement, but he had heard nothing. He wondered what could be taking so long. Did this antipope not realise who he was? Suddenly, they heard footsteps, and the old wooden door, swollen with dampness, was shoved open at the top of the steps, letting some light in from the large chamber above. Scaravaggi and the monks drew their swords. Even the boys clutched the hilts of their daggers in alarm. A voice whispered, 'Scaravaggi, are you there?' Monseigneur Besson was a local but important cleric in the Pope's household. 'Yes, come down here. We have been waiting for you,' he replied in a censorious tone.

The cleric descended and glanced around in the gloom at the pinched white faces who stared back at him. Whatever Scaravaggi was doing here in Avignon, he knew he wanted no part of it. He had heard that Piers De Chatillon was in the city with two famous Horse Warriors and that they were searching for someone. The rumour was that a young boy had been stolen from them. The warrior monk towered over him as he reached the last step, so he retreated slightly to put himself on a level with the man's face. He owed a debt of honour to Scaravaggi for removing a troublesome merchant in Rome. A man who would have stopped his advancement in the church. He had been carrying on an affair with the merchant's wife, but Pope Gregory's strict reforms meant it was taboo. Unfortunately, the merchant had found them together and would have gone to the Pope. Scaravaggi solved the problem for him, and the merchant's body was found floating in the Tiber the next day.

'I have arranged a private audience with Pope Clement at dawn tomorrow morning. He does not want people to see you entering the monastery. He is aware that there are people in the city searching for you. So I will meet you outside the monastery walls and take you through the postern gate. Then we can go through the servant's quarters and up the back stairs to the Pope's chambers. He only sees you because of your influence and the power you wield, although he did admit that he was intrigued by the little I had told him of your plans.' Scaravaggi had bridled at first at being taken like a beggar through the servant's quarters, but the result was worth it. He needed Clement to sanction his plans and secure funding from Holy Roman Emperor Henry IV. He slapped the cleric on the shoulder and thanked him. 'One more thing, Scaravaggi, when I have taken you to the Pope, I expect my debt to you to be paid.' Scaravaggi's cold, pale eyes narrowed, but he nodded, and Besson gave an audible sigh of relief as he mounted the stairs back to the light and warmth of the outside world. The Master turned to the assembled group, 'Father Franco put on the black habit and find some food, buy lots of food, meat bread, cheeses with some good red wine to wash it down. Tonight will be our last night in this place so let us celebrate.'

At the end of the first day, Chatillon was convinced they must have searched the whole city. His mire splattered boots and aching feet certainly told him that. His bruised and stinging knuckles were also a testimony as one burly baker had tried to deny him entry to his premises. They had found no sign of the boys or monks, and no one admitted to seeing them. However, Chatillon wasn't disillusioned as they headed to bed. Tomorrow they would gather at an early hour and continue. The boys were still in the city, he could feel it.

Morvan and Luc were equally hopeful as they sat down to break their fast with warm bread, honey, cheeses and ale. Suddenly, a hammering on the outside doors penetrated up to the Great Hall, which was unusual at this early hour. Edvard showed in a pock faced young man just as Ette and Chatillon joined them. 'He says he has information,' said Edvard as a way of explanation while pushing the thin man forward. 'Come here and tell me,' Commanded Chatillon as he waved him over to stand beside him. 'I saw him, Sire, the big monk he told us to look for,' he spluttered, pointing at Edvard, his hand shaking in nervousness. 'Where did you see this monk?' asked Chatillon while spearing a piece of cheese. 'At the monastery, Sire, this morning.' Chatillon heard the rush of chairs pushed back as they all rose to their feet. 'I was coming out of my dormitory on the servant's backstairs to help in the kitchens, Sire, and there he was going up the private stairs to the Pope's chambers with Monseigneur Besson. I stepped back into the shadows quick like, but he turned and grabbed me by my tunic. He lifted me clean off the ground. 'Say a word about this, and you're dead,' he hissed at me, and then he dropped me over the stairs, and I rolled to the bottom, fair bruised I am.' Chatillon looked across at Edvard, 'Well done, boy, make sure you pay him well, Edvard. We need to leave immediately. Edvard will gather a dozen men and follow us swiftly to the monastery.'

They rode to the city's southeast, heading for the outskirts where the monastery was situated just inside the old city walls. They could see the outline of the Dominican monastery in the distance, rising out of the early morning ground mist. Chatillon called a halt in a large copse of trees. 'Edvard, you and the rest of the men stay here. Ette, you'll act as my mounted messenger. We will move closer and follow Scaravaggi on foot when he emerges from his meeting with Clement. Hopefully, he should lead us straight to Conn and the boys.' Morvan took Ette's hand, 'Stay safe, no unnecessary risks, do you hear?' She grinned at him and then watched as they dismounted, tied up their horses, and headed towards the monastery before disappearing into the mist. She gave them a good start, and then she moved forward to stand her horse in a high clump of bushes, from where she could see the dark shapes of the main gates and archways. As she watched, Morvan climbed the wall and lay prone along the top so that he could see in several directions. Meanwhile, Luc and Chatillon hid in the lee of an old stable hut where the mist was high, and the shadows were deep.

Ette prayed that Scaravaggi was still in there and they had not missed him. She scanned around and noticed the ruins of the old bishop's residence that Chatillon had mentioned in the distance. The roof was long gone, the shingle tiles used for building elsewhere, no doubt, but most of the church's structure was still there, rising eerily from the thick mist. Suddenly there were several sounds, and two men emerged from a smaller postern gate. One of them was much taller. They stood for a few moments, and then there was only the smaller man, and he turned and went back inside—the sound of the gate being closed and barred carried to them. Ette stared until her eyes hurt, but she couldn't see the taller man no matter how she searched for him. Suddenly she had him. A figure was running along the walls in a low crouched position, hidden most of the time by the mist. He stopped at the western corner and flattened himself against the wall, scanning the area in front, and then he was off racing across the ground and through the bushes towards the ruins.

Scaravaggi was triumphant as he emerged from the chambers of the antipope, Clement III. The Holy Father had listened intently to what he had to say. He had sat and considered what he heard and asked searching questions about the boys and their training. Finally, he had agreed to sponsor the project and bring it to Henry IV's attention when he left for

Cologne shortly. He advised the Master to take the boys and establish them there, under the protection of the Holy Roman Emperor. Besson had been waiting for him and took him to the gate. 'From the smile, I must assume that your audience went well?' he asked the warrior monk. 'Yes, Besson, we are in the ascendency again. You would do well to support us.' The cleric inclined his head and added as he opened the gate, 'Take care, they are saying that Chatillon and his Horse Warriors searched most of the city yesterday.' Scaravaggi narrowed his eyes at the cleric, who seemed to know too much, but he said nothing and said farewell outside the gate. He thought he had caught a flash of light, on metal, near an old rundown building as he turned away. He sank to the ground immediately, welcoming the ground mist. He clung to the base of the walls as he ran at a crouch.

Scaravaggi was too close to the wall for Morvan to see him. He saw him emerge from the gate but thought he had gone right, so he ran along the top of the walls, leaping the main gates and almost losing his footing on the slippery mist drenched stones. He now sat on the wall at a loss before he cursed and dropped down. He ran towards the stable to join with the others. 'Did you see where he went?' he asked. 'We saw him disappear. Chatillon, at that point, thought he was coming straight at us under the mist. We drew our blades.'

They searched for several minutes to no avail around the walls until they heard a horse trotting towards them. Ette had decided to risk leaving her cover to tell the warriors what she had seen. 'I saw him, he was running low around the walls and then ran towards the old ruins. He was right under your feet, but you couldn't see him, Morvan.' He gave a rueful smile. 'Well done, my love. At least one of us is eagle-eyed, thank goodness.'

Chatillon cut in, 'Ette, ride to Edvard and the men. Get them to meet us over at the old palace. We will search the ruins there. Meanwhile, the mist is dropping, and the grass is so wet we may be lucky and see his tracks.' Morvan looked sceptical, 'Would he hide that large group in there? Isn't it too open and accessible?' asked Morvan. Chatillon shook his head, 'Some parts are, but this was the original residence of the Bishop of Avignon. The old palace may have lost its roof, but there are many rooms, nooks, and crannies where they could hide. We will have to split the men up and search it thoroughly. Come, we must hurry as I feel that he has been alerted to our presence and may try to take the boys out in the mist.' With that worrying thought, the three of them broke into a run, swords drawn, towards the old palace.

Chapter Thirty-three

Scaravaggi had stood in the palace ruins behind a crumbling wall and watched the horse break cover and trot across to join a small group of men. They were too far away for him to see who they were but inside, he knew. He raced up the long nave towards the large stone altar of the deserted church. Hidden behind and within it was the door that would lead down to a series of chambers and crypts. He had taken the boys down to a deeper crypt through another door and staircase. He knew he had to get them out of there now, or they would all be caught like rats in a trap. He was aware of no other entrance or exit to the crypts. He pulled the door on the altar tightly closed behind him and ran down the narrow stairs two at a time. He raced across the first much larger chamber to yank open the second much older door. As he descended the stairs, he was shouting instructions, 'Put your daggers and cloaks on, roll up your blankets, and leave nothing essential behind. Father Franco, quickly pack up any food we have left. We will take it with us. We must leave now, they have found us, and they will kill us all.' The boys hurried to obey when a clear, loud voice rang out unexpectedly.

'No, they won't! They will not kill us all, and those Horse Warriors are only here for Conn De Malvais. It's his father and his uncle out there. Hand Conn over to them, and the rest of us will live!'

Conn glanced around. In the dim light, he could see his shock registered on the faces of the other boys and even the younger Warrior Monks. They were speechless that anyone would dare to challenge the Master like this! Scaravaggi, who had one foot on the stairs, slowly turned around to face Father Franco, disbelief on his face. 'You dare to tell me what to do, to hand over a boy I have spent nearly seven years training. Have you any idea who he is or how important he is to us as a brotherhood? Can't you see the influence we will have with him as the leader of our Army of Christ?'

Franco bravely stepped forward, 'Yes, I do. He is the grandson of King William. His mother is Princess Constance, now the Duchess of Brittany. His father is the leader of the northern Horse Warriors, Sir Morvan De Malvais.'

The boys and monks all looked at Conn as if seeing him for the first time as Father Franco continued. 'However, I know they will come down here and take him if you do not hand him over. They won't kill the boys, they are not savages, but they will kill all of the Warrior Monks down here, including me, to avenge what you did to Sir Gerard. I heard what you told Bruno. You had the injured knight thrown off the walls of the Hermitage, while he was still alive.'

Conn stood frozen to the spot. He felt real fear as he dreaded what Scaravaggi would do. The Master's lips were white with anger. The only sound in the chamber was the flickering of the tallow lamps and the fast breathing of Father Franco as everyone waited....

'I would rather cut his throat here and now than hand him over to them, and you're nothing but a traitor to the brotherhood. Kill him.' he yelled, pointing at the brave monk, but nobody moved. Scaravaggi looked around at their faces in astonishment. He was so used to blind obedience. Fury filled him, and drawing his sword, he ran Father Franco through. A cry of dismay from the boys and many young monks went up, as Father Franco fell sideways to the ground. Scaravaggi pulled his blade out. Sensing the mood, he turned to face them. 'Does anyone else want the same?' he asked, glaring around the dim crypt. Conn stood in silent fury as he watched Franco's blood run down the blade and onto the Master's hands. 'Now move, we must go,' shouted Scaravaggi as he ushered them up the stairs into the much larger chamber full of tombs and stone coffins.

Chatillon, Luc and Morvan had searched all of the buildings and ruins above, but there was no sign of the boys, no handprints or footprints in the dust. Many of the rooms had lain undisturbed for years. They seemed to have reached a dead end. Ette, Edvard and the other men had arrived to join in the search to no avail. 'I only saw him run in this direction. He may well have gone further afield. Perhaps he only hid here for a while before moving on to a farmstead on the outskirts again.' she offered. 'No, the goat farmer admitted that they were inside the city, that means within the walls which are only down there,' said Luc pointing southwest to clusters of buildings built up and around the high sand-coloured walls of the city.

Chatillon turned to Edvard, 'Send the mounted men and search the bushes around here and the buildings near the walls. There are lots of tanning yards and warehouses near the river.' Edvard went to relay his master's orders and watched his men canter off while he decided to stay close to Chatillon. Ette lingered with Morvan, reaching out, she put her hand on his arm. 'I was sure that he was here. I felt it.' Morvan gave a thin smile and put his hand over hers. 'We are so close, Ette. I know we are. We will find him.'

Edvard, who had sat quietly watching them and thinking, now had a thought, and he leaned forward to whisper to Chatillon, 'Have you searched the tombs or vaults. This palace was riddled with underground chambers. I remember from the early days when I came here as your messenger.' Chatillon whirled around, 'We did not search the vaults. Luc, Morvan, come, let us try to find an entrance to them. I know they will be underground because Scaravaggi will know of the vaults. He spent several years here in Avignon. Edvard ride quickly after them. I know they split up, but find and call back half of the men.'

Chatillon ran back towards the main building shouting over his shoulder, 'The vaults will always be under the church or chapel because that is sacred ground. Luc, Morvan go left, Ette and I will go right, search the floor for any stone slabs that lift, search the walls for any handles or iron rings set into what could be a door. They scanned every inch of the church while Ette wandered around through the chancel towards the sanctuary where the large stone altar stood. She could see the small carved gravestones set into the floor, but there was no sign that they could be moved. She stood by the altar and gazed around the floor and walls. It was then that she heard shouting. She presumed it was the riders returning outside, but then it was louder and came from under her feet. She shouted for the others to be quiet, and then she could hear and feel the reverberation of running feet. She went behind the altar and gave a sharp intake of breath, for steps leading down to a solid door were built into the back of the wide stone structure. It would usually have been hidden behind a long altar cloth to deter grave robbers.

'Morvan, Luc, it's here,' she shouted. The Horse Warriors ran up the nave towards her, followed by a grinning Chatillon. Luc grabbed the ring set into the door and pulled it open, further steps led down, and he drew his sword. Morvan turned to face his wife, 'Ette, you stay up here and wait for Edvard to guide him and the men down. No matter what happens, you stay here. Do you understand?' She nodded, but she was terrified for him as he followed his brother and Chatillon down into the darkness to face God knows what or how many Warrior Monks. At first, she prayed that Edvard would be back soon with some of the men, but then she ran to her horse and galloped off towards the city's walls, determined to help Edvard find them.

Chapter Thirty-four

Scaravaggi glanced around, his eyes passing over the body of Father Franco without a second thought, before he followed the boys and other monks up into the much larger chamber above. It was high and wide, stone coffins were stacked at the sides, but the middle was littered with larger stone tombs of past bishops and local dignitaries. They should have been moved when they abandoned the palace years ago, but it never happened.

Scaravaggi suddenly heard voices above him, and he knew he was too late. They would have to fight their way out. He climbed onto one of the high flat tombs and waved the group over, 'We can't get out! They are above us. Father Franco was wrong, and he listened to the poison dripped into his ear by the spy we killed at the Hermitage. These men above us are killers and mercenaries, paid to wipe us out.' He looked directly into the eyes of his young Warrior Monks. He had trained every one of them. 'I know that you're loyal to the brotherhood. You have proved that you're the chosen ones to protect The Seven. You must protect these boys with your lives, we lost one, and we must lose no more. At least three of you must stay with them at all times. Boys, go to the far sides of the chamber into the crevices behind the stone coffins and hide there. If they attack you, come out fighting in pairs and try to kill or wound your attacker. You have trained for this.'

There were the distinctive sounds of the door above being opened, followed by booted feet descending the steep staircase as light flooded into the chamber. The boys raced to hide with their protectors, the rest of the monks spread out in a semi-circle behind Scaravaggi, who, sword drawn, remained on top of the tomb.

Two-thirds down the stairs, Luc stopped and held a hand up for those behind him. It was a large chamber, much bigger than expected. There was light from the door above, but there were deep shadows and passages everywhere. At a glance, Luc took in the sight of Scaravaggi standing on one of the large tombs, his lips drawn back in a rictus grin. 'You will never get out of here alive,' his shout, reverberating around the chamber. Around and behind him stood half a dozen Warrior Monks, swords drawn, waiting for them. Luc knew that they were outnumbered and would have to act with speed. He half-turned, reluctant to take his eyes off the men in front of him, toward the two men behind him. He could see from their faces that they had taken in the scene at a glance. 'I will go left,' whispered Chatillon. 'Where are the boys?' asked Morvan.

'They are hiding at the sides. They may attack us as well. If so, try to disarm them and knock them out with the hilt of your sword or a punch. They will recover.' Before Luc could say another word, Scaravaggi spoke, 'See how they hesitate. They are afraid of us, these killers, and these bandits.' Without warning, Morvan pushed past Luc and Chatillon, 'He is mine,' he shouted as, with an ear-splitting Horse Warrior roar, he ran down the steps leaping straight at Scaravaggi, who still towered above him on the high tomb. The Master went into a crouch, throwing his sword from one hand to another, the grin still on his face, which was soon erased as Morvan drew his second sword with his left hand and delivered a sweeping cut at the man's legs. He leapt back but not quickly enough, and the blade sliced deeply into his left calf. 'You're too old and too slow, monk, so who is afraid now.' he yelled as Scaravaggi jumped backwards to the floor, putting the tomb between them.

Luc had raced to the right, drawing both swords as he took on two of the Warrior Monks at once, beating them down and back with powerful blows and inflicting several wounds. They had never seen or experienced such speed, accuracy or skill. As he shook the sweat out of his eyes, he noticed the uncertainty and fear in the eyes of the third monk, who hovered back, and he played on it by beheading the monk on his left. It was killing them or being killed, and he knew these trained Warrior Monks. They may be young, but he had faced them before. They wouldn't hesitate.

With a sword in his right hand and his long carved dagger in his left, Chatillon was having a harder time. He was being attacked by two monks, one of which had a stave. At one point, the monk delivered a numbing blow to his right arm, and Chatillon nearly dropped his blade, which would have been the end of him. Fortunately, Chatillon had trained with the best in Paris. Although no one could match Luc De Malvais, the Papal envoy could certainly see off most swordsmen. Morvan saw that his friend was in difficulty, and with Scaravaggi still on the other side of the tomb, he whirled and attacked the third monk who was swinging the stave at Chatillon's head. Morvan ran him through from behind, and with a surprised gasp, the man dropped to the floor. Chatillon threw a smile of thanks to the Horse Warrior. He stared through the chamber's gloom at the monks guarding the boys. 'Surrender,' he shouted. 'You can't possibly win against Horse Warriors led by Luc De Malvais. There are another dozen men up there waiting for you. Do you want to die down here?'

Scaravaggi, in blind fury, rolled swiftly over the top of the tomb, dropping silently behind Morvan, who was still facing the white-faced boys and their guardians. The monk delivered a downward killing blow with his sword that Luc saw, and he shouted a warning. Morvan just raised his blade in time, but the powerful impact on his right arm made him drop the blade.

Conn and the boys were watching all of this wide-eyed. There had been a sudden jolt of recognition when Luc De Malvais had come down the steps. At first, with the light behind them, he could only see the menacing outline of men with swords coming for them. However, when Luc had turned to the men behind, the sunlight had lit his face. Conn gave a sharp intake of breath, and he whispered the word 'Papa' unbidden. He knew he had called this man by that name. Suddenly, he could see a huge dappled black stallion called Esprit Noir. He could remember sitting on the horse in front of this man who laughed, as Conn kicked his legs to make it go faster. He stood up behind the coffins and drew his dagger. He was confused and torn. The Hermitage and the Master had been his life for so long that he had a loyalty to them and had to protect the other boys. What if these men killed them all?

The other Horse Warrior was engaged in a fierce fight with the Master. Conn watched as Morvan threw the sword from his left to his right hand. They seemed to be able to fight with both hands, his other blade lay on the ground where he had dropped it, but Conn could see that he couldn't reach for it with Scaravaggi circling him. Georgio reached out a hand and grabbed Conn's arm firmly. 'What are you doing?' he hissed. 'I think that might be my father, but I don't know,' said Conn, staring at the man fighting Scaravaggi. Beside them on the ground, Gustave was cowering and covering his ears. The clashing blades, grunts, screams, the strong tang of blood and groans of dying men who had soiled themselves filled the chamber. This all created a cacophony of noise and smell that terrified the boys.

At that moment, Scaravaggi caught Morvan off guard and forced him backwards across the lower tomb. Morvan still had his blade, but it was being forced down towards his face by the pure weight and power of Scaravaggi's sword. The Master was a big man, heavy with bone and muscle. He was on top of Morvan, pinning his thighs down and putting all his force onto his sword, as the crossed scraping blades dropped towards Morvan's throat. Scaravaggi delivered several punishing blows to Morvan's head with his left fist, to force him to relinquish his blade. Morvan knew that he was in trouble for the first time in many years. This powerful man had him pinned to the tomb, and if he didn't manage to throw him off or dislodge him somehow, he would die here in this mausoleum. From the corner of his eye, he saw two boys emerging from the shadows, as he strained every muscle to keep the blades from slicing into his throat.

Chatillon was also in trouble. The Warrior Monks guarding the boys had joined the fray, and the first one ran at Chatillon, already engaged in a vicious fight. Chatillon saw him coming, arm outstretched with a pointed blade. He quickly turned sideways to give the man less of a target while still trying to keep the other monk at bay. Chatillon had not been fast enough, and the blade plunged through his shoulder, knocking him off his feet onto his knees. The other monk crowed in triumph and raised his sword to take off Chatillon's head. There was a sudden clattering of feet down the stairs, and a roaring Edvard came flying down to Chatillon's aid.

Luc, heavily engaged with the last of the young Warrior Monks, could see what was happening with Morvan but couldn't help until he despatched at least one of them. Morvan could feel the strain on his arms beginning to tell. He could also feel Scaravaggi's hot breath on his face. He knew he couldn't hold this for much longer. He tried again to kick his legs free or bring his knees up to no avail. He glanced right, the two boys, daggers in their hands, were much closer. He closed his eyes for a few moments. It would soon be over as soon as they sank their blades into him. 'Luc,' he shouted hoarsely, but the chamber's noise was too much. The larger of the two boys raised his dagger over his head, holding it with two hands, and as he came into the light from the doorway, Morvan found he was staring into the large blue eyes of Constance. 'Conn, Conn,' he whispered, but the boy's face did not change. Only his eyes narrowed as the dagger descended.

Ette was slowly coming down the stairs. The mercenaries followed behind her. The scene that met her eyes was a bloodbath. Luc was in the fight's final moments with a skilled young swordsman. Chatillon was wounded and on his knees, blood dripping from his fingers as he leant against a tomb. Edvard launched a vicious assault with his long carved sword over on the left into two monks. She could see frightened boys cowering in the shadows, but it was the scene in the centre that made her release an ear-piercing scream of 'No,'

Scaravaggi had both blades pressed against Morvan's throat, and blood ran down his neck. Beside them were two boys and the taller had a dagger raised over Morvan's head. She drew out her smaller sword and ran at them, screaming, but she was too late as the dagger descended.

Chapter Thirty-five

Chatillon sat on a ruined wall outside the palace in the autumn sunshine. His shirt had been torn off, and his shoulder and arm were blood-smeared as Edvard expertly bound the wound with the torn strips of his shirt. 'You're fortunate, Seigneur, that it hasn't done too much damage. It seems to be a clean wound. We will summon a physician back to the house to stitch and poultice it to prevent infection or rot. Chatillon grimaced at the thought but thanked him for saving his life and bandaging his wounds. As self-effacing as ever, Edvard just gave a smile in recognition of the services rendered to his master.

Chatillon felt fortunate to be alive. He considered himself a consummate swordsman, but taking on two trained young Warrior Monks with swords and staves had almost ended him. When a third joined in, he knew he was done for, as he was exhausted. Fortunately, Morvan had despatched one of them, but he was still outnumbered and wounded. He remembered being on his knees and becoming so angry, because he did not want to die in this tomb, when he had so much living to do. Then suddenly, Edvard was there, killing one immediately and holding others at bay, so that Chatillon could escape. He could remember Ette's sudden scream, and then he was staggering

283

up the stairs, past the mercenaries, gasping in the cooler fresh air before he sank gratefully onto a wall.

Now he gazed around at the scene in the sunlit ruins. Weary bloodstained men sat on the stones or grass, some with their hands tied behind them. A group of young boys looking lost and confused sat on the grass. Nearer to him, Luc stood with his arms tightly wrapped around a dark mop-haired young boy sobbing uncontrollably. He could hear Luc repeating that it wasn't his fault. Conn could not have known. Chatillon quickly scanned around the ruins as he realised that he couldn't see Morvan, Ette, or Scaravaggi. He closed his eyes for a moment, praying that Morvan had survived. They had taken on ridiculous odds down there to save these boys, the type of odds that only Luc De Malvais would consider acceptable. He shook his head at the madness of it all, and pushing himself to his feet, he walked towards Luc, who had calmed the boy but was still holding him close. He nodded at the Papal envoy, 'Well met, Chatillon, you fought like a lion down there.' Chatillon smiled, 'A compliment indeed from the great Luc De Malvais.'

Chatillon turned his attention to the boy. 'I presume this must be Conn De Malvais I am addressing.' The boy turned and looked up at him through blue tear-drenched eyes. 'You have no idea how pleased I am to see you,' he said with relief. 'We have searched all over Europe for you for years, and you have cost me a fortune.' The boy straightened up, 'Thank you, Sire, for your perseverance, but I think we were probably too well hidden at the Hermitage.' Chatillon looked at the boy in surprise just as Georgio shouted Conn over. The boy bowed his head to both men and ran to his friends.

Both men watched him go. 'He is so intelligent, astute, and

polite, but I shouldn't have been surprised given his lineage. However, even I could see the pain in those eyes. The boy has been damaged by his experience, and he'll take time to heal.' Luc agreed as they stood and watched the group of boys for a moment longer, as Chatillon scanned the ruins again before turning to Luc with one questioning word, 'Morvan?' he asked. Luc shook his head and indicated the crypt. He is down there. Chatillon went cold and raised shocked eyes, 'Dead?' he asked, in a voice breaking with emotion.

Luc gave him a keen glance. This man cared for his brother. 'No, God be thanked, Morvan is with Ette. He is wounded badly in the thigh, a thrust he hardly noticed until the blood pooled at his feet. Ette is dealing with it, and then we will help him up those stairs.'

'And Scaravaggi? Did Morvan kill him? Please tell me he did not escape!' Luc's gaze went to the two friends now running together over the grass in the sunlight. 'He was stabbed in the neck by Conn and numerous times in the back by little Georgio. That enabled Morvan to push him off.'

Chatillon nodded in satisfaction, 'So Conn saved his father's life!' Luc nodded, 'He is still shy with him as he has never met him, but that will improve with Ette's help.' Chatillon grasped Luc's arm with his good hand and left him to go down to the crypt. As he descended the stairs, he could see Ette had bandaged Morvan's neck, and she was now kissing him. It was a strange sight as they sat on the tomb, highlighted in the sunlight, but surrounded as they were by blood and dead bodies. He coughed to get their attention. They laughed when they saw it was Chatillon and Ette told him he looked very dashing, bare-chested, in his bloodstained sling. 'It's such a shame that Isabella can't see you now. She would be very impressed. Women always love a blood-stained hero.' Chatillon gave a rueful smile. 'Remind me to play on it when I return to Genoa, Ette.' She gave her tinkling laugh as she watched him. Sometimes, she forgot just how handsome Chatillon was because of who he was and how people feared him.

'I'm delighted to see that you're alive and with us, Morvan. I did fear for you once or twice when I saw that Scaravaggi had you pinned down. Luc tells me that Conn and his friend stabbed him.' Morvan nodded, 'To be honest, Chatillon, he almost had me. He had such strength, and I was at a disadvantage, in a position where I could no longer use the sword skills that would have beaten him.

When I saw a boy with a dagger raised over his head, I feared the worst. Then Ette's scream, which reverberated around the chamber, distracted Scaravaggi. He glanced over at the stairs and did not see the dagger plunging towards him. I will never forget the fury and shock on his face when he saw it was Conn. He clutched at the dagger in his neck and began to choke, then the other boy attacked, and I could push and disengage the sword cutting into my throat. Ette then arrived and stabbed him again several times. Do not tell her this, but I think she gave me the wound in my thigh. She was so fierce, she did not see where she was stabbing.' Ette turned and looked at him in horror, and he laughed with Chatillon joining in.

'At that moment, Luc came over, and Conn ran into his arms, which wasn't surprising as he was the only father he had known. Luc explained to him who I was.'

'So what now Morvan De Malvais?' asked Chatillon, with a raised eyebrow.

'We will take Conn home to Morlaix where we can recuperate, and we can only hope that his years at the Hermitage have not scarred him too much. We will wrap him in love and kindness, teach him how to ride and fall off well, of course.' Chatillon smiled. It always came back to horses. 'I'm to marry Isabella in the spring. I have decided to put it off again as I refuse to walk down the aisle in a sling, and I would like you two to be there beside me in Genoa if possible?' Morvan glanced mischievously at Ette. 'We will certainly try, Chatillon. After all, it's only a short boat ride away.' They all laughed at that, knowing Ette's habit of minimising any distance. Edvard appeared on the stairs to tell them he was there to help Morvan up the steps and that he had found several wagons, to take them back to the house.

At Conn's request, Luc had brought Father Franco's body up from the lower crypt, and the men had buried it in the sacred grounds of the old church. They decided that the rest, including Scaravaggi, could lie and rot where they dropped. Now, the boys clambered into the wagons, chattering and laughing. They were happy to be out and away from the harsh control of the Master and the monks. Chatillon stood and waved off the wagons. Edvard stood beside him. 'Do you think it wise to ride back? After all, even the great Morvan De Malvais is in a wagon?' Chatillon narrowed his eyes and gave him a withering look. 'If you think I am riding in a wagon through the city like some travelling group of players, you do not know me as well as I thought, Edvard.' His manservant smiled but was surprised to see his master heading back down into the crypt.

The smell hit Chatillon as he descended the stairs, and he blanched, but he had to see it for himself. He walked towards the large tomb. Scaravaggi's body lay face down in a pool

287

of blood. Using his foot, he managed to flip the body over, and he stood and stared down at the blood-soaked body of his arch-nemesis, who hated him and had tried to kill him several times. He felt a small satisfaction. After all, it was rare that his enemies were not vanquished, but this had been different, more dangerous, more of a challenge. This vision of Dauferio's, this plot, and the stealing of hundreds of boys would have affected the church and the princes of Europe. He knew he still had much work to do to crush this. He had to find the other groups and free the boys, this Army of Christ. The power of seven would be no more.

No distance away from the crypt, another man thought differently. Scaravaggi had given the antipope, Clement III, the locations of all the groups he had set up in Europe. Clement had already sent messengers to each location and ordered them to move to the Monastery De Canonici Lateranensi near his home town of Ravenna in northern Italy. He did not expect Scaravaggi to survive his pursuit by Luc De Malvais and Chatillon, so he would find someone else to lead the plan. Clement himself would leave Avignon in a week, and then he intended to give all this information to the Holy Roman Emperor.

Chapter Thirty-six

Later that evening, back In Chatillon's spacious house, Ette and Edvard arranged hot tubs of warm water for the boys to bathe. Their skin was encrusted with grime, and she was convinced they had head lice in their hair. She left them to it and went to find blankets and cloths to dry them. She stood in the doorway when she returned, and her mouth dropped open in shock. She retreated and went to get Luc. 'You have to see this,' she said, tears in her eyes. Chatillon had risen to his feet. Morvan had his leg propped up on a small bench, but their faces reflected their concern. She waved them down as Luc followed her down the stairs and along the stone corridor to the huge kitchens. Here two massive fires were blazing, and the meat was roasting on several spits. At the far end, lit by a bank of candles, were two large waist-high wooden tubs where the boys scrubbed themselves with lye soap as they'd been ordered.

They were laughing joyously as they had never been immersed in warm water before and they shrieked in pretend alarm as the servants topped it up with hot water. It was such a positive heart-warming scene, but Luc and Ette stood in the doorway's shadows grim-faced. Edvard saw them and shook his head to warn them not to say anything and spoil the moment. Ette nodded and took the pile of blankets into the kitchen, laying them on the benches before smiling at the boys and leaving. 'She is a woman, really,' whispered Conn to his friend Georgio who looked after the young man in amazement. 'She is my father's wife and is a warrior!' he said proudly.

Luc made his way back upstairs to the two men, talking quietly. They both saw the expression on his face. 'What is it?' asked Morvan. It took Luc a few moments to answer. 'If you discount the bruises, the cuts, the marks left by being beaten by a knotted rope on their bodies, then what Scaravaggi has done to them is barbaric!' He had to pause and look away for a moment. 'Each boy has an identical tattoo on his back, not a small cross on his neck, but a coloured tattoo. It goes from the neck to the base of their spines and from shoulder to shoulder. They must have suffered agony having this done, and they now have it for life. Try not to be shocked when you see it. We will warn those at home as well.' Both men nodded, Morvan's face was white with anger that someone could have done it to his son. Soon after, the boys appeared at the table with blankets knotted and belted, toga style, by Ette. The boy's mouths were watering with the smell of the roasting meats in the kitchen, and it was a happy and noisy crowd that sat down for dinner.

'What are we going to do with them all?' asked Ette looking at the six smiling faces as they tore into the roast fowls and large loaves of bread. 'I have asked Edvard to question each boy about what they remember of their families and where they lived. We will return them to their families if possible. Others we will put up for adoption. I want to keep them out of the monasteries if possible.' said Chatillon. 'One died on the dreadful walk over the Alps, I believe?' Ette nodded, 'Conn told me his name was Verruchio. He was from Milan. We think that Giorgio's parents died in a raid on their village, and if so, we will take him to Morlaix with us, as he and Conn seem to be inseparable.'

Listening to her, Morvan smiled, 'I have decided that we will stay at Morlaix for the next year, to give him some stability, in a place he may remember. I intend to take over the Breton Horse Warriors. Luc tells me that he is retiring to do nothing but breed horses and more children.' Everyone laughed at the thought of Luc ever retiring. 'Seriously though, our mother Marie will be heartbroken to hear of Gerard's death. She'll need our love and the support of her family around her.' Luc smiled, he was pleased if it meant that he and Merewyn would be there to help with Conn, giving him time to get to know and love his father and Ette. Like Chatillon, he was concerned about the shadows and pain he saw in the boy's eyes at times. He glanced down the table to see that Conn was watching him. He smiled, and the boy left his seat to come and stand beside him. Luc put his arm around him and pulled him to his side.

'Are you ready to go home, Conn? Home to Morlaix? Home to your cousins, grandmother, and aunt, Lady Merewyn, who have all missed you? Do you remember Merewyn?' Conn frowned for a moment and then shook his head. 'She has the most beautiful long silver-blonde hair and the biggest green eyes you have ever seen, and she loves you dearly.' Conn's mouth dropped open, Luc described his angel, but Conn was too shy to share that. 'Of course, your father will have to pick you out a beautiful horse of your own, a horse for a young warrior.' Conn looked over at his father, who nodded and added, 'We will also be taking Georgio with us.' Conn grinned and raced down to tell his friend. Luc and Morvan looked at each other in understanding. It would take a while, but he was back with his family. Before long, the boy's heads were nodding, warm, cared for, and well-fed. Ette ushered them off to their beds. Soon after, Ette helped Morvan up to bed, and only Luc and Chatillon sat by the great fire.

Chatillon swirled the ruby red liquid around in his Venetian glass. 'You do realise that Conn will still be a target because of his parentage! King Philip was asking questions about the missing boy.' Luc closed his eyes for a second. Did it never end, he wondered. 'We will protect him, Chatillon. We won't be caught napping again, and he is older. I need to send an urgent message to Morlaix, a bittersweet message. I have tarried too long in doing this. I will tell them of Gerard's death, which will devastate my mother and the family. Then I will tell them that we have found Conn, and we will be bringing him home.' Chatillon gave a rueful smile. 'It's always difficult to break that news, but I will arrange a series of riders, and the message will be with them in just over a week.' They sat for a while longer, poignantly remembering the man Gerard was and his role in their lives.

'I will tell you one thing, Malvais, there was a moment down there, in that crypt, when I thought we had bitten off more than we could chew.' Luc laughed before looking around the hall conspiratorially, leaning forward and saying. To tell you the truth, Chatillon, as I stood on the stairs with only the three of us facing Scaravaggi and a dozen Warrior Monks and another half dozen unknown but trained boys, I was sure that we had.'

Chatillon looked up in surprise at that admission but then

saw that Luc's eyes were sparkling with amusement, and he burst out laughing. 'If ever I'm in a tight corner, I will call on you, Luc De Malvais!'

Luc shook his head, 'Please don't. I think you managed to get us into more dire situations than I ever have, and you heard, Morvan, I am going home to my family to breed warhorses. On that pleasant thought, my bed is now calling me.' He bowed to his host and headed for the stairs.

'Wait, there is something you need to know before you go.' Luc turned back and placed his hands on the back of the chair in expectation—he wasn't sure he wanted to hear it, looking at the papal envoy's face.

'I received a message today from one of my priests in Nantes….' He paused and looked away for a moment, and sighed. 'Constance, the Duchess of Brittany is dead.'

Luc frowned. 'Constance? She was no age, thirty or so. Was it childbirth?'

Chatillon shook his head. 'She swore that she would never bear Alan's child, making sure it never happened. I think that may have been her undoing. My man is sure that the servants poisoned her on the orders of Alan Fergant.'

Luc ran his hands through his hair in anger and dismay. 'I can't tell Morvan yet, not on top of Gerard's death and my mother's grief. I will wait until we are back at Morlaix. Also, Conn has only just found out who his parents are now his mother is dead. Do not breathe a word to them, Chatillon.'

'My lips are sealed, Luc. I know how this will affect him, although I warn you that the news may come out as you travel home. Perhaps you should tell Ette to give her a prior warning'

Luc stood, pensive for a moment. 'I will think on it. Now I will retire, but probably for a restless night after what you have shared.' He reached the bottom of the stairs and added, 'She was so beautiful, Chatillon, inside and out. So full of life, and she loved Morvan so much.' Chatillon gave a rueful smile and sympathetic salute. Then he watched him ascend the stairs, another weight on his shoulders.

Chatillon sat for a while longer, pondering the day's events. His enemy, Dauferio's creature, Scaravaggi, was no more, and the Warrior Monks would be leaderless for a while. They had found and saved Conn and the boys in Avignon with minimum loss of life and few injuries. He knew that he couldn't have achieved this without the Malvais brothers. They were truly formidable, and he did not doubt that they would both ride out to war again with the Breton Horse Warriors if called. For now, though, they all deserved a few years' peace, not least Morvan and Luc De Malvais. And... for himself... he was to be married to the beautiful Isabella Embriaco.

It would be a new beginning.

End.

Thank you for reading **Vengeance**, I hope you enjoyed it as much as I enjoyed writing the series. Reviews are important to us indie authors and I would be very grateful if you would find the time to rate or review it. Thank you. **SJ**

List of characters

Fictional characters in *Italics*

Morlaix

Luc De Malvais.
Merewyn De Malvais - his wife.
Lusian, Chantal & Garret – their children.
Conn Fitz Malvais – son of Morvan and Constance.
Morvan de Malvais – Luc's younger brother
Marie De Malvais – their mother
Minette De Malvais (Ette) – Morvan's French wife
Gervais De Malvais- their son
Marie De Malvais – their daughter
Sir Gerard de Chanville– their mentor, sword master and family friend
Garret Eymer – Merewyn's Saxon brother and Captain of the Caen Horse Warriors
Benedot – Captain of the Horse Warriors
Brian Ap Gwyfd- horseman (now deceased)
Hildebrand – children's nurse

Caen

King William of England and Duke of Normandy
Queen Matilda- (now deceased)
Robert Curthose – eldest son heir to Normandy
William Rufus – heir to England
Henry – youngest son
Constance – daughter now Duchess of Brittany at Nantes
Alan Fergant – (Iron glove) Duke of Brittany
Earl De Clare – acting Regent of Normandy in William's absence.
Roger Fitz-Richard De Clare – his son and Morvan's friend and comrade.
Hugh De Grandesmil – Earl of Leicester
Aubrey De Grandesmil – his youngest son

Ghent in Flanders

Piers de Chatillon – Papal envoy, spy and assassin
Edvard – Chatillon's manservant and Vavasseur
Bianca da Landriano – wealthy Italian Contessa-(deceased)

Paris

King Philip of France
Gervais de la Ferte – Seneschal of France
Etienne de la Ferte – his eldest son

Rome

Dauferio – Abbot of Montecassino, Cardinal of Saint Cecillia (Pope Victor III 1085)
Odo de Chatillon – Cardinal and Prior of Cluny, uncle of Piers. (Pope Urban II 1088)
Pope Gregory VII– the Vatican, the Holy See (1073-1085)

Genoa

Signori Guglielmo Embriaco
Isabella Embriaco – his daughter
Signora Di Monsi – a wealthy merchant widow
Marietta Di Monsi – her daughter
Conrades Di Mezzarello – Bishop of Genoa

The Hermitage

Scaravaggi – The Master of the Warrior Monks
Father Bruno – his secretary and right-hand man
Father Franco – a tutor
Father Mezzi – a talented Warrior monk, tattooist and physician
Conn De Malvais – son of Morvan and Constance
Gustave –one of the seven
Verucchio- one of the seven
Georgio- one of the seven, Conn's best friend

Glossary

Acolyte – A follower

Bailey - A ward or courtyard in a castle, some outer baileys could be huge, encompassing grazing land.

Braies - A type of trouser often used as an undergarment, often to mid-calf and made of light or heavier linen.

Castello – A large building or palace in Italy strengthened against attack.

Chausses – Attached by laces to the waist of the braies, these were tighter fitting coverings for the legs.

Cog – wider flat bottomed trading ship used from the 10th century.

Coif – A chain mail hood and collar.

Dais – A raised platform in a hall for a throne or tables, often for nobles.

Destrier – A knight's large warhorse, trained to fight, bite and strike out.

Dock Wallopers - A labourer who loads or unloads vessels in a port.

Donjon – The fortified tower of an early castle later called the keep.

Doublet – A close-fitting jacket or jerkin often made from leather, with or without sleeves. Laced at the front and worn either under or over, a chain mail hauberk.

Factor – A person who manages estates and operates as a mercantile agent for products or goods.

Fealty – Sworn loyalty to a lord or patron.

'Give No Quarter' – To give no mercy or show no clemency for the vanquished.

Gunwale – The widened edge at the top of the hull of a boat.

Hand-fasting – A legally binding ceremony for a couple that could replace marriage.

Hauberk – A tunic of chain mail, often reaching to mid-thigh.

Hermitage – A place of religious seclusion with strict self-discipline, often in a remote setting.

Holy See – The jurisdiction in all matters relating to the Catholic Church by the Bishop of Rome – the Pope.

Lateran Palace – The main Papal residence in Rome.

League – A league is equivalent to about 3 miles in modern terms.

Liege lord – A feudal lord such as a count or baron entitled to allegiance and service from his knights.

Monseigneur – A title and honorific in the Catholic Church.

Motte – An earth mound forming a secure platform on which a donjon would be built; initially, this would be made of wood until the earth settled and compacted.

Neophytes – A new convert to a religion or belief.

Palazzo – A large imposing building or residence in Italy.

Pallet Bed – A bed made of straw or hay. Close to the ground, generally covered by a linen sheet and also known as a palliasse.

Palisade – A defensive fence made from high wooden stakes or tree trunks.

Patron – An individual who gives financial, political, or social patronage to others. Often through wealth or influence in return for loyalty and homage.

Pell – A stout wooden post for sword practice.

Pell-Mell – Confused or disorganised action, often in street riots or battles.

Pottage – A staple of the medieval diet, a thick soup made by boiling grains and vegetables and, if available, meat or fish.

Prelate – A high ranking member of the clergy.

Quarrel – A large, often square-headed bolt for a crossbow.

Retainer – A dependent or follower rewarded or paid for their services.

Rout - A disorderly withdrawal from a battle.

Seneschal – A senior advisor or Principal Administrator of the royal household.

Serjeant – The soldier serjeant was a man who often came from a higher class; most experienced medieval mercenaries fell into this class; they were deemed 'half of the value of a knight' in military terms.

Signori – A lord or individual powerful enough to preserve peace in a city state. It often became hereditary.

Vedette - An outrider or scout used by cavalry.

Vellum - Finest scraped and treated calfskin, used for writing messages.

Author note

It is always sad coming to the end of a series…. but wow, just look where this series has taken me. As a historian, this period of history in Europe has proved fascinating. The deeper you delve, the more stories are revealed, leading you down paths you may never have explored.

William the Conqueror, the King of England and the Duke of Normandy proved to be a highly complex character. One of the greatest warrior kings in Europe, he spent most of his life at war or quelling rebellions as he tried to hold his Anglo-Norman kingdom together.

He loved his wife, Queen Matilda, very much, they had nine children who all survived to reach their adult years. There is no record of mistresses or illegitimate children during his marriage. However, she was the glue that held his family together, including his brother Odo and his errant son Robert. Matilda healed the rift between them after the disastrous rebellion and siege at Gerberoi, and father and son were reconciled for some time. In the later years, with Matilda dead and his brother Odo imprisoned, the constant threats on the borders of both Normandy and England must have been exhausting. During those years, his eldest son Robert was a thorn in his side. Robert was being manipulated by other forces, whether by his uncle Count Robert of Flanders, King Philip of France or by several popes in the Holy See. They all wanted William to fall, and Robert was the tool they used to try and bring him down.

William was indeed fatally injured during the attack on Mantes. He had burned the town and churches, but he did send payments on his death bed as reparation for his damage. Unfortunately, when he died, he did not get the burial that a king of his stature deserved, and his son Robert did refuse to go to his deathbed or funeral. The stone sarcophagus made for him was found to be too small, and they tried to force his body in with disastrous results.

Then during the ceremony, the family who owned the land on which the Abbaye-aux-Hommes was built arrived (you may remember them from Book Three - Betrayal), forbade William's burial in their land as it was stolen from their father by the Duke. According to sources at the time, Prince Henry paid compensation so that his father could be buried in the Abbaye, approximately one hundred pounds, according to sources at the time. Then a disastrous fire broke out in Caen, and everyone left the ceremony to try and extinguish it except for a few monks.

His son King William Rufus finally built his father a noble tomb that shone with gold, silver and precious stones. Unfortunately, it was destroyed during the French Revolution, and King William's remains were thrown into the River Orne. Several years ago, I stood beside the marble slab that marks his final resting place in the Abbaye-aux-Hommes in Caen. I was suitably awed, not realising that the only remains of William that still exist beneath that slab is a single thigh bone!

The Holy See built its power during this period and flexed its muscles. Pope Gregory was a great Benedictine reformer, and he did excommunicate the Holy Roman Emperor Henry IV for appointing his own bishops. In retaliation, Henry did elect another pope, and there was a schism in Europe as Princes and rulers supported one or the other of the popes. This split continued for hundreds of years, with a papacy being established at Avignon.

Dauferio did become Pope Victor III; although I must apologise for slightly blackening his character, he died of a protracted illness at Monte Cassino. Odo de Chatillon become Pope Uban II. He was responsible for establishing the First Crusade against the infidels in Palestine, using Knights of the Cross, who became known as crusaders.

The Hermitage of San Colombano does exist in the Italian Alps and is built into the cliffs. It is just as stunning and inaccessible as it is in the book.

Constance, the daughter of William and Matilda, was kept at home much longer than her sisters. There was an arranged marriage between her and Alan Fergant, the Duke of Brittany. She bore him no children. William of Malmesbury, one of the more reliable historians of the period, alleges that her husband had her servants poison her. She was approximately thirty-two years old.

Genoa did become a maritime republic under the control of the Signori Guglielmo Embriaco. He is a fascinating character in his own right, fighting several battles at sea against the Saracen corsairs and being instrumental in relieving the siege of Jerusalem during the crusades. The Embriaci tower is still standing today, one of the only remaining towers of this height in the city's historic quarter.

So with this last book, we say goodbye to the Breton Horse Warriors, who found fame led by Alan Rufus in the Battle of Hastings, helping King William win the battle. They were responsible for developing and spreading the great War Destriers, which became necessary as armour developed and became heavier. They went on to become a lethal fighting force in Europe.

As I move on to another series, I will certainly miss Luc De Malvais and his brother Morvan De Malvais. However, Piers De Chatillon, papal assassin, could not possibly die. He will live on in his own series....

Maps

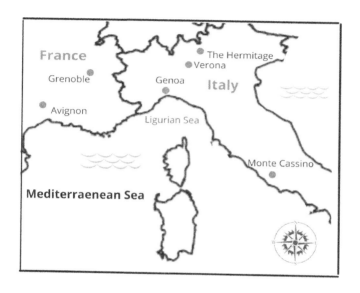

About the Author

S. J. Martin... is the pen name of a historian, writer and animal lover who lives in the north of England. Her abiding love of history from a very early age influenced her academic and career choices. She worked in the field of archaeology for several years before becoming a history teacher in the schools of the Northeast, then in London and finally Sheffield.

Having decided to leave the world of education after a successful teaching and leadership career, she combined her love of history and writing as an author of historical fiction. She particularly enjoys the engaging and fascinating in-depth historical research into the background of different historical periods and characters, combining this with extensive field visits.

Always an avid and voracious reader herself, she decided with her partner and a close friend to establish Moonstorm Books, publishing her first highly successful series to tell the story of 'The Breton Horse Warriors.'

When she is not writing or researching, she walks their two dogs with her partner, Greg, on the beautiful beaches of the North East coast or in the countryside. She also has an abiding love of live music and festivals, playing and singing in a band with her friends whenever possible.

You can connect with me on:

🌐 https://www.moonstormbooks.com/sjmartin

🐦 https://twitter.com/sjmarti40719548

📘 https://www.facebook.com/SJMartin-Author

🔗 https://www.instagram.com/s.j.martin_author

Subscribe to my newsletter:

✉️ https://www.moonstormbooks.com/sjmartin

Also by S.J. Martin

The Breton Horse Warriors Series

Ravensworth

Rebellion

Betrayal

Banished

Vengeance

The Papal Assassin Series

The Papal Assassin

The Papal Assassin's Wife

The Papal Assassin's Curse

The Papal Assassin Series

The Papal Assassin Series follows the adventures, life and times of the darkly handsome swordmaster Piers De Chatillon. A wealthy French noble, the young influential Papal Envoy of several popes and a consummate diplomat, he spreads his influence, favours and threats around the courts of Europe.

He is an arch manipulator, desired by women and feared by men; he is also a lethal assassin used by Kings and Princes alike. His adventures take him back and forth across Europe in the turbulent seas of politics and intrigue in the 11th century.

Meanwhile, an array of enemies plots his downfall and demise. With the help of his close compatriots and friends, he manages to keep them at bay, but time is running out for Piers De Chatillon, and danger draws ever closer to his beautiful wife, Isabella and their children.

Printed in Great Britain
by Amazon